Goose Island
Black Jack

A Kate Houlihan
Mystery

G. R. Kinra

GOOSE ISLAND BLACK JACK
Copyright © 2019 G.R.Kinra.
All rights reserved.
ISBN: 978-0-9913213-3-9

~~~~~~

~~~~~~

Published in the United States of America
June 2019.
G.R. Kinra, PO Box 863462, Plano TX 75086.

~~~~~~

~~~~~~

May you always hear the whisper of the ocean's kiss,
On the beach beside you, to grant a wish.
May you always find treasure amidst the golden sand,
From the Dry Tortugas to the Rio Grande.

≈≈≈≈≈≈

Goose Island Black Jack is the second book in the Goose Island series featuring Kate Houlihan's amazing crime solving abilities and passion to protect and preserve the Texas Gulf Coast.

~~~~~

Contents

Into The Mist.. 1

Sea Breeze... 3

Dead Man's Chest.................................... 27

Breaking And Entering......................... 44

Black Jack.. 66

Dolphins.. 96

Dry Dock... 131

Mesquite Bay.. 159

Fool's Gold... 188

Ferdies... 205

Batten Hatches..................................... 224

Cast Off.. 237

Key Largo.. 263

Indian Key... 280

Alligator Reef....................................... 296

Home Sweet Home.............................. 330

Spyglass Hill... 347

Into The Mist

On a warm summer evening in 1821, Jean Lafitte and his motley crew sailed quietly out of Galveston Bay. They vanished quickly into the night, heading south towards Mexico with no plans to return. As their ship rounded the tip of the island, they could see flames shooting up behind them.

Jean and his brother Pierre had once operated a legitimate business as traders in New Orleans. However, everything changed with the Louisiana Purchase in 1803. As the American Government gained control of New Orleans, it continued to increase its influence in the area. The Embargo Act of 1807 prohibited American ships from docking at foreign ports. This made it unlawful for the Lafittes to continue their mercantile business from New Orleans. In response to the embargo, the Lafitte family moved their operations further south to Barataria, Louisiana.

Barataria Bay is a narrow passage between the barrier islands of Grande Terre and

GOOSE ISLAND BLACK JACK

Grande Isle south of New Orleans. Jean's ships could now slip in and out of the area in defiance of the control imposed by the Governor of New Orleans. Branded as pirates, Pierre rolled the dice and remained in Barataria. However, Jean moved his base of operations to the Spanish territory of Galveston. When the Americans continued their expansion into Texas, they gave Jean an ultimatum to surrender in 1821. In response to this ultimatum, he set fire to his garrison on Harborside Drive in Galveston and disappeared into the night. Many believe that he died at sea.

Jean Lafitte vanished into the mist outside Galveston in 1821, but his presence continues to be felt along the Texas Gulf Coast to this day. From time to time, sailors in the Gulf have reported seeing a shadowy schooner in the early morning mist floating serenely across the water. Jean was intelligent, resourceful, friendly, and handsome. He had been educated at a military academy in St. Kitts and had an excellent knowledge of the Gulf Coast. He was a ladies' man who spoke Spanish, French, and English fluently. In other words, he was a complete scoundrel.

≈≈≈≈≈≈

Sea Breeze

The evening sun bloodied the edges of the clouds that hovered over Aransas Bay. The clouds that morphed across the horizon gave a clear indication of an approaching storm. Across the bay from Shipwreck Beach, the sky was a brilliant mix of orange and red with dark, foreboding crimson hues. The incessant rush of the surf echoed in the air with the ebb and flow of each wave that crashed upon the rocks at the end of the beach. Sand pipers skittered silently across the sand foraging for food.

Kate Houlihan, the owner of the Golden Goose B&B, made her way down the narrow path that meandered beside the sand dunes to Shipwreck Beach. Her friend Shirley followed close behind her. They walked carefully past the sea oats and the abandoned, mismatched, flip-flops that lay half buried in the sand. Kate paused next to a large piece of driftwood to allow Shirley to catch up with her. Her hair streamed behind her in the sea breeze that wafted over the water. The wind picked up

Kate's skirt and it billowed past a pair of perfectly sculpted legs. The artist who had created her had used a generous supply of clay in all the right places. Her active lifestyle helped preserve her amazing figure.

Shirley was a little shorter than Kate and slightly larger at the waist. She was the owner of the Goose Island Bakery, an island institution that she had inherited from her mother Bridget. Her figure was a reflection of the fact that she was never more than a few feet away from her next chocolate muffin. Her cherubic profile was pleasant and very easy on the eyes. She wore her blonde hair in a ponytail hanging through the opening in the back of the USS Lexington baseball cap. Shirley was the star catcher on the Goose Island Women's Softball League. She looked as if she could spit clear across the sand dunes into the surf. You did not want to get caught stealing second base with her at the plate.

Kate had helped Shirley close up her bakery on the Goose Island Town Square for the evening. They had just ridden their bicycles to the beach from the Square. It was late in the day and the lifeguard station on the beach was deserted. Kate and Shirley loved nothing better than the walk along the sandy shores of Shipwreck Beach. It always amazed Kate how different the beach looked each time they visited it depending on how angry or calm the seas were. One day the water could be raging with six-foot swells, a rush of emotion that crashed along the rocks at one end of the shore. The next day it could be as flat as a pancake, just a shimmering sheet of glass.

*   *   *

Goose Island is a small seaside community on the Texas Gulf Coast, where everybody knows everyone else, and everything about each other. A place where all the secrets on the island come foaming out of the beer steins of the Swamp Shack beside the causeway by midnight. Secrets that retreat into the morning fog drifting slowly past the fading deck chairs and folded umbrellas outside the restaurant. Where the seagulls and pelicans sleep with one eye open in order to keep a watchful eye upon the entrance to the causeway. A place where the warmth of Texas BBQ and blues connects you to everything that had ever happened at Goose Island before and after your time.

Kate and Shirley had no doubt been the subject of many conversations at the Swamp Shack. The idle chatter around the bar about Kate was mostly about Kate's boyfriend Ray, a fellow from Odessa. The scuttlebutt about Ray was that he wasn't hanging around Goose Island just to drill for oil. He was clearly besotted with his love for Kate, and the Goose Island community had quickly accepted him as one of their own.

Where Shirley was concerned, the talk about her involved the local sheriff, Troy, who had a soft spot for Shirley. Everyone in town seemed to know whenever she had been pulled over for driving too fast or running a stop sign without coming to a complete stop. It did not help that Troy had once pulled Shirley over for leaving the parking lot of the Swamp Shack going a few miles over the speed limit while a group of lackeys from Rockport had driven out the back with a refrigerator full of gulf shrimp from the Swamp Shack. Bar-room chatter at the Swamp Shack became more convoluted and ribald with each re-telling of the tale and pretty soon entire fleets of fishing trawlers had gone missing while sheriff Troy had Shirley spread-eagled against her car while he searched her person for concealed weapons.

Shirley and Kate could do nothing to prevent the pre-adolescent humor at the Swamp Shack. However, they did not hesitate to toss a few poison darts across the room while sipping on a tall glass of Goose Island Flash. In addition, Shirley and Kate had an uncanny knack for fixing anything that threatened their island lifestyle. Their friendship had blossomed as they often joined forces to campaign the city for minor improvements such as better sidewalks and lighting in the area near the Goose Island Town Square.

The residents of Goose Island wanted no part of the annual Spring Break festivities and debauchery that descends on the Gulf Coast each year. They liked the simplicity their town offered and worked concertedly to defeat any altruistic endeavor that threatened to change their life style in any significant way. They were determined not to attract the pleasure seekers who drove noisily down the highway, en route to Port Aransas.

The revelers who visit the Texas Coast every year during Spring Break are a rowdy bunch of students who seem to get younger and more obnoxious each year. Thankfully, Goose Island lacked the hotels, restaurants, neon signs, nightlife and wet-T-shirt contests that lure these pre-pubescent teenagers to the area. The township did its best to discourage unwanted visitors by making itself invisible each year through the month of March.

The sign on the highway that showed the way to Shipwreck Beach was cleverly re-directed each year to point the way to Mustang Island instead. The sudden gust of wind that turned the sign askew each year was no one other than the local sheriff, Troy, doing his sworn civic duty to keep the residents of Goose Island safe from harmful influences at all times. That is only when he wasn't cruising through the Square in his police car in order to catch a glimpse of his sweetheart Shirley driving her bicycle to or from work. Troy kept a close watch on everything she did. He made sure that she knew his evil intentions were honorable. He was determined to earn her trust one small gesture at a time.

*   *   *

Kate began each day by checking her mobile phone for messages for reservation requests from her small clientele of 'snowbirds'. As the owner of the Golden Goose B&B, Kate experienced a steady stream of maintenance and repair adventures to meet the ongoing needs of her establishment. Her routine included confirming new reservation requests, changing linens, cleaning windows, rearranging the furniture, serving breakfast, and any one of the many tasks needed to operate her B&B establishment. She had become an expert at painting rooms, sheetrock repairs, replacing sprinkler heads, trimming branches, and a myriad of general repair and maintenance skills. Some days disappeared in the twinkling of an eye. These were the days when she felt completely satisfied and fulfilled, as if she had accomplished a great deal in the short span of time from sunrise to sunset. At other times it seemed as if nothing had gotten done all day, through no fault of her own.

Shirley was at work before dawn every day. She made sure the muffins that she served her customers were always baked to perfection, with nicely browned edges. Folks came from miles around to pick up a box of her blueberry lemon, carrot raisin, or poppy seed muffins. There were four muffins in each box, and she always added a tequila-mint flavored honey glaze on top of each muffin. Each of her signature chocolate chip pirate cookies was decorated with an outline of a skull and X shaped cross bones. The small dining area in the bakery was often filled to capacity by sunrise. A cup of steaming hot coffee from the Goose Island Bakery was the perfect way to start the day.

One of the hazards of owning a bakery was that Shirley had to sample and taste test her confections several times each day. Over the years, Shirley's figure had filled out more than she cared to admit. She was getting a little out of breath as they made their way to the beach.

"I really must work out more," she said. "I need to lose about fifteen pounds."

"Yes you must," Kate replied. She made a mental note to give Shirley a gift membership to the new fitness facility that had just opened in

Rockport. It had a really nice pool. Perfect for swimming laps.

The path that led past the sea oats to the beach was just wide enough to let one person through at a time. Shirley tiptoed gingerly past the sand reeds next to the path leading to the beach. As they approached the water, the sound of the waves crashing along the shore echoed in the air. It was a sound Kate loved, the sound of the ocean on tap. It was impossible to come within a hundred yards of the beach without hearing it in every direction. As they walked along the narrow footpath that meandered through the sand dunes to Shipwreck Beach, Kate could not wait to see the clear blue water along the shore. The sound of the surf made her pick up the pace and walk faster, impatient to see the ocean, even as her feet sank into the dry sandy path making each step more laborious than the previous one.

The sound of the ocean was a never-ending orchestral melody that subsumed Kate's spirit. It helped her relax and think things through more clearly. It was a welcome change from the pedestrian sounds at the Goose Island Town Square a half mile away where the only natural sound was the occasional screech of a sea gull foraging for food.

Then suddenly they were past the sand dunes and the ocean lay before them in all its blue vastness. It never failed to take Kate's breath away. A flock of geese trailed across the bright orange, red and blue sky. The ground became firmer and easier to walk upon as they got closer to the water. Kate walked past the swath of seaweed that stretched along the length of the shore. She held her sandals in her right had so she could let the water wash over her feet and ankles.

They walked towards their favorite spot. It was next to a rocky outgrowth of boulders at one end of the beach that routinely got splashed by the frothy waves at high tide. They left their sandals and a beach bag with towels perched next to a large brown, weathered boulder and rolled up their slacks. Kate loosened the buttons on her blouse and let the sea breeze caress her body. The beach was deserted. There were no catcalls or raised eyebrows as she stepped into the surf and began walking at a leisurely pace towards the other end of the beach. The girls could have been completely naked and no one would have noticed.

It was a far cry from the foolishness being enacted on Mustang Island just a few miles down the coast from Goose Island. The islands were a magnet for college students from all over Texas during Spring Break beginning in the first week of March and continuing almost to the end of the month. Hotels were packed to capacity and grocery stores routinely ran short on beer and other essentials. The folks who could not afford to get a hotel room camped out on the beach having wild parties that often continued for days. The typical campsite usually had a roaring fire, a guitar player, and a large collection of empty beer cans surrounded by drunk teenagers in various stages of alcohol or drug induced nudity.

"I've heard some of the girls are walking around topless on the beach at Corpus with nothing on but body paint." Kate said. "The Mustang Island Brewery has a girl behind their drink station wearing an air-brushed island scene with a tropical sunset and wild orchids wrapped around her torso. .With the palm trees and flowers covering her body it's hard to ascertain where one part of her anatomy starts and where it ends. I saw her on the news the other day. Aside from the paint, all she had on was a thong and a pair of skin colored stickers on her nipples. "

"It would have to be a pretty big sunset to cover me up," said Shirley.

"You know what they always say about living in Texas," Kate said. "Everything's bigger here. Bigger sky, bigger sunsets and ..."

"Bigger boots," said Shirley with a smile completing Kate's sentence for her.

Kate laughed. "Always!" she said nodding in agreement.

"I agree!" said Shirley, warming up to the idea. As always, her thoughts returned to baking. "Do you think it could be done using an edible paint? A late evening sunset using dark chocolate with some orange confectionery sugar mixed in. Maybe even a map to some hidden treasure."

Kate laughed. "Did you know that in some cultures in the world the bride's arms and torso are painted in mystical patterns using henna," Kate said. "That's a reddish brown colored dye and one of the traditions is that the grooms name is hidden within the pattern. On the wedding night the groom has to find his name on his bride's torso before their marriage can be consummated."

"It could make for a very interesting evening if your partner had to get to know you from head to toe before he could possess you," Shirley replied. "I'll have to remember to put Troy's name on my thigh next to the dessert selection."

"Yes, that would be very interesting," Kate replied. Something about Shirley's remark about Troy was a little unexpected. Kate narrowed her eyes and looked at her friend carefully. "Is that a diamond ring on your right hand?" Kate said suddenly. She had just noticed what looked like an engagement ring on Shirley's finger.

"Troy proposed," Shirley said bashfully. Shirley was standing a few feet away from Kate and stood looking intently at the waves. She had rolled up her blue jeans above her knees. The waves swirled around her feet as they washed up on the shore behind her. She was wearing the ring on the middle finger of her right hand.

"Wow!" said Kate. She had not noticed the ring until then. "Congratulations! Have ya'll set a date for the wedding?"

"No, not yet," Shirley said.

Kate reached instinctively for the ring she wore and twirled it around her finger a few times. Kate remembered the intense feeling of excitement she had felt when her friend Raymond had proposed to her. Kate and Ray had not set a date for their wedding either. The ring was a symbol of their commitment. She often slept with nothing on but her ring.

"I think you'll make a great couple Shirley," Kate said. She paused. "Have you told your Mom yet?"

Shirley did not answer. She looked as if she was a million miles away.

"Is something wrong?" Kate asked. Shirley had not answered her last two questions. Kate was not sure what to make of Shirley's predicament.

"I'm not sure if I want to marry him, Kate," Shirley replied.

"Oh!" Kate said. "What did you tell him?"

"I told him I'd think it over".

"Makes sense," Kate replied. She waited for an explanation.

"We had just barbecued some hamburgers on the grill outside my apartment," Shirley continued. "I was inside fixing his favorite drink, a shot of Tullamore Dew on ice with a twist of lemon. While I was inside he put the ring on my plate next to the French fries."

"Okay," Kate said, still waiting for more details. It was just like Troy! Hamburgers, French Fries, Tullamore Dew and a bodacious barmaid. It did not take much to keep that boy happy.

"I returned with the drinks," Shirley said. She lowered her voice as she imitated Troy. "I got something for you," she said in a deep voice. She paused.

"That's nice," Kate said, noncommittedly. She was not sure where this was going.

"Well I never realized there was a diamond ring on my plate next to the fries. Before I knew what had happened, I had ketchup all over it. I wasn't expecting a ring with my French Fries. It was such a mess," Shirley said tearfully.

"Yes, I see," Kate, replied. Troy would have had a better chance of impressing Shirley if he had simply taken her out on an ice-cream date. One scoop of peanut butter crunch with a diamond ring next to it would have done the trick. A drive to Austwell along the hilly road that runs along the Gulf Coast would have been fine. They could have stopped at the scenic overlook along the way to look at the sunset. The old Spanish Mission near the airport would have been perfect. It was right in the glide path of airplanes coming into land at Corpus Christi International. Kate liked to visit it with Ray and feel the thunderous roar each time another 737 came in to land. The sound of the airplanes and the smell of jet fuel always got her a little excited. Troy's French Fried proposal seemed to be severely lacking in emotional creativity. A woman needs to feel that she is being courted as an object of intense desire, not like a bargain purchase at a flea market or the First Friday Trade Days in Canton.

"I guess he didn't get down on one knee?" Kate asked her.

"Ha!" Shirley said. Her response told Kate all she needed to know about what had transpired between Shirley and Troy. They leaned against the boulder and gazed silently at the water for a minute or two.

"Or tell you that you were the most beautiful girl in the universe and that he could not live without you?" Kate continued.

"You are too funny, Kate," Shirley replied. "No, he didn't."

"He should have!" Kate said.

Kate had a flash back of her ex-husband James and the three bags of trash that had sat at the top of the stairs in their house for a week before she had hauled them off to the garage. That was just before she had decided to leave James forever. James was always too busy to help around the house. Too busy to help clean up after dinner; too busy to do his laundry; too busy to iron his shirts or to take them to the cleaners; too busy working in Houston on an environmental pollution case to come home to Goose Island for the weekend. Just hard at work with the legal secretary at the office in Houston. When Kate found out about the affair between James and the bimbo-bitch she had spent the entire weekend in a rage. She considered her options with the help of a freshly opened bottle of eighteen year old Scotch whiskey that James had been saving for a special occasion. There were no good choices. Divorce is never fun, never easy. All she could think of at that time was that no matter what happened she planned to stay on in Goose Island until she could put her life back together again. Afterwards, she carefully super glued the fly to all the boxer shorts in his closet. It was just a small gesture of goodwill as they parted ways. The next day she held a garage sale of all his personal items. When he returned to Goose Island there was nothing for him to pack. Later, she got a real chuckle when she heard how he had wet his pants when he had gone to the restroom to relieve himself after a meeting with a client.

"It's the little things that make the difference," Kate added.

"I know," Shirley, replied, tearfully.

"Well I am very happy for you, Shirley," Kate said. "I know Troy is not as romantic as you would like him to be. However, I do think he is a good man who will stay by your side and love you forever," Kate said. "You should give your Mom a call"

"I'm sure Mom would approve," Shirley said. "She likes Troy a lot."

"Yes, I agree," Kate replied. Shirley's mother, Bridget had always had a soft spot in her heart for Troy. "You are really fortunate. My mother never liked my first husband, James, and looking back I guess she knew something about James that I was too blind to see when the two of us were getting ready to tie the knot."

"Dad likes him too. They get along just fine." Shirley said.

"That's a great start," Kate said. "Most folks don't realize that a marriage spawns a relationship with a whole slew of relatives, not just the one person you are marrying."

"I'm just not sure if he's the right one. I don't know what to tell him, Kate," Shirley replied. "I don't want to hurt his feelings. He's a good friend, but he just doesn't make my heart beat any faster than it did before I met him."

"You have to decide what you want Shirley," said Kate. "Only you and you alone, are the one who has to accept or reject his proposal. No one else can do that for you," she added. "Marriage is an aspect of the rest of your life where you have to be the one making the final decision. What will it be like to wake up with him in your bed every morning, 'till death do you part'"?

"It could get a little tiresome," Shirley said. "But then again, it might be okay."

"Most men think they are going to come home every night, throw you on the bed, pull your bloomers off and have their way with you," Kate replied. "Just remember that the bedroom is one area where a woman can rule once she learns how to satisfy her man." She winked at Shirley knowingly. "What you say and do when the lights are turned off is between the two of you. If you take care of him in the bedroom he'll never feel the need to go anywhere else. When he comes home tired and beat up by the world outside, you have to recharge his batteries so that he can't wait to go back to work once more the next morning to fight for his family."

"Oh!" Shirley replied as she contemplated the meaning of Kate's remark. Most of what Shirley knew about love came from the pages of her women's magazine subscription.

"Marriage is like a treasure chest that you share with your beloved," Kate continued. "It's just an empty box when you start your voyage together. You fill it up as you go along. It doesn't matter what you put into it so long as you both put something into it."

"Like a pair of pirates traveling through uncharted waters on the ocean of life" Shirley added.

"In a certain sense, yes. As a team of two that works together to survive life's trials and tribulations," replied Kate. "Not in the sense of plundering, pillaging, and going around killing innocent people. The things you put into your treasure chest are the special moments that take your breath away." Kate had had a few of these recently with Ray.

"We haven't had too many of those," said Shirley. "Not yet, anyway."

"It hardly matters whether it's pieces of eight or bits of sea glass," Kate continued. "Just as long as you both contribute and put a few treasures into the treasure chest every now and then. My first marriage ended up on the rocks because my ex-husband, James was too busy working to notice if I was around."

"Oh I wouldn't describe you as a round Kate. You have more of a dumbbell shape than a round," Shirley said with a twinkle in her eye.

"I'll dumb belle you," Kate said, realizing that Shirley was having a little joke at her expense. "But seriously, I felt that the treasure chest I shared with my ex-husband James was pretty empty. I felt that I was the one putting things into the treasure chest and he was the one taking them out," she continued.

"He was gone much of the time wasn't he?" Shirley asked.

"It wasn't so much being away from home so much, as being gone when he was in the same room right next to me," Kate said. "One time we were having dinner at the marina in Port Aransas. He had just returned to the island after spending the week defending an oil company in Houston and we decided to get some supper on our way home. We were seated at a table on a wooden deck outside the restaurant. We had a plate piled ever so high with crawfish and a bucket of beer on the table in front of us. There were some fishing boats in the bay, clouds in the distance, some seagulls squawking overhead and the most beautiful sunset in the sky. I was hoping he would turn around, give me a kiss on the lips, say those three magic words and tell me how much he had missed me. Guess what he said instead."

"I don't know," Shirley replied. "What did he say?"

"Well his exact words were "I don't know what you see in this place Kate. There is nothing here. Nothing at all! It's just so far from everything."

"Really! You could not have been more than a few feet from the water. That's how far you were from everything that matters! Just too far from the hustle and bustle of the big city. I guess he wanted to smell some diesel fuel and hear the sound of eighteen wheelers shifting through their gears on the highway," Shirley exclaimed, turning a little red in the face as she empathized with Kate. "Did you toss him overboard?"

Kate didn't answer right away. "Not till the divorce," Kate said quietly, brushing at a strand of invisible hair against her face as she wiped away a silent tear. "He was always planning to do things, like planning to pick up around the house, planning to wash the dishes, or planning to take out the trash. He never actually did anything to help me with the housework or make me feel valued, or beautiful or special. I was just there to cook and clean and serve his drinking buddies pancakes at three in the morning."

"With pancakes like a harvest moon in August, and a cleavage to match the Palo Duro Canyon, I bet there were plenty of blokes who wanted to die in your arms," Shirley said with a laugh. "What was the breakfast special? Legs over easy?"

"It was more like rocky road with granola!" Kate replied with a touch of sarcasm.

They turned to go back to the beach access area where they had left their bicycles. The waves were a little bigger and had a few more flecks of white than usual. The jagged edges of the clouds suggested that it was raining in the distance. It was time to go home. They were far enough from the rocks to avoid being splashed with water and close enough to feel the power of the approaching storm. It seemed as though every third wave was slightly larger than the two before it and resulted in a bigger splash when it crashed against the rocks. The wind from the Gulf streamed past them as it rushed towards the sand dunes. They could see the street lights flicker once before they came on to illuminate the Copano Bay bridge that straddled

Copano Bay at the east end of the beach about a mile from where they stood.

A flock of geese flapped effortlessly in a Vee formation across Copano Bay, headed north for the summer. The bird at the head of the Vee must contend with greater air resistance and work harder than the one right behind. After some time the lead bird changes position with another bird, who then moves to the head of the Vee. The same change in position occurs at both the extremities of the Vee and birds move from the extremities to the middle of the Vee.

Kate loved to watch the fluidity with which geese move in and out of these constantly changing positions, while still maintaining the Vee. "A good marriage requires the same kind of teamwork," Kate thought to herself as they made their way back through the sand dunes to their bicycles. It was dark by now. The shadows cast by the sand reeds made it difficult for them to see the trail as clearly as when they had crossed it earlier that evening. They picked up their bicycles and rode down along Shore Drive pedaling into a light head wind.

"I was thinking of going to the police auction in Corpus Christi on Friday," Kate said as they pedaled down Shore Drive. "Ray's coming into town for the weekend and I'm going to meet him at the airport. I might pick up a few knick-knacks at the auction on the way to the airport."

"I'd come with you but I have to work," said Shirley.

They turned right on Marlin drive. Shirley veered over to one side as they went past the entrance into her apartment complex. She disappeared down the circular driveway that led to the front entrance of The Breakers. Kate continued down Marlin Street to the Golden Goose Bed and Breakfast at the corner of Marlin and Azalea Street. Her last houseguests had checked out that morning. The next customers were due to arrive the following day, giving her an evening to herself. She hummed the lyrics to the theme from Mondo Cane as she entered her driveway, her heart overflowing with love and the crazy relationship she had with Ray.

Ray lived near Odessa and came to visit Goose Island as often as possible. They did their best to stay in touch when they were apart. Kate viewed each message that she received from Ray as a soulful shout across the miles that warmed her heart and made it race. His text message to Kate this morning had been a welcome request for a ride from the airport the next day along some home brewed hugs and kisses.

"You sure are asking for a lot," Kate had replied. "Do I really know you? It's been so long since you were here that I'm not sure I remember what you look like. You know how much I dislike blind dates. Besides, I have a lot of important things to do with my time."

"Oh please Kate, can't we just go dancing to the same place we were at last Friday?" Ray replied. He sent her a text message with a recent photograph of the two of them at the beach in Goose Island. They were seated in beach chairs next to a small ice chest that threatened to float away with their beer as the surf dappled the shoreline. It brought back some very special memories.

"Has it only been a week since you were here?" Kate inquired. "I must be getting old. It feels as if it's been ten years since I saw you wearing your super hero underwear."

"I'll take that as a yes, Wonder Woman," Ray said. What followed next was a string of uninterrupted X's and O's. Even when he was miles and miles away, she could feel his presence right beside her. Sometimes she expected him to appear magically each time she went down the hallway, or up the stairs to her bedroom. Naked.

≈≈≈≈≈≈

Dead Man's Chest

The annual police auction ended just before noon on Friday. Its venue had been in the Lincoln conference room of the Bay Area Convention Center in Corpus Christi. The items in the auction consisted of objects that had been confiscated during police investigations in Nueces County. There were also a few lost and found items that had remained unclaimed for months. The Corpus Christi Police Department simply didn't have the facilities to keep these items in storage indefinitely. Kate had learned about the auction from her friend Shirley, and Shirley had heard about it from her buddy Troy. Shirley had wanted to accompany Kate to the auction but she simply could not get away from work. So Kate had come by herself with explicit instructions from Shirley to buy a boat if one came up for auction.

A fifteen-minute recess followed the auction. After the recess, it was necessary for the winning bidders to settle-up and pay for their purchases. Kate Houlihan followed the other bidders out of the Lincoln Room. Most of them were leaving for the day. However, Kate would have to return to complete the paperwork on her purchases shortly. She walked down the hallway to look for a quiet area to make a few quick phone calls on her mobile telephone. She found a lounge about halfway down the hall. There was a large bank of windows on one side and a balcony nearby with a view of the atrium and the lobby area on the ground floor of the Convention Center below her. Her mobile phone showed several bars of service with excellent reception and afforded a great view of Corpus Christi Bay. The water was a slightly darker shade of blue than the clear blue sky. There were a few sailboats making their way slowly across the bay, their colorful sails billowing in the warm ocean breeze. The picture postcard scene outside was interspersed sporadically with an occasional puffy white cloud, just begging for a postage stamp and a terse greeting on the reverse that said "Wish You Were Here".

It was all Kate could do to keep from walking down to the parking lot, getting her swimsuit from the beach bag in her station wagon and heading out toward the beach along Mustang Island looking for seashells. That would have to wait until she picked up her friend Ray from the airport. She settled into a comfortable armchair overlooking the bay.

It was Kate's first auction experience and she had found the proceedings extremely interesting. Everyone who attended the auction was issued a small paddle with an identifying number. Kate had received number "53" affixed to the back of her paddle. In order to place a bid, she simply had to raise the paddle so that the number was clearly visible to the auctioneer at the appropriate time.

The bidding process had been a cacophony of sounds. A continuous flow of words emanated from the auctioneer's mouth in a rush. As if he had swallowed a tidal wave and had to regurgitate it in a fraction of the time it had taken going the other way.

Kate's most recent purchase consisted of an old wooden seaman's trunk. The intricate carvings on its sides and the worn out appearance of the trunk had fired Kate's imagination and transported her back to the eighteenth century. As she dialed the telephone number to speak with her friend Shirley, she recalled the auctioneer's voice crowding her mind once again.

It had all started with a brief promotional statement from the auctioneer, stating that "The next item is a one of a kind, unbelievable opportunity to own a piece of history, with a minimum bid of fifty dollars. I have fifty dollars from number 91 in the back of the room. Give me sixty, give me seventy. Give me seventy-five, give me eighty. Give me one hundred and fifty, give me one hundred and sixty. Do I hear a two hundred?"

Kate had raised her paddle at two hundred dollars. She recognized its intrinsic value immediately and planned to use it within her bed and breakfast establishment to store linens and other household items. The trunk would make a great conversation piece. It seemed unlikely that she would ever find another one just like it at this price.

The auctioneer continued the bidding in a rapid staccato voice. "Going once for two hundred dollars, going twice. Raise to two hundred and fifty from number 78. Do I hear three hundred? Three hundred dollars from number 22 over on the left aisle. Three fifty from the young man in the third row. Do I hear four hundred? Four hundred from number 78 in the back row. Four hundred and fifty from number 91."

Kate raised her paddle. She was probably going to regret this purchase.

The auctioneer recognized her immediately. "Five hundred from number 53 in the back of the room. Do I have five hundred and fifty? Five hundred once, five hundred twice. Five hundred three times. Sold to the young lady with number 53 for five hundred dollars."

The young lady that the auctioneer was referring to, was no other than Kate. She was wearing a maroon scarf over an ivory colored shirt with the one and only blue suit that she owned. It made her look more like a banker than the owner of the Golden Goose Bed and Breakfast.

The top of the trunk had a curved appearance. It must have been hewn from the rounded wooden planks that are used for old whisky barrels. Its edges were reinforced with tin and there was a row of rivets running along each edge to hold everything in place. It was the kind of trunk that one could envision hoisted above a sailor's back as he carried all his worldly possessions. The kind one sees in old photographs just as the sailor is about to board a ship that is due to set sail for a destination that lies on the other side of the equator. All four sides of the trunk had been carved very carefully in a nautical theme by someone who had obviously had a lot of time on his hands. The carvings were exquisite.

Kate was very satisfied with her purchases at the auction. In addition to the final purchase of the seaman's trunk, earlier that morning Kate had purchased a beautiful oil painting, a porcelain table lamp with a relief of a flock of geese flying over a marsh on the side, a ceramic planter in the shape of a wishing well and a few other treasures.

The painting was a very serene looking beachscape featuring the Port Aransas Lighthouse in the background. Kate had mixed feelings about purchasing the painting at auction. One could never tell if the artwork was just a pleasant landscape or whether it had been commissioned by a pirate to help remember the location of buried treasure, or by an ax murderer to remember where he had buried the dead bodies of all the people who had double-crossed him. There was always a chance that the owner would come looking for his painting after being released from the penitentiary.

She could scarcely contain her excitement as she dialed Shirley's telephone at the Goose Island Bakery to tell her the news.

"Hello Shirley," Kate said, as a woman's voice answered the phone. "You'll never guess what I purchased today".

"Did you buy a boat?" Shirley asked.

Kate laughed. "Sorry Shirley, there weren't any boats for sale at the auction, today. What kind of boat did you have in mind?"

"I just thought you might have found a nice sturdy boat that we could use for our next trip to the Port Aransas Lighthouse. Something with lots of masts and rigging to hang our swimsuits upon to dry. Maybe an old pirate ship to fly the colors of the Goose Island B&B."

"We'll just have to keep searching for an old pirate ship a little longer. However, if we could use one of your swimsuits every now and then, then we wouldn't need a mast," Kate said with a chuckle She had a sudden vision of sailing past the dolphin docks at Port Aransas using one of Shirley's double, extra-large, swimsuits as a main sail billowing in the breeze.

There was a deafening silence at the other end of the line and Kate quickly proceeded to describe her purchase at the auction. "I did get this gorgeous wooden seaman's trunk at the auction today. I bet the person whom it belonged to originally was a pirate."

"A wooden sailor's trunk?" Shirley asked. There was a buzzing sound of a timer going off in the background. "That's cool. Hold on while I get some muffins out of the oven." There was a brief pause for a few seconds until Shirley returned on the line. "Does it come with a wooden sailor? I've been looking for a wooden sailor all my life. How big is it?"

"It's really not that big," Kate said. "I can't wait for you to see it. It's probably been all over the world. There are all sorts of carvings and inscriptions on it. There is even a hand-carved etching of an old sailing ship on the front of the trunk and a dragon on the other. I think it's going to make a great conversation piece for the Golden Goose Bed and Breakfast."

"Sure," said Shirley. "I'd love to see it. She could tell Kate was brimming with excitement."

*   *   *

Kate got up from the armchair that she was seated in. It was almost time to return to the auction room. As she glanced out the windows, she noticed a small commotion at the entrance to the convention center. Three well-dressed individuals dashed in through the entrance to the lobby. They left their car, a black Chevrolet Avalanche, parked in the circular driveway much to the chagrin of the convention center staff on duty.

After a brief delay, they re-appeared through the elevator door at the end of the hall. Moments later, they went rushing down the hallway going directly past Kate towards the Lincoln conference room where the auction had just ended. She flattened herself against the wall to avoid getting run over by a young man in his late twenties. The other two men followed hard on the heels of the fellow in the lead. They rushed into the auction room and rushed out just a few moments later. The passed her again almost immediately, headed back out towards the lobby. Kate resisted the urge to stick her leg out and trip them as they went rushing past her. They were talking animatedly and Kate recognized a few words in French. They did not look happy at all.

"I guess they just found out that the auction just ended," Kate thought. "You snooze, you lose!"

Earlier that morning, Kate had run into bumper-to-bumper traffic near Emerald Cove. Several lanes of traffic had been closed for repairs making it very difficult to negotiate. Only one lane of traffic was getting through and traffic through that area had slowed to a crawl. Each change at the traffic light at Emerald Cove was only able to let a few cars through each time it turned green. The situation had probably gotten progressively worse as the day wore on. It had probably contributed to their tardiness of the three men who had just passed her in the hallway.

As soon as Kate settled-up with the auctioneer and his staff, Kate received a slip of paper authorizing her to pick up the trunk from the dock. The auctioneer who handed her the sales receipt gave her directions to the loading zone, and provided telephone instructions for the staff on duty to help pack and load her purchases into her car.

GOOSE ISLAND BLACK JACK

As Kate turned to leave the area, she noticed that the three individuals who had rushed past her in the hallway were standing in line behind her, waiting to speak with the auctioneer. Two of the men were older, and probably in their fifties, and the third fellow was much younger, probably in his mid-twenties. The young man looked very athletic and wore a gold chain around his neck. The two older men were looking at her intently, just like some of the geezers at Goose Island who were always trying to look up her skirt or down her shirt. Kate had always tolerated the lecherous glances at Goose Island in a good-hearted way because she knew they were quite harmless. However, the attention from these individuals was most unwelcome. It was a very different type of gaze and she did not find it flattering at all. In fact, it was making her downright nervous. She ignored them and headed towards the door.

Kate walked to her station wagon, which was parked in front of the building. She got into her car and drove around to the loading dock behind the convention center. By the time she backed her car into the loading zone and walked up to the receiving area of loading dock, the three Frenchmen materialized seemingly from nowhere. They must have taken an alternate route to get there since they were waiting at the dock when she arrived. One of the older men approached her as she stepped out of the car. He was clean-shaven and wore his hair in a ponytail. He resembled her Chemistry teacher from High School. However, instead of being comforted by his appearance Kate found herself feeling intimidated by his demeanor. It had nothing to do with not being able to recall the value for Avogadro's constant, or the chemical reaction that occurs during photosynthesis. She watched him warily, feeling a sudden rush adrenalin. Her sixth sense warned her to keep her distance from him. She could hear the sound of klaxons going off in the distance.

His other two companions seemed content to observe her from across the loading zone. One of the men was looking distractedly at the items in the loading dock. The youngest of the three was trying to strike up a conversation with one of the female workers at the dock. He looked ill at ease in his suit and the stubble on his face suggested that he had not shaved for several weeks. He looked like a rogue and there were no two ways about it. The girl on the loading dock was smiling and seemed to be enjoying the attention. Judging from her body language, she seemed quite willing to accept a dinner invitation to go home with him to look at his etchings.

"Pardon me Madam, you are Miss Houlihan. Yes?" said the older man with the ponytail. He approached her just as her purchases were being wheeled towards her on a small flatbed cart. Like the young man on the other side of the loading dock, he was wearing a small gold cross on a chain around his neck. He had a heavy accent.

"Yes," she replied. It bothered her that he seemed to know who she was. "I'm not sure if we have met. Can I help you?" Kate wondered if the three men were priests, or members of a religious cult. Most priests that she knew were clean-shaven, and did not sport ponytails. With his blonde hair and blue eyes he seemed to be of Scandinavian origin. However, he could just as easily be Russian, or Croatian, or from any one of a dozen other countries in Europe.

"I would like to purchase the wooden storage chest you bought at the auction earlier today," he said. "It's very similar to one that used to belong to my family and it is of great sentimental value to me. Would you consider an offer of one thousand dollars."

"Thanks for the offer," Kate said quickly, not really sure how he knew who she was or what she had purchased. She had passed them in the hallway after the auction had ended so they would normally have no way of knowing what she had acquired. "I'll have to think it over and get back to you at a later date". There had once been a time when Kate would have jumped at the offer. She had gone through some financial hurdles when her fledgling B&B was just getting off the ground. However, times were much better now, and she really did not need the money. Besides she did not appreciate the manner in which these individuals had followed her from one end of the Convention Center to the other.

He continued to stare at her as the staff at the loading dock brought her purchases out to the car. He took out his cell phone and proceeded to take a series of pictures of the trunk without her permission. This did nothing to endear him to her. As far as she was concerned, he had worn out his welcome by now.

"It's not for sale at this time," she added quickly. "No more pictures, please, or I will have to charge you for each one that you take." She held up her hand and stepped between him and the trunk. She motioned for him to depart, making her displeasure as clear as possible without raising her voice.

He looked crestfallen and handed her a business card. "If you change your mind Mademoiselle, you know how to find me. Just call me at any time."

Kate accepted his card and gave him one of her own business cards. She turned to walk away.

"Thanks, Henri" she said, trying to cut the conversation short. He was not deterred.

"Do you live in this area?" he inquired.

"Not really," Kate replied. "I live just outside Corpus Christi, it's a little ways down the road from here."

"You look familiar" said the blue suit scratching his forehead with his left hand.

"I'm not sure I know what you mean" Kate said. It was time to end this conversation. She turned and walked away.

The man with the ponytail returned to his friends and they had an agitated conversation. Kate glanced in their direction. They were having a heated debate, and clearly, she or the trunk she had purchased was the topic of discussion. They kept turning around to look in her direction. The younger fellow was quite athletic and his muscles seemed to bulge out from underneath his suit. "Either he spends the whole day working out at the gym, or he's packing a loaded pistol under his arm," she thought. The blue suit with the ponytail showed the other fellows the business card that Kate had given him. After another brief discussion amongst themselves, they turned and walked away from the loading dock.

Kate picked up the old seaman's trunk and the other paintings she had purchased earlier that day. There was plenty of bubble wrap and packing supplies at the loading dock. Kate made sure everything was nice and snug before she departed. She felt a cloud lift away as she left the loading dock. It was good to get away from the Russians on the dock.

It was two o'clock in the afternoon by the time she reached Rockport and almost another thirty minutes later before Kate made her way back home to Goose Island over the Copano Bay Causeway. She waved to Deputy Sherriff Troy, who was parked under the palm trees at the entrance to the bridge, his radar gun pointed in her direction as she approached him. The wave turned into the bird with her middle finger once she was well beyond Troy's speed trap traveling much slower than the legal speed limit.

Troy was not very forgiving when it came to breaking the law. He would just as soon give a speeding ticket to one of the residents of Goose Island, as he would to a complete stranger. However, at least he had the courtesy to stay in the same spot every day so the islanders always knew when to slow down. He waved back at Kate as she passed by. A few seconds later she was going over the center section of the causeway with a field of view that seemed to stretch for miles. In the distance she could see a couple of large ships out in the harbor.

GOOSE ISLAND BLACK JACK

A small pigeon flew alongside her vehicle and passed her as she drove over the end of the causeway doing well over 45 mph. Kate always felt warm and at peace with herself when she was entering Goose Island. "There's no place like home," she thought to herself. As she drove past the highest point of the causeway she could see a small marina jutting out into the water, and a few boats tethered to the dock. Seagulls swarmed around the marina, foraging for food.

She slowed down when she reached the end of the causeway and entered the Township of Goose Island. She drove past the Goose Island Town Square where her store, the Goose Island Curiosity Shoppe had once been located. Kate had never regretted her decision to move. The move had allowed her to keep falling behind in her rental payments to her landlord, Kenneth Porter. Ken had been very understanding of her situation. On a number of occasions he had offered to finance her rental payments on the shop. However, Kate had declined all his offers of assistance. The rumor on the island was that once you were in hock to Ken you never got out of debt until he either owned your business, or you were sleeping with him. Kate was sure that if she had agreed to his terms, then she would still be making payments of one type or another to Ken today. She drove past the courthouse on

Main Street, and turned right onto Shore Drive.
It was a short distance to Shipwreck Beach and
then she turned right again on Marlin Avenue,
entering her neighborhood with a happy and
untroubled mind.

≈≈≈≈≈

Breaking And Entering

Kate pulled into her driveway at the Golden Goose Bed and Breakfast and reached for the bag of doggie treats that she kept behind the passenger's seat. Milo, her next door neighbor's pet Border Collie wagged his tail and came barking up to the fence to greet her.

"Woof," he said, approaching the chain link fence that separated Kate's driveway from his back yard. "Do you want to play?" He had balanced both his front paws on the fence and looked directly at her, wagging his tail from side to side. Then Milo dropped his tennis ball over the fence. It rolled into her driveway. Kate gave Milo the treat. He was delighted. "Woof". Milo said. "Got any more where that came from?"

When he had finished the morsel Kate threw his ball as far as she could over the fence. Milo raced along after it and caught it on the first bounce. He brought the ball back to Kate and they did this several times before he sat down on the ground with the ball between his front paws. As he paused to catch his breath, Kate made her way to Charlotte and Jerry's front door to ask for some help in unloading her vehicle.

Charlotte and Jerry had lived next door to Kate for over a decade and they were like family to her. Kate was a frequent guest at their house and sometimes felt as though she was a member of their family. There were few things she liked more than going over to help them finish off a broiled Gulf Flounder, Sea Trout, or Blackfin Snapper that Charlotte had prepared after one of Jerry's fishing trips. Most of the time he fished from the Copano Bay pier on the old Highway 35 bridge that spanned the entire length of Copano Bay, a distance of well over a mile. Sometimes, if the weather demanded that he do so, he would rent a boat and take it out into the Gulf. Jerry insisted that it was cheaper to rent a boat by the hour, than to be burdened with the responsibility of ownership. "Salt water will rot just about anything it comes into contact with and I just cannot afford the maintenance expenses," Jerry had explained one evening after dinner.

That made sense. Kate had just replaced the HVAC unit at her house the previous year. Constant exposure to the moisture from the salty air had probably reduced its useful life by at least a third. The squirrels chewing through the power cord on the unit had not helped either.

Jerry came over to help Kate unload her car. "Cool!" he said admiringly, as he studied the carving of the old Spanish galleon on the right side of the trunk. "What did you do, run into the Ancient Mariner on your way home?"

"It's just something I purchased at the police auction earlier today," Kate replied.

"It looks really awesome," Jerry said, as he stepped back to admire the craftsmanship.

"I think it must be quite valuable," Kate said. "There were three suspicious looking men who came late and missed the auction. They came rushing in right after the end of the proceedings. One of them approached me as soon as the auction ended and offered to buy it from me before I had even taken delivery of it. He offered me five thousand dollars for it. That's ten times what I paid for it."

"It's beautiful," he said. However, his eyes had narrowed and the lines on his forehead furrowed. "You don't suppose there's anything of value hidden inside, do you? I hope no one tries to steal it from you. In any case, I'd say that the price just went up a little more than that. If they offered you five thousand then it's probably worth double that if not more."

"I think it has a lot of character," Kate replied. "I plan to keep it as a conversation piece in the living room. It looks as if it's been all over the world."

"That carving of the ship looks like the work of a sailor who probably spent his whole life on the ocean," said Jerry. "It must have taken a month of Sundays to get it to look like that." They carried it into Kate's living room. The chest was fairly light and was probably empty. "Mind if I look at it?" Jerry asked.

"Not at all," Kate replied. "I have a few more things to bring inside. Knock yourself out while I finish unloading the car". She made a few trips back to her station wagon and brought in the table lamp and the paintings she had purchased.

"Looks like it might be a pirate ship," he added. "There is a black jack flag on the bow."

"It sure does," Kate replied. "There is a skull and crossbones on it. Anything interesting inside it?" she asked.

"I haven't been able to open it," Jerry replied.

Kate came over to give Jerry a hand, but it was quite securely locked and their attempts to open the chest were to no avail. "Perhaps we should take it down to the Gutmann brothers' locksmiths in the Elk Grove shopping center," Jerry suggested. "Between the two of them I suspect they will be able to figure out how to get it open. The tumblers are probably rusted inside and may need to be lubricated in order to get them moving again".

"I won't be able to attend to it today," Kate said with a disappointed look on her face. "I have to pick up Ray from the airport. He's coming in from Odessa for the weekend."

"I don't mind taking it down to Elm Grove if you'd like," Jerry volunteered. "Maybe let the Guttmann's work on it for a spell?"

"Sure," said Kate. "That would be wonderful."

The two of them picked up the trunk and carried it over to Jerry's house. Even though it was bulky, it was surprisingly light. Kate left the trunk in Jerry's hands and made her way to the airport to meet Ray.

*   *   *

Kate's face lit up the moment she saw Ray walk through the revolving door that led from the terminals to the baggage claim area at the airport. As soon as he walked through the security gate she enveloped him in her arms. They held each other for a long time while a steady stream of passengers made their way around them. Kate gave Ray a big "Don't ever leave me again, I can't live without you!" hug and kiss. Ray blushed as he noticed a few of the onlookers smiled knowingly in his direction. Then he closed his eyes and allowed himself to drift away to a far off place with the love of his life. He was in love with Kate and didn't care who knew it.

Ray knew that this was one of those moments that take your breath away, more precious than anything else in the world. It wasn't just because Kate had her tongue down his throat just about as far as it could go. Ray had never spent a moment with Kate that had not failed to amaze him, even when he was just sitting next to her at suppertime.

She was the greatest hostess in the living room, the best cook in the kitchen and the most amazing courtesan in the bedroom. Every moment he had ever spent with her had been an adventure that he would never forget. Even the most mundane things they had done together like standing in line at the ice cream parlor, or meandering through the booths at an antique mall seemed fresh and exciting when she was with him. Everything they did, every time their eyes met, every kiss, every touch, was filled with the promise of what lay ahead.

"It's so good to see you Kate," Ray whispered softly as Kate continued to hold him pressed tightly against her. She kissed him again. Very gently at first and then with a fierceness that took him by surprise.

"Mm mmm," murmured Kate. She could feel him press against her and released him slowly, allowing him to breathe once again.

"I do believe you may have missed me more than you care to admit."

"I'm not sure how I survived without you," said Ray as they collected his things and walked out to the parking lot holding hands. There was always something very special and amazing, a feeling so warm and welcoming about Kate's hug. The way she wrapped her arms around him and enveloped him with the softness of her body. Her fragrance and the loving kiss that followed her embrace always made him feel immensely loved and happy whenever he was with her. It was as if nothing else mattered when he was with her.

Kate smiled. It felt very nice to be appreciated.

Ray was an engineering consultant for an Oil and Gas Company in the Permian Basin. He was an expert in designing specialized drilling strategies to maximize the amount of oil that could be extracted from an oil field. He planned to continue working these for a few more years before retiring to live on Goose Island with Kate. In the meantime, he spent every other week with her counting down the seconds until he would see her again.

Kate and Ray had known each other for several years. They first met at Kate's store, the Goose Island Curiosity Shoppe. Ray had purchased a gift for his mother and struck up a casual conversation with Kate to inquire about the area. As Kate described Goose Island and the historical landmarks in the area near Port Aransas, Ray could not help noticing how beautiful she was, with her brown eyes, auburn hair and friendly, welcoming smile. Her love for Goose Island was evident in the way she described her hometown. Ray fell in love with her instantly and eventually with Goose Island as well.

For Kate and Ray, the breakers on Shipwreck Beach were infinitely more beautiful than any other place on the Texas Gulf Coast. The two of them loved to sit on the beach and watch the tide come in while they sipped on some Goose Island iced tea. Ray found it infinitely satisfying to hold Kate's hand and watch the clouds float across the horizon at sunset. An occasional stolen kiss reminded him how special it felt to be loved by her.

After the initial encounter that had taken Ray's breath away, their friendship had blossomed as they had gotten to know each other better. Ray had helped Kate remodel her house and transform it into the Golden Goose Bed and Breakfast. They had converted the patio to house the Goose Island Curiosity Shoppe and relocated it from the Goose Island Town Square for financial reasons.

They left the airport and walked to the parking garage across the terminal to her station wagon. Ray stowed his gear in the back seat and sat down next to Kate.

"Do you have any guests staying at the Bed and Breakfast this weekend?" Ray asked as Kate started the ignition on her station wagon.

"Nope," Kate replied with a twinkle in her eye. "Just you and me. My last visitors checked out earlier this week. They wanted to get back home to Chicago before all the kids showed up for Spring Break. My next guests arrive on Monday, so we have the place to ourselves this weekend. You might remember them from an earlier visit. Courtney and Glenda live on a farm in Nebraska and visit Goose Island every year around this time. They are wonderful houseguests. Sometimes I think they love Goose Island almost as much as I do myself."

"That's great," Ray replied. "I'm planning to stay until Monday night. Maybe I could catch a ride back to the airport with you when you go to pick them up."

"That should work," Kate said.

"If you don't have anything planned this weekend we could get started on the project to replace your kitchen counters," Ray added.

"I'd love that," Kate replied. "I want to get something in pink granite, if possible."

"I think that would look wonderful," Ray said. "That should match your unmentionables!" They listened to the radio playing songs from the sixties as they drove down the park road from Mustang Island to Port Aransas. "We have a lot of catching up to do, don't we?" Ray remarked.

"Yes," Kate agreed. She knew exactly what Ray had in mind.

"I can't wait to get home and throw you on the bed, pull your bloomers off and have my way with you." Ray said.

"I see that you've had a lot of time to think this through," Kate replied. "There's just one problem. I'm not wearing any."

"Good grief!" Ray exclaimed. Clearly, Kate had just thrown down the gauntlet, and there was no turning back now.

They stopped at a seafood restaurant overlooking the Laguna Madre on the way home. They ate on the patio watching the sunset over the water.

*   *   *

Kate and Ray knew something was amiss the moment they walked up to the front door. It was ajar and pretty much swinging freely in the breeze.

"Blue blistering barnacles! What in tarnation happened here? Did I forget to lock the door?" said Kate with a puzzled expression on her face. She had a sinking feeling in the pit of her stomach.

"I doubt it," said Ray pointing to evidence of splintered wood near the lock next to the door handle. "It looks as though someone forced the door open with a crowbar." Ray pushed the front door gingerly with his toe and stepped into the foyer tentatively, afraid to touch anything. He had once been arrested for having inadvertently picked up a gun that had been used as a murder weapon in a homicide. It had been a little inconvenient to have his fingerprints on the murder weapon.

Kate dialed 911. "Hello," she said. "I think that my house has been broken into." She proceeded to give the operator her street address.

"They sure made a mess," Ray whispered as he proceeded to go from room to room to check for strangers hiding behind the furniture.

Kate followed close behind him. She nodded in agreement. She had a very simple lock on her front door and if she wanted to get in it would have taken her less than sixty seconds to jimmy it open with a credit card. The intruders, whoever they were, were no longer on the premises. It was clear that whoever had broken into Kate's house had been searching for something. The doors to the closets in the bedrooms had been opened and left ajar. The door to the Golden Goose Curiosity Shoppe adjacent to the Bed and Breakfast had been kicked open. There were some shattered glass fragments on the floor. Whoever had been there had been in a hurry and had knocked over a crystal vase.

The sound of an approaching police siren and flashing red and blue lights interrupted Kate's thoughts. Deputy Sherriff Troy stepped out of the police cruiser and took her statement. He walked slowly through every room in the house and took some photographs of the damage to the front door and the door leading to the Curiosity Shoppe.

"It's very strange," he said, after studying the situation carefully. "They did not take anything of value. They didn't pick up the ear rings decorated with some reddish colored semi-precious stones or the matching necklace that you have on your dresser. Whoever came here went through your house as if they knew what they were looking for. It's almost as though they left when they did not find what they wanted. They were not in any hurry since they went through the house without making any attempt to ransack the place."

"I agree," said Kate. "Those are garnets," she added, pointing to the earrings. Kate was convinced that the thieves had not taken her jewelry, or opened her dresser drawers because the object they were looking for had been much larger. Perhaps it had been the seaman's chest that she had purchased earlier that day. They had not found it because it had not been at her house when they had broken in. The Russians might have figured out where she lived, but they still did not have the chest that they wanted.

Kate hesitated to tell Troy about her suspicions. She wondered if she should tell Troy about the three men whom she had met in Corpus Christi earlier that day. She decided against doing so. It was too complicated and she did not want to be viewed as being racist or discriminatory against the strangers. It had probably been a mistake to let them know that she lived on Goose Island. However, she had no evidence that they were involved and it did not seem right to jump to conclusions. It just seemed surprising that they had located her residence so quickly.

"Well, as long as nothing's missing, I guess there's no harm done," he said.

"I guess you are right Troy," she said. "Thanks for coming out here so promptly. I hope I didn't interrupt your evening."

"Not at all," said Troy. "It's always a pleasure to be of service."

There was nothing more to be done. Troy departed and the front door flapped uselessly in the evening breeze behind him, refusing to close. The taillights of the police vehicle disappeared down the street.

"I guess we better take care of that door tomorrow," said Ray. They pushed a large armchair against it to keep it closed on the inside.

"Maybe I'll borrow Milo from Jerry and Charlotte for protection," said Kate.

"That sounds like a good idea," said Ray.

Despite the late hour, they went next door to Jerry and Charlotte's house.

They need not have been concerned about disturbing the neighbors.

The light was on in the kitchen and Kate could see Charlotte peering out of her window trying to figure out what had happened next door.

*   *   *

"We were just about to come over to see if you needed any help," said Charlotte as she opened the front door. Jerry was standing right behind Charlotte and the look on his face echoed the concern that his spouse had just expressed.

"Come on in," Charlotte offered. "I've got some fresh coffee in the kitchen if you care for a cup." It wasn't long before she asked if they had had any dinner. Then she proceeded to prepare some fish tacos for them.

"Thanks Mom," said Ray as they traipsed into Charlotte's kitchen. He loved her homemade salsa.

"Thanks Charlotte," Kate said as she proceeded to explain what had happened. "It doesn't appear that they stole anything. The earrings and necklace my grandmother gave me are still on my dresser. They didn't even bother with them. I think they were looking for something else."

"You don't suppose they were looking for that sailor's trunk, do you?" Jerry asked Kate.

"If that is all they were looking for then it has to be the man who tried to buy it from me earlier today. I even gave him my card with my address on it," said Kate. "That was not very smart, was it?"

"Well, I'm glad they didn't get it," said Jerry. "I've never seen anything like it. Whoever owned it went to a lot of trouble to decorate it. It's been hand carved, probably with a mallet and a chisel. It must have taken years just to carve the ship on the trunk."

Jerry went on to explain that Bernard Gutmann had been able to open the locked trunk without difficulty. At Jerry's insistence, neither Bernard nor Jerry had taken a look inside the trunk after he had unlocked it. They walked into the den where Jerry had the trunk placed squarely in the center of the room. There was a hush in the room as everyone stopped to admire the exquisitely carved ship sailing serenely on the front of the trunk.

"Wow," said Ray finally. "That's a beautiful piece of work."

"Is there anything inside?" Kate asked, turning to Jerry.

"I'm not sure," Jerry replied. "I was waiting for you to return before taking a peek inside. Just wanted you to be the first to see what was inside."

"Thanks Jerry," Kate replied. "That's very thoughtful of you." She had not really considered the possibility that the trunk actually contained anything inside it. However, if it did then Jerry was right, she did want to be the first to see what was inside the trunk.

"But we do need to be careful!" Jerry added quickly. "The flag on the ship that's carved on one side of the trunk has a skull and crossbones design on it. The Gutmann brothers warned me that there could be a booby trap inside. It's not unusual for a pirate to protect his belongings with an extra dose of security."

"You're right!" whispered Kate, bending down for a closer look at the side of the trunk. "It does have a skull and crossbones design! So this really is a pirate's chest."

"Not just any pirate, Kate," said Jerry. "The carvings on the trunk are so exquisite that this could hardly be the chest of an ordinary pirate."

Ray couldn't keep his eyes off Kate. He loved watching her when she got interested and excited by something. He could sense the awakening of her spirit of adventure by the way she was breathing. It was evident that she was trying to soak in every detail on the carved trunk.

"I do think the idea of a booby trap seems a bit excessive" Kate said. "I guess pirates are just adolescents who never tire of playing games. What do you think I am going to find? A poison arrow held in place by a piano string that shoots me right through my heart when I open the lid?"

Jerry and Ray smiled.

"I'd certainly booby trap the trunk with a poisoned dart or two, especially if I was travelling in the company of other pirates. There are a lot of thieving blaggards out there, you know," Jerry said.

"If this trunk is as old as it looks, then it must have been handed down from one generation to the next. What if some small child was just curious and decided to open the trunk to see what was inside it?" Kate asked. "You wouldn't want to hurt your next of kin just for being curious would you?"

"If it belonged to me I would disable the booby trap," Ray replied. "I wouldn't want to harm anyone in my family."

"I guess that explains why it was locked," Charlotte said.

With all the talk about booby traps, the trunk had suddenly taken on a more ominous appearance. No one made a move to open the trunk and look inside. Due to the late hour, Kate decided to wait and open the pirate trunk the next day. It just didn't seem to be urgent enough to warrant keeping everybody up into the wee hours of the morning.

Jerry assured Kate that it was perfectly okay to leave the trunk with him and Charlotte. There was a light drizzle and Kate did not want to risk getting the trunk wet. As they walked back home, Kate and Ray could see the shadow of a police cruiser glide by them on Marlin Ave. with its lights off. Troy had called in a little extra protection for them and it was unlikely that the robbers were going to be back anytime that night. Besides, the trunk was not like jewelry that they could stuff in their pockets and then make a quick getaway. They would need to have virtually unrestricted access to the house for several minutes to haul the trunk out of the house and load it into their getaway vehicle.

Milo was a frequent visitor at Kate's house. Kate had borrowed him a few times in the past for added protection. He wagged his tail joyfully when he realized he was going to spend the night with Kate. It was going to give Milo an opportunity to chase the squirrel who lived in her backyard and who kept taunting him as it hopped across the limbs of the oak tree in Kate's yard. The squirrel took full advantage of the tree branches that reached well over the backyard fence.

Then Kate and Ray retired to the bedroom upstairs. It had been a long day and they were both tired. Kate was the first one in bed while Ray was still brushing his teeth. She watched him with anticipation as he walked over to the bed in his boxer shorts. Kate moved to make room for him to slip under the covers. He finally turned out the lights and jumped into bed before it was dark. They lay motionless next to each other for a minute listening to the blades of the fan turning steadily above them.

"What do you think is in that old pirate's trunk?" Ray asked Kate, giving her hand a small squeeze.

She turned to look at him and bent her left arm at the elbow to get closer to him. She leaned over and trapped him under her right arm. The twins looked down at him expectantly. Kate put her finger to her lips to silence him. She did not want to talk about the pirate trunk.

"A genie," she said finally biting her lower lip with a smile. "Here to grant you three wishes".

"I was hoping you'd say that," Ray whispered.

"The first wish is for me to be naked and in bed next to you," Kate replied. Leaning forward over him she gave him a long soulful kiss that seemed to last forever.

"How did you know what I always wanted?" he asked.

"That's easy," Kate replied. "I always know what you want because I can read your mind," she replied. She sat up and unbuttoned her shirt.

"Now there's a treasure map I know how to read," Ray whispered. He leaned forward to kiss her.

Kate swatted him away. "Now before I grant your other two wishes, are you going to behave or do I have to tie you down to get you to listen to me."

"But you don't know my other two wishes," Ray protested.

"Oh yes I do," Kate said firmly. She gave him a shove so that he fell back on the bed, quite unprepared for Kate's next move. Suddenly she was on top of him and her hands and lips were everywhere. Kate leaned over and yanked him towards her. She planted her lips against his and gave him a kiss with the surprise fury of a December squall that blows into town without warning, and leaves a calm in its wake that suggests that everything is all right with the world.

Ray could feel the room spinning around him. Oh, how he had missed her. The electric feeling that he had experienced when they had met at the airport returned with a vengeance. His senses were filled with her fragrance, the smell of lilacs, rose, jasmine and honey that enveloped him like the morning mist rolling over the water. It felt wonderful to be next to her again and to feel her warm, succulent body meld against his.

They separated for a moment and then Kate tumbled towards him in a rush and she kissed him repeatedly. She rose to ascend the solitary ray of light cast by the moonbeams shining through the bedroom window. When she fell back down, she was drenched with perspiration. Beads of sweat formed on her forehead and she could taste the salt water as it rolled down her cheeks. She lay prone on the deck of a pirate ship riding through the swells of the raging sea with waves crashing all around her. Just then it started to rain fiercely and the ship she was riding rose and fell with each new wave that rolled in across the ocean. Then it was just her and Ray riding out the storm, lashed to each other with invisible cords. Their ship kept moving out towards the open sea riding crosswise over the swells until the moon came out from behind the clouds and the sea was perfectly calm once again. They lay prone on the deck, holding hands, unable to move, drenched in each other's perspiration.

≈≈≈≈≈

Black Jack

Early Saturday morning Kate rode her bicycle over to the Goose Island Bakery for a cup of freshly brewed coffee and one of Shirley Winters' delicious carrot, raisin and walnut muffins. Shirley always added nutmeg and cinnamon to add to the flavor. Shirley had sprinkled chopped pistachios on top with a honey glaze that said "Eat Me" to anyone who saw them. The only thing better was the sliced blueberry, lemon cake with chocolate mint glaze that said "Eat Me First". That was before Kate rode up to the bakery, looking very hot in a well-balanced sort of way, in her cut-off jeans and sleeveless pirate T-shirt. She came to a brisk halt beside the bench in front of the bakery, leaned across the handlebars and parked her bike against the side of the building.

Despite the burglary attempt at her house the previous day, everything seemed downright cheerful. Birds chirped around her as she made her way past the trees in her neighborhood on Marlin Street. As she turned the corner onto Shore Drive, she was greeted by the sight of a flock of geese silhouetted against the morning sunrise slowly illuminating every corner of the sky. Kate could not help thinking about how much she loved living on Goose Island. She drove down to Goose Island Town Square, a small shopping area with stores along a set of Tic-Tac-Toe cross streets that surrounded City Hall in a checkerboard pattern. Kate locked her bicycle and chained it to an iron railing outside the store as the smell of freshly baked bread and freshly brewed coffee wafted out into the street.

Shirley had recently expanded the seating area in her bakery. The original store that Shirley and her mother Bridget had operated had room for only two small tables. Now the seating area opened up into an adjacent room she had leased from Kenneth Porter, the owner of more than half of all the property in the Goose Island downtown district. There was a small step down between the bakery and the adjacent room, which had formerly been an accountant's office on the corner of Shore Drive and Main Street. There were two large windows along the wall. The new windows had opened up the bakery and allowed Shirley to look across the street at the people passing by on the sidewalk outside. The additional space had allowed her to add four nice tables along the windows that faced Shore Drive.

Ray and Troy had done most of the construction work at the bakery. They had installed new double-paned windows overlooking Shore Drive, tiled the floor, painted the walls and generally reworked the interior. Kate had to admit that the expansion was nice.

She was not happy about Shirley's lease agreement with Kenneth Porter. Kate was convinced that Ken had been dealt from the bottom deck of life's gene pool. Left to herself she would never have entered into any type of relationship with Ken. "You can't trust Ken any further than you can throw him," Kate had told Shirley when she had first heard of the plan. "He'll do his best to make you believe he's your best friend, but if you ever fall behind on a single payment you will regret it for the rest of your life."

"It's strictly business, Kate," Shirley had replied. "Besides, it's not a lease. It's a lease-purchase. Someday I'll be the sole owner of both sides of my bakery. And if anything happens in the interim, I'll have to go back to the way it was before."

Kate knew that life was just not that simple. Shirley could no more go back to her earlier bakery accommodations than she could go to a Vegan diet after having lived on meat and potatoes most of her life.

Kenneth Porter was a large man. Kate had no idea how much he weighed, but he was remarkably agile for someone his age and weight. His well-rounded belly was quite an unforgettable sight on the beach whenever he appeared in his slingshot swimming briefs. If you happened to be present at the time, it was always a relief when he entered the water. Then you could turn your attention back to what you were doing before he had clouded your vision with his torso as it did the calypso to the sound of the waves.

"So when do you make the last payment on the lease-purchase?" Kate inquired.

"Just a shade less than twenty nine years," Shirley said. "It's the best I could do Kate," she protested. "It's not as if I could walk into a bank and get a loan. Ken Porter was more than willing to work with me."

"Just keep a rolling pin handy in case he decides to come on your side of the counter, Sis!" Kate replied. "There's a lot of other things that he'd like to help you with, Shirley, such as helping you step out of your jeans."

*　　*　　*

GOOSE ISLAND BLACK JACK

As Kate entered the bakery, she saw Ken sitting at a table by the window. They nodded to each other like wrestlers entering a ring and Kate walked over to the counter to place her order. Ken gave his 'Mona Lisa' smile, the one that made Kate wonder if she had forgotten to put on her bra. She reached inside her T-shirt for the reassuring grip of the elastic strap. Ken's face broke into a broad grin as he blew her a kiss. Not to be outdone Kate blew one right back at him. As she greeted Shirley, she could see Ken's reflection in the mirror behind the counter, observing her movements surreptitiously as he pretended to drink his coffee. He was a completely incorrigible, prototypical, dirty old man of sixty-five regardless of whether he was slurping down his coffee, licking his lips, or gazing hungrily at the nearest female figure over the top of his bifocals. Kate bent down provocatively to adjust her sandals and watched in the mirror as the coffee cup slipped out of his hands. "Mission accomplished," she thought and smiled with satisfaction.

Ken had dated Jan, one of the servers at the Italian restaurant on the other side of the Goose Island Square. Jan was drop-dead gorgeous and Kate could never figure out why someone like Jan would condescend to spend fifteen minutes with Ken, let alone go out with him for an entire evening. He was a compulsive liar who could not be trusted any time there was food or money involved. Or sex. That was never going to change. A year after they had been living together, Jan found out that Ken was having an affair with one of his tenants. Heartbroken, she had left Goose Island and moved back home to Albuquerque. Ken had lost the best thing that had ever happened to him and the irony of it was that he did not even know it.

Kate brought Shirley up to date on the recent burglary at the Golden Goose B&B. It was not the sort of thing that happened very often on Goose Island. Shirley listened attentively even as she bustled around behind the bakery counter. She had French braided her hair in a very unusual style with a loose bun and had on a pair of large silver earrings. She looked like someone from the fifteenth century Renaissance period. Kate couldn't help noticing that she looked very professional and aristocratic.

Kate was just about to take Shirley into her confidence and describe the carvings on the pirate trunk when she saw a shadow outside the entrance to the bakery. She paused and looked away immediately as soon as she recognized the person who had just entered. She moved away from the counter just as the door opened. It was Henri, the elderly man with the ponytail from the police auction in Corpus Christi". His other two colleagues shuffled in behind him and took up their places at the bakery counter.

Shirley seemed to be falling over herself to serve the trio from Europe. Kate was sure she was going to trip over her dress. "Oh my goodness," Kate thought to herself. Her dress! It had suddenly dawned on Kate that little Miss T-shirt and blue jeans was actually wearing a beautiful white dress with frills and lace. Something in her demeanor had definitely changed. She was more attuned to serving the Russians than she was to giving Kate the time of day. In fact she seemed to have forgotten that Kate was still in the bakery. Kate wandered over towards a table at the end of the room and sat down to drink her coffee.

"Hot in here," Ken remarked, as she walked past his table. He paused to put down his blue berry muffin and offered Kate the vacant seat at his table.

"Yes it is," Kate replied, sitting down across from Ken without stopping to consider what she was doing. "Rather warm for March, isn't it."

"It's warm enough for July," Ken said. "Why don't you take your shirt off and cool down?"

"Why stop there?" Kate said. She rose and sat down several tables away.

"Why indeed," Ken replied with a smile. "I must hand it to you Kate. I heard you were the big winner at the auction down in Corpus this week. What's all mystery about the nautical antiques that you purchased?"

"I have no idea what you are talking about, Ken," Kate replied.

"Yes you do," Ken remarked. "We are all family here Kate. Any artifacts that you find here belong to all of us no-name cave dwellers and you know that. Please think of me as one of your friendly coastal Uncles. I have known you from the time you were a baby."

"Really, Ken," Kate said. "I think I would know if I were related to you. As I recall you didn't exactly do me any favors when I rented the storefront across the street. The only attention I received from you was when you were trying to rub up against me behind the cash register or look down my shirt whenever you stopped by the store for your rent."

Ken wilted before Kate's thinly veiled look of contempt. Kate wondered what he knew about the trunk she had purchased at auction. It was funny how quickly word got around in a small town like Goose Island. By tomorrow morning everyone on the island would be looking at her as if she had won a billion dollars in the Power Ball Lottery and lining up outside her front door for their share of the prize.

"What would you like to have today, Louis," said Shirley in a cheerful voice addressing the tall, young, unshaven Frenchman who was standing before her. Louis was looking disinterestedly at Shirley. She was looking at him as if he was a blueberry stud-muffin. His older companions were studying the selections in the bakery display.

"Bonjour Mademoiselle. How are you?" said Louis. He had not noticed Kate as his eyes were still adjusting to the change in lighting inside the bakery.

"Just ducky!" said Shirley. "Tally ho to you too." She was positively beaming at him.

Louis was wearing a pale blue cardigan that looked very stylish and European. Kate wondered how he managed to keep the stubble on his face always looking as if he had not shaved for a week. Did he shave periodically and just let it grow back, or did he trim it with some type of special trimmer? "He probably has a girl friend to take care of all his special needs," Kate thought. He did not look like someone who had ever owned a shaving razor.

The cardigan was a huge turn off for Kate. It looked very European, perhaps even a little effeminate. However, it seemed to be having the opposite effect on Shirley who seemed to be attracted to him in a 'bad boy' sort of way.

"Would you care for some fresh coffee and a muffin?" Shirley asked Louis.

"Yes, please," said Louis. "You don't have any éclairs, do you?"

"Not today," said Shirley. "We are all sold out of éclairs and apple tarts. However, if you check back with me next week I promise we'll have some fresh fruit tarts".

Kate could not help thinking that there was at least one fresh tart behind the bakery counter. There was definitely something going on between the two of them. Something in the way Shirley had served Louis seemed out of character. She had taken the time to dip a fresh strawberry in molten chocolate and place it next to the muffin. As Louis reached for the plate, she had paused to lick the excess chocolate off her index finger in a most provocative manner. Her finger seemed to stay in her mouth far longer than necessary.

"Thank you. That's wonderful," said Louis as he reached over the top of the bakery counter to take his plate.

"Ah Mademoiselle!" he exclaimed turning as he noticed Kate for the first time.

"Why hello Louis," said Kate in the sweetest voice she could muster. "How nice to see you again." This was a most unpleasant surprise! Kate thought to herself. She was sure his other two companions were not far behind.

"He's from out of town," said Shirley helpfully. "From 'Boredough', France. The place that makes the best wine in the world, right?" she added, looking at Louis admiringly.

"France! Of course. They were French, not Russian," Kate thought to herself. She realized that she would have to tell Shirley about Napa Valley over a bottle of Cabernet some evening. Perhaps she could organize a weekly wine tasting event at the Golden Goose Bed and Breakfast. There was no doubt in her mind that her new houseguests, Courtney and Glenda would love the idea and she could invite Charlotte and Jerry over as well. A few sips of the warm cherry flavors of her favorite Cabernet from Napa Valley, would leave no doubt in Shirley's mind about where the best wines in the world were to be had. Kate had often thought about bottling her very own brand of Goose Island Houlihan hooch, but had just never gotten around to it.

"Yes," said Louis who seemed to be a very taciturn person with very little to say for himself.

"Louis was telling me that it's real close to the coast of France," Shirley added. "Near a place called 'Rose Biscuits', or 'Biscuit Rows'. They have some places there where people walk around naked on the beach without bothering to cover up their biscuits," she whispered.

"I see," Kate replied. "We have a few places like that right here in Texas." She smiled at Shirley's Texan pronunciation of Biscarosse, a town in France she had heard about in college. In ancient times, girls who were judged to be 'promiscuous' by city officials were forced to stand naked on a barrel underneath an elm tree in Biscarosse for a day. It seemed like a clever way for a bunch of perverts to get some free adult entertainment at someone else's expense. Legend has it that one girl had died of exhaustion in the fifteenth century before the practice had eventually been discontinued.

"So who are Huey and Dewey?" she asked Shirley after a pause.

Shirley frowned. She could tell that Kate had not accepted the newcomers from France as warmly as she had.

"Louis is visiting Goose Island with his Dad, Henri and Uncle Sebastian," added Shirley helpfully.

"How nice," said Kate. "Have you seen Troy?" she asked Shirley pointedly.

"Not today," Shirley replied dismissively. She seemed more interested in consorting with strangers than in her fiancée.

"Never mind," said Kate. She wondered if Shirley had been the one who had directed these unsavory individuals to her house the day it had been broken into. She had probably told them all about the trunk as well. It was quite evident that Shirley had gussied up her appearance for Louis' benefit. She had even unbuttoned the top of her blouse so that the contour of her breasts was clearly visible as she went about her business behind the counter. Kate shrugged. It was spring. If Shirley's pheromones had decided to kick it up a notch there was nothing anyone could do about it. Shirley seemed to be determined to straighten the muffins in the display case every time Louis was around to glance at her cleavage. The only question was how Troy would react to this sudden change in the woman he had courted for the better part of the last decade.

"What have you done with the beautiful wooden trunk you bought at the auction?" Papa Henri asked Kate.

Kate's eyes narrowed. Was this just an innocent question, or was he asking about its whereabouts because he had broken into her house the day before and been unable to find it anywhere? She saw no reason to explain that it was in her neighbor, Jerry's house. Henri's interest in the trunk suggested that there was something very special about it.

"Why it's in my living room, of course," she replied glibly.

Henri was not convinced. His demeanor suggested that he knew Kate was not telling the truth.

"Henri's the owner of an antique store in Victoria," Shirley added by way of explanation, as if she could read the unasked question in Kate's mind.

"How very interesting," Kate said. The information did not endear him to her. "Do you by any chance own the Antique Mall on Maple Street?" she inquired. "I just love that place!"

"Thank you so much!" Henri remarked. "It is so nice to be appreciated. We have been dealing in Antiques for years."

"Liar, liar, pants on fire!" Kate thought to herself. "I see," she said. She had just caught Henri in a barefaced lie. There was no Antique Mall on Maple Street in Victoria, Texas. Kate had just made that up. For all she knew there was no Maple Street in Victoria, either. Kate had never liked the Antique Malls in Victoria. She was pretty sure she did not like Huey, Dewey and Louie very much either. As far as she could recall, the Antique Malls in Victoria specialized in antique reproductions and inexpensive imitation pieces that were significantly more economical to stock when compared to the original artifacts that they were based on. A genuine, Depression glass bowl could easily retail for fifty dollars. However, the Antique

Malls in Victoria and the other larger cities in Texas seemed to have an endless supply of similarly designed glassware for sale at a substantial discount.

"Of course, Mademoiselle," Henri said, turning to Shirley. "We have been the suppliers for a number of antique stores throughout the Southwest. Not long ago we saw a tremendous opportunity in Goose Island and plan to open a new store here within few months with some help from Mr. Porter."

Kate's eyes widened. Ken Porter's involvement in the venture changed the equation. There was something fishy going on and Kate could not help wondering what it was. Ken never got involved in anything unless there were large sums of money changing hands or pretty women involved in the transaction. Preferably, both! Since there were no hot looking women hanging around the three stooges, Kate was not surprised that Ken had just weaseled his way into another lucrative business deal.

Kate was convinced that Henri and Sebastian were after the sailor's trunk and the secret that it contained. She had a strong suspicion that they were involved in the recent burglary attempt at her house. The break in had occurred immediately after the auction, even though she had told Henri that she was willing to consider his offer to purchase the trunk when they had met at the convention center. The timing suggested that the intruders either did not want to pay what the trunk was worth, or they had wanted to take the trunk away from her before she had had a chance to look inside. Jerry was right; the trunk was worth way more than a thousand dollars.

"We are still getting settled into the area," Henri continued. "I hear that you have a wonderful Bed and Breakfast establishment close by. Do you have a room available for lease for a few weeks?"

"I'm so sorry Monsieur," Kate replied. "I'm completely booked right now."

"And thank goodness for that!" she thought to herself. Her skin bristled at the thought of giving these villainous individuals carte-blanche access to her house. There was simply no way she was going to entertain the notion of Henri traipsing through the Goose Island Bed and Breakfast with a hall pass to meander through her boudoir at all hours. Good Grief! The thought of having him stay at her place made her skin crawl. As the sole proprietor of the B&B, thank goodness she could refuse the right to serve anyone she considered a blaggard, thief or no good villain.

"I understand," Henri replied. "Do let me know if you decide to put the trunk for sale.

I believe it may be of French origin and quite possibly that it belongs to one of my ancestors. It has a great deal of sentimental value for me."

"I'll call you immediately if I decide to sell the trunk," Kate replied. "However, honestly it looks more Irish than French to me. Sorry, I have to rush off. It was so nice to meet you again, Henri."

"Yes please Mademoiselle," said Henri. "I would be willing to pay you any reasonable amount for the trunk," he said.

"That's so very generous. It was nice to meet you both," said Kate. She waved goodbye to Shirley and Louis who were still chatting at the counter. Henry and Sebastian sat down at a table by the window as she stepped out of the bakery. She gave them the finger as soon as the door closed behind her.

Shirley had done a super job of placing potted plants strategically around the bakery. She had picked plants that required infrequent watering such as the bromeliads near the tables by the window. Out of the corner of her eye, she could see Ken using his X-ray vision to stare at her profile admiringly. She sucked in her stomach. You had to admit that a man of his girth and appetite for blueberry muffins was the Goose Island Bakery's best friend. He was a walking advertisement for her establishment. She really did not mind him as long as he was helping her pay off her loan with every donut and muffin he purchased from her.

*   *   *

"So how much exactly was 'any reasonable amount'?" Kate wondered. It had to be more than the five thousand dollars Henri had originally offered her immediately after the auction. If she doubled the offer, it would be ten thousand dollars. That was twenty times what she had paid for the chest. That was actually a lot of money. Kate could not wait to return home and look at it again. There was something very peculiar and mysterious about it. She was sure it held the key to some long lost secret.

She drove back to her house on Marlin Street. The Golden Goose Bed and Breakfast had blossomed into an iconic Goose Island establishment since Kate had first opened her doors. It already had a steady set of repeat customers who typically stayed for several weeks while on vacation at Goose Island. Her next houseguests, Courtney and Glenda were due to come into town from Nebraska within a few days. They were planning to stay with her for about six weeks, through the end of April. They had stayed with her every year since she had been in business. It was very comforting to have their approval and to see them come back every year.

Turning her house into a Bed and Breakfast had been a big change for Kate. Getting the place decorated and ready for use had been a lot of fun and hard work. Kate had had lots of help from all her friends and neighbors. Ray had helped remodel her patio and it now housed the Golden Goose Curiosity Shoppe. She had traded her personal privacy for financial freedom. Business had been very good. The extra income had even helped finance a few small improvements to the establishment, the most recent being the granite counter tops that she was having installed in her kitchen.

Ray made short work of the muffins that Kate had brought home from the bakery. They sat in Kate's kitchen watching Milo dart around happily in their backyard. Milo came up to greet Kate and Ray as they entered the patio with their coffee and sat down at the table next to a small fountain that Ray had engineered during one of his earlier weekend visits. Milo had a puzzled look on his face as if he was wondering why the squirrels were always on the other side of the fence.

It took Kate the rest of the morning to apprise Ray of the events that had transpired at the police auction the previous day, including her encounters with the cloud of three

Frenchmen who suddenly kept appearing wherever she went. "Wow," he said when she finished bringing him up to date. "I can't wait to see this trunk you have acquired. It must really be something special."

"It is," Kate said, beaming. She was very proud of her recent acquisition. We will have to go over to Charlotte and Jerry's house tonight. Jerry's keeping an eye on it for me, on account of the break-in.

"That's mighty nice of him," Ray said. He knew that Charlotte and Jerry treated Kate like a daughter.

Kate and Ray took a bottle of red wine to the trunk opening ceremony at Charlotte's house in the afternoon. Ray let out a low whistle when he saw the trunk in the middle of the living room.

Charlotte brought out her best crystal flutes. Technically speaking they were champagne glasses, but they worked just as well with red wine. Then they began the serious business of opening the trunk.

Kate allowed Ray to do the honors. He used a broom handle to push open the lid, lying on the floor beside the trunk for added safety. He opened the lid easily and very, very slowly.

"Any pirate would know that you were going to do that and shoot the poison arrows out the sides of the trunk," Kate said jovially trying to boost Ray's morale as he began this delicate operation. He paused and placed some pillows from the sofa between himself and the trunk.

Ray was going at it rather slowly and Kate, Jerry and Charlotte were peering into the trunk from the sides rather impatiently. Suddenly the lid sprang open and startled them all. There was a puff of smoke when the trunk opened and Kate had visions of everything disintegrating into a cloud of sand right before her eyes. However, the smoke was simply the dust that had accumulated inside the trunk over decades of neglect. There was a brace to hold the lid in place and they affixed it to the stop inside the trunk.

Kate looked inside the trunk. Inside there was nothing but a few seashells on a bed of sand and the remains of what had once been a handsome bouquet of flowers. From all appearances, the flowers had once been roses. They were faded with grey and pale reddish-brown hues. Perhaps the flowers had once been red and white. The trunk must have been completely air tight for the flowers to survive for so long, or perhaps they had been added to the trunk. It made sense for a sailor's trunk to have a nice tight seal, to keep out humidity and to preserve the contents from the elements. "Were these the flowers from a wedding on the beach?" Kate wondered.

Kate was not sure what she had expected to find in the trunk. The flowers were definitely a surprise. She brushed the sand aside and tried to see if there was something else inside the trunk. However, that was all. Everybody looked a little disappointed. After the first rush of opening the trunk, this seemed a little anticlimactic. Kate and Ray, and Jerry and Charlotte looked at the trunk and then back at each other as if to say, "Well, I guess that's it, then".

It was Charlotte who first noticed the etching of the mermaid at the base of the trunk. She was sitting on a rock looking out over the water. Ray and Jerry went into the garage to fetch a tarp and then the two of them emptied the sand out of the trunk so that they could get a closer look at the mermaid. It was a beautiful carving and every detail of her lithe figure was carved in the most life like manner possible. The mermaid was wearing a ruby necklace and a diamond encrusted white hibiscus flower in her hair. Her long hair streamed behind her and seemed to meld into the waves beneath the rock.

"My goodness, she is really beautiful," Jerry said.

"I agree," said Ray.

Charlotte and Kate looked at each other. The boys were hypnotized by the mermaid's voluptuous figure and seemed to have just one thought in mind. Charlotte was looking at the trunk quizzically and Kate realized that she had noticed something else. They both reached for the black onyx rock that the mermaid was perched upon and pressed it at the same time.

Suddenly the base of the trunk flew open. The mermaid split apart unevenly at the waist with the two sides following the contour of the scales along her body. Underneath was a small secret compartment. Folded neatly at the very bottom of the trunk was a large black, white and gold canvas sheet. Kate removed it carefully, spilling some of the rose petals on the floor. She opened the sheet carefully and placed it on the dining table. They all looked at it in silence.

"Wow!" said Ray finally. "That's got to be a pirate flag."

"Indeed it is," said Kate.

"I'll be darned," said Jerry.

"Oh my goodness," said Charlotte.

The flag that lay before her was magnificent. It was made of a white canvas material that had been painted painstakingly in black and gold. She could picture it billowing on top a mast on a pirate ship bouncing jauntily over the waves on the open sea.

The skull wore a black and white cap with gold trim. There was a golden eagle emblazoned on front. The hollowed out eyes on the skull seemed to jump off the canvas material. The teeth were arranged in a cheerful, rakish smile. The skull seemed to be foaming at the mouth as though a waterfall was spewing out of the skull's mouth. The water cascaded out of the skulls mouth and seemed to flow to the right side, wrapping itself over and over the pirate sword on the right.

There were flecks of gold in the water and all over the flag. The eye sockets in the skull seemed to have been brushed with gold dust because they had a sheen that glistened in the light. The mouth on the skull was a broken, jagged opening that curled up toward the right side in a wicked smile. Something about it suggested a madman swinging through the air on a rope, with a knife between his teeth was "coming to get you mate". It gave Kate the chills just to look at it.

There were even some moderately sized crystals sewn into the flag that sparkled like diamonds. There was a baguette diamond sewn in the middle of each eye socket and one humongous baguette on one of the pirate's front teeth. Kate looked at it carefully. "My goodness!" she said. "These look like real diamonds." As she studied the irregular shape of the eye sockets she realized each eye was a mirror image of the other eye.

GOOSE ISLAND BLACK JACK

It took her breath away just to look at it. She wasn't sure which one of the two artifacts was more breathtaking, the seaman's trunk, or the pirate flag. The latter made it clear that it wasn't just any seaman's trunk. It was a pirate's trunk, one that had perhaps belonged to the pirate King of the Gulf Coast, himself, Jean Lafitte.

The colorless, round cut diamond tooth on the pirate flag alone was probably worth far more than ten thousand dollars. Kate might not have known very much about old wooden trunks, but she certainly knew a high quality rock when she saw one. It had to be at least five carats. The baguette diamonds in each eye were smaller, but not by much. The flawless artisanship of the carvings that adorned the trunk and the quality of the diamonds in the flag was astounding. Taken all together it made the flag worth more than a hundred thousand dollars even before taking into account its vintage, or whom its original owner may have been.

"Oh my! It's really beautiful," said Charlotte after everyone had had time to catch their breath. "It takes me back at least a hundred years just to look at it, maybe more. The chest looks like it must be French. Antique French furniture seems to have more hand-carved motifs on it than furniture from any other region."

"It does look French," Kate agreed. It must be a long way from home. The owner must have been a pirate of French origin.

"Maybe not so far," countered Charlotte. France owned large swaths of land in North America at one time. That was before they sold it to us for little or nothing.

Kate recalled hearing about the Louisiana Purchase when she had studied American History in school. It had accounted for all the land that comprised fifteen states within America and a small part of Canada. Napoleon had agreed to sell it to the United States after France had failed to put down an insurrection in the island nation of Saint-Domingue.

"You can almost imagine a sea captain taking it all over the world with him. Someone like Captain Cook," Jerry said. "I think he was the first man to sail around the world. Can you imagine what an adventure that must have been?"

"Especially when you consider that he had to navigate with no maps, just a sextant and the stars," Ray said"

"I suppose he must have stopped at every port on his way and talked to the locals to learn the lay of the land. The risks and uncertainty of traveling into uncharted waters must have been tremendous," Kate added.

"What do you think the trunk is doing here in Nueces County?" Charlotte asked. "I know we have a lot of talk about finding pirate treasure here, but isn't that just an urban myth? Isn't all the pirate treasure located further along the Gulf Coast, north east of here?"

"You mean like Galveston, or New Orleans?" Kate asked, referring to the hot bed of piracy from the eighteen hundreds. Her mind was racing nineteen to the dozen as she tried to connect the dots in her mind. Having dealt with antiques much of her life she could not help recalling that Jean Lafitte had once based his pirate operations in Galveston, and before that in the swamplands of Barataria just south of New Orleans.

The elaborate design of the skull and crossbones on the pirate flag was breathtaking. It was more than just iconic. Each element of the flag seemed to flow to the next such as the water spewing out of the mouth and wrapped around one of the swords. Could this possibly be a map of some kind? Kate wondered. This could be the map to Jean Lafitte's hidden treasure! The thought was chilling. It made the hair stand up on her arms and the nape of her neck.

"Exactly" replied Charlotte, answering the question Kate had just posed before stepping off the gangplank and falling into the water without making a splash. "New Orleans was overflowing with pirates about two hundred years ago. Pirates controlled most of the outlying areas, especially the islands and marshland just south of New Orleans."

"You must mean Barataria," said Kate. "I think that was Jean Lafitte's stronghold in New Orleans."

"There you go," replied Charlotte.

"I guess that's possible," said Kate. However, she was clearly not convinced. It seemed unbelievable that her purchase of a trunk at a police auction could be a map to the buried treasure that every teenager on the Gulf Coast must have dreamed of finding at some point in his or her life.

Kate recalled that unlike the other pirates, Jean Lafitte was bolder and more brazen than the rest. Women loved this quality and were drawn to save him from self-destruction. It would be just like him to flaunt the map to his treasure openly for all to see on the mast of his ship. The more Kate studied the pirate flag the more she became convinced that it contained a hidden map of some kind, with the diamonds sewn into the fabric of the map representing the pirate treasure hidden at that location. Since there were three large diamonds sewn into the flag, one on the pirate's tooth, as well as one in each eye it suggested there were three locations where the treasure was distributed. She would be delighted to unearth just one of these.

They folded the flag neatly and replaced it in the chest. As they placed it back upon the bed of dried rose petals inside the chest, Kate realized that the four persons present in the room, including her, were probably the first people to view the flag in decades. Otherwise the rose petals would have been below, not above the flag when they had removed it from the chest a short while ago. It also explained the inordinate amount of money she had been offered for the trunk after the auction, and the subsequent break-in attempt at her house to prevent her from access to its contents.

Kate was reluctant to take the pirate chest and pirate flag back to her house because of the robbery attempt the previous day. It was obviously worth more than she had ever dreamed of, or imagined. However, since the burglars who had broken into her house had failed to find it there the previous day she decided to take her chances with it. Under cover of darkness Ray carried it out the back door of Charlotte and Jerry's house and they snuck it into the Goose Island B&B. The carried it upstairs to Kate's bedroom and sat down briefly to catch their breath.

"I don't think anyone saw us", Kate whispered.

"How could they?" Ray inquired. "They were too busy watching the most beautiful girl in the world float across the lawn."

"Hold that thought while I get my broom," Kate said, getting up to freshen up.

"We'll need that for our trip to the moon and back," Ray answered.

≈≈≈≈≈

Dolphins

Ray was still asleep when she awoke. He looked adorable, sleeping so peacefully in her bed. Kate drew the blinds to keep out the daylight. She was going to let him rest-up for a bit. She tiptoed quietly downstairs and started a pot of coffee.

The first thing that she noticed as she sat down at the kitchen table and took the first sip was a message on her answering machine. It was from an someone in New Orleans, offering to purchase the seaman's trunk. No way! Kate did not intend to sell the trunk without first uncovering whatever secrets had remained hidden within it for so long. She picked up the phone and dialed the telephone number on the recorded message. After a few rings, it was evident that the party she had dialed was not available. She left a message indicating that the trunk was not for sale.

Kate was determined to find out more about the trunk. It amazed her that the previous owner had not discovered the trunk's secret compartment or the flag at the bottom of the trunk. Both the trunk and the flag were priceless artifacts that deserved better care and handling. It must have been a family heirloom that had been passed down across several generations. Had no one before her noticed the rock beneath the mermaid that unlocked the secret compartment within the trunk? Kate felt certain that determining the identity of the previous owner could provide one of the keys to finding the treasure.

Kate observed the trunk carefully, looking for clues to help establish its identity. A small coat of arms had been engraved in one corner of the trunk's surface. It portrayed a cross emblazoned on a shield and embellished with a floral motif. She sat down at her computer desk and did a search on the internet to see if she could discover one with a similar design to match the carvings on the top of the chest. There was a pair of dolphins facing each other in each of the upper quadrants of the cross and a mermaid perched around an anchor in the quadrant on the lower right side of the coat of arms. To the left of the mermaid was a single tropical flower that resembled a hibiscus.

Kate settled down at her desk and did her best to interpret these nautical symbols with the help of the internet. As she browsed the internet, she realized that the dolphins are often viewed as a symbol of charity. In ancient Greece, Arion, a musical prodigy, was rescued at sea by dolphins. Legend has it that Arion had just won a music competition in Sicily. He was returning home from the tournament when he was attacked by pirates, eager to steal his prize money. The pirates allowed him to play his instrument one last time before they threw him overboard. Some dolphins were drawn to the music he played, just before he jumped into the sea. They carried him safely to shore. In early Christian times, the symbol for Christ was the fish. The Greek word for FISH was comprised of the first letters of each of the words for Jesus Christ, Son of God, and Savior. Christians in Greece used this as a symbol of recognition amongst themselves whilst hiding their true identities from Roman authorities.

Kate found a number of family crests on the internet that were similar to the one that she was looking for, but none that was an exact match. Dolphins appeared on the crests of the Dolphin family, in Ireland and the royal coat of arms of the French D'auFin until the time of the French Revolution. The carvings on the trunk indicated a family that was committed to protecting the weak from harm. Kate recalled that Jean Lafitte had been such a person, a modern day Robin Hood. His reputation as a gentleman pirate and a ladies' man was also legendary. He loved his children as much as he had loved the women who had borne them for him. No doubt, this had endeared him even more to the women who had chosen to give themselves to him. If Jean Lafitte was indeed the original owner of the chest then he must have created his own unique family crest to pass down to future generations.

Under normal circumstances, a trunk like the one she had just acquired should never have appeared at a police auction. Something very unusual must have happened to the previous owner of the trunk for it to fall into the hands of the authorities. Kate scoured the obituaries on the web pages of several area newspapers, including the Rockport News. There were so many entries to go through. It seemed like an insurmountable task until she decided to look for someone who had passed away within the last six months and who had an Irish or a French surname. It was not long before she felt that she had a match.

Mr. and Mrs. Zachary Dubois had both died recently in a fiery car crash during the first week of the year, just two days after New Year's Eve. Kate remembered the accident because it had closed down Highway 35 between Rockport and Fulton for hours. Zachary and Nicole had been on their way home when their car had gone out of control, spun across the highway, overturned and gone careening down Highway 35 on its roof. Their car had some to a halt only after it collided with a guardrail on the other side of the highway, narrowly missing the path of the oncoming traffic. The guardrail had prevented it from ending up in Copano Bay. Both the occupants of the car had died almost instantly. Kate recalled hearing the sirens as emergency vehicles had rushed to their rescue in a futile attempt to save their lives.

Something about the way Zachary and Nicole's lives had ended seemed very wrong. There seemed to be no good reason for an elderly couple to be going that fast. Kate located a newspaper report that provided a summary of the crash without giving any specific reasons for its cause. The reporter had speculated that perhaps the driver had fallen asleep at the wheel. Readers were left to presume that the elderly couple driving peacefully along Highway 35 on a pleasant January afternoon had just dozed off with his foot on the accelerator, lost control, flipped over and died. This smacked of age discrimination. It was such a stereotypical response to suggest that an accidental highway death should be accepted because of they were obviously an old and feeble-minded couple. Even though there are thousands of individuals who come to an unexpected end each year on the highways across Texas, they don't all have an antique trunk worth a small fortune in their car at the time of the accident. Kate was sure that someone in New Orleans, or Huey Dewey and Louie had something to do with the accident. They were either directly responsible for Zachary and Nicole's death or vultures who had descended on the scene of the accident to pick apart their carcasses.

Kate checked the weather conditions at the time of the accident and found that traffic conditions were about as normal as they could get, sans ice, fog, rain, construction closures or any other extenuating circumstances. The crash had not occurred on a particularly busy day, and the driver of the vehicle had not suffered from a heart attack, stroke, or any other unexpected ailment that could have caused the accident. Kate could not help wondering if they had been the victims of foul play. If Zachary and Nicole Dubois had been of sound mind and in reasonably good health, then they should not have died in this manner.

Why had the police not investigated the accident more thoroughly? Was it just negligence or were they in on it too? Kate respected the authorities and was very thankful for the services they provided, but she did not trust them implicitly. Perhaps due to all the fake news propagated by the media and the movies, Kate was convinced that there were a fair number of corrupt individuals masquerading as police officers. It had taken her some time to get used to Troy, and he was the only person who was about as honest as the day is bright.

As she studied the obituary in the newspaper, Kate noticed that the survivors included Zachary and Nicole's daughter Lucy Matthews of Galveston, a local artist who had grown up in Rockport. This came as a huge surprise. Kate knew Lucy personally. Lucy had had been one of the very first guests at Kate's fledgling Goose Island Bed and Breakfast enterprise. Lucy loved to paint and she had gone down to Shipwreck Beach several times when she had stayed at the B&B. Kate had one of Lucy's paintings on display in the lobby of the Goose Island Bread and Breakfast. Kate loved the tranquility of the palm trees next to the water in Lucy's painting. The beige sandy beach, greenish-brown palm trees and a myriad of blue hues in the water made the ocean flecked with white tips come to life under a spectacular red sunrise on a cloudy morning. Lucy had moved away from Goose Island after losing her husband a few years earlier. What a shame for her to have so many tragic events occur in her family. She would have to contact Lucy and let her know about the trunk.

*   *   *

The front door of the Golden Goose was still in need of repair and so a trip to the neighborhood hardware store seemed to be in order. Kate and Ray made a quick trip to the hardware store and picked up a brand new pre-hung door. Ray picked up an assortment of steel plates to reinforce all of the front and the back entrances to Kate's house.

While Ray was picking up the supplies they needed to repair the front door, Kate browsed through the remodeling section of the store looking at various samples of granite for the kitchen counter. There was a dazzling array of choices. Granite was available in hundreds of colors depending on its origin and the mineral deposits in the local area where the stone had been mined. There were also several edge finish options to choose from, ranging from a rounded finish to one with the edges squared off.

She narrowed down her selection to a pair of alternate granite choices, both with a rounded edge finish. The store gave her a small four square inch sample of each to try out at home to try out at home before making a final decision. Ray joined her as she was making her final selections. They located a counter top planning guide, which allowed them to measure and plan the sizes, shapes and amount of material needed for the project. The planning worksheet also provided an estimate of project expenses. Kate scheduled an appointment for the hardware store to send a professional installer out to confirm the measurements of the pieces to be delivered.

Kate's first choice was a reddish-pink colored granite that is mined from an area in Central Texas called 'Granite Mountain', near Marble Falls, Texas. The same material is still present in an undisturbed, natural state at the Enchanted Rock, near Fredericksburg, Texas. The stone is called Sunset Red and it adorns the Texas State Capitol in Austin, Texas. However, because of the heavy mining, Granite Mountain is more of a granite heap that no longer looks like a mountain. Kate was advised that there could be a delay due to availability of Sunset Red.

Her alternate selection was a yellowish-brown Amarillo Bamboo quartzite granite that is quarried in Brazil. Kate loved the dark golden color that had a touch of red in it. If the color of the reddish-pink Texas granite could be described as a Sunset Red, then the Amarillo Bamboo quartzite was more of a Golden Sunrise.

When they returned to the Golden Goose B&B, Ray installed the new front door without much difficulty. He added the steel reinforcement plate to the front and rear entrances to the house. After some discussion, they both decided that they liked the Golden

Sunrise quartzite better than the Sunset Red. The decision may have been influenced by the fact that both Kate and Ray loved going down to the beach at sunrise and watching the sun come up over the horizon. It also seemed to match the golden oak color of the cabinets in the kitchen, whereas the Sunset Red was more of a contrasting rather than a complementary color.

Kate was so sure that she liked the Golden Sunrise granite for her kitchen that they went back to the hardware store and placed an order for delivery and installation the following weekend. The hardware store assured her that they would come by and take measurements immediately so that the granite could be cut to size in advance of the installation. Ray assured her that he could easily remove the old counter tops and the back splash on his next visit to Goose Island.

"Now if you find a gun or any other deadly weapon hidden underneath the old countertop or behind the backsplash I don't even want to know about it," Kate said.

"Absolutely," Ray replied. "I'll just put on my gloves to make sure I don't leave any fingerprints on it when I toss it into the Gulf on my way out of town," he said with a laugh.

The last time he had helped Kate with a small patio project at the Goose Island B&B they had found a gun hidden behind one of the walls in the house. The gun had been used to murder one of Goose Island's residents. It had really troubled Kate that there was a murderer loose in the small, tightly knit community of residents at Goose Island. Zachary and Nicole's death left her with the same cold, clammy feeling. All the sunsets and walks on the beach at sunrise were somehow less wonderful if there was a murderer in their midst. Solving the mystery of the murder weapon hidden in her patio with the help of her friends and neighbors, Shirley, Ray, Troy, Charlotte and Jerry had helped reassure Kate's faith in the human spirit. It reinforced her feeling that she had made the right decision when she had decided to live on Goose Island. She simply had to find out what had happened to Zachary and Nicole.

Kate and Ray were sweating profusely by the time they finished installing the new door. Once the new door was securely fastened and closed, they were finally able to turn on the air conditioning once again. Ray was scheduled to return to Odessa the next day. Kate did not want to give him up so soon, but at least there was still time for a leisurely walk along Shipwreck Beach. It was a sunny day and the water was nice and warm. There were several people out by the beach and Kate waved hello to everyone she knew. They stopped a few times to exchange pleasantries with the island residents.

Several of the island residents were enjoying the sunshine at the beach. Charlotte and Jerry were out taking a walk and they soon joined Kate and Ray. They left Shipwreck Beach as a group and stopped off at Island Pizza for dinner. Shirley and Troy joined them at the pizzeria. They ordered the house special. An extra-large BBQ chicken pizza with fresh roasted artichokes, hot peppers, and pineapples that was absolutely scrumptious. The island lager was nice and frosty. Over dinner, Kate answered Shirley's questions about the break-in. No, nothing was missing. Yes, everything was all right. Everything was going to be just fine. Ray had replaced the front door and reinforced all the other entrances to the house.

*   *   *

Monday morning appeared in the twinkling of an eye. The weekend had gone by in a flash and Ray was headed back to Odessa later that afternoon. Kate was going to drop him at the airport and wait for her new houseguests to arrive on a flight from Lincoln, Nebraska.

Ray was worried about leaving the trunk out in the open in Kate's Living Room. As a precaution, they decided to place the trunk in a more secure location. Kate and Ray lowered the retractable stairs that led to the attic of the Goose

Island B&B. Between the two of them, they were able to haul the pirate chest up the stairs and placed it behind the HVAC unit, the attic monster that controlled all the heating and cooling for the house. It was almost invisible in the darkness of the attic as it lay underneath the myriad of ducts leading to and from the ventilation openings in the walls and ceiling below. They rearranged some of the insulation so that by the time they were finished it looked like an extension of the HVAC unit covered with insulation.

Kate dropped Ray back at the airport in Corpus Christi for his return flight to Odessa on Monday afternoon. She held his hand tightly as they walked into the departure lounge at the airport. Letting go was the hardest part about leaving him each time he disappeared past the security checkpoint at the airport. She took him aside just before the security checkpoint and wrapped her arms around him. She did not want to let him go. She gave him a long kiss, one they would both remember and then she turned abruptly and spun him towards the security checkpoint with a tear in her eye. Anything more and she would be forced to take off her belt, tie him up and take him back home with her.

Ray walked through security in a daze, wondering where this amazing, beautiful woman had been all his life. The one who had just groped him in public, and whose tongue had just darted into his mouth and out of his ear. At least that was what it had felt like. He turned and waved to her from the other side of the security checkpoint, gave her a silly smile and then turned to walk down to the gate where the airplane was located. Kate smiled as she saw him walk away hoping no one would notice he was holding his baseball cap strategically in front of his trousers.

After he was completely out of sight, she started to tear up, feeling a knot well up in the pit of her stomach. It was always the same. As she walked back to her station wagon she knew that it would not be the same until they could meet again. She was bawling helplessly by the time she started the car. This would never do! She turned the engine off and waited in the parking lot to catch her breath. It was a good thing that he could not see her like this. She knew that she had to respect his space and allow him the freedom to come and go as he wished. It was just so hard to watch him leave, never knowing if she would see him again.

*   *   *

Kate had about an hour to herself before it was time to meet and greet her new houseguests, Courtney and Glenda, who were due to fly in from Nebraska that day. She drove to a small gas station near the area and picked up a newspaper and some bottled water. Then she returned to the cell phone lot outside the airport terminal and waited for their flight to arrive. While she was waiting, she received a text from Ray who had reached Odessa safely.

Courtney and Glenda arrived tired and a little worn out from their journey. Their flight had left from Lincoln, Nebraska at six am. They had actually awakened much earlier and left for the airport by 4:30 am. They had had a very long day, and were delighted to find Kate waiting patiently for them when they arrived. They tumbled into the back seat immediately. Courtney fell asleep shortly after they left the airport. Glenda sipped on the bottled water and glanced at the newspaper.

As she drove back to the Goose Island B&B, Kate couldn't stop thinking about the pirate's trunk she had purchased just a few days earlier. It amazed her that the trunk had remained unopened for decades until she had looked inside it earlier that weekend. This could only have been possible if the trunk had remained in the possession of the original family that had owned it until shortly before her purchase. Kate surmised that Zachary and Nicole, and their daughter Lucy were the direct descendants of Jeanne LaFitte. Wow! She had a new found respect for Lucy, the pirate's daughter!

Courtney woke up from her nap fresh as a daisy just as they pulled into the driveway at the Goose Island Bed and Breakfast. Kate introduced them to Jerry and Charlotte who were relaxing in their back yard. Kate invited everyone over to her place to share a bottle of red wine and enjoy watching another incredible Texas sunset from the vantage point of her first floor balcony. Jerry helped Courtney and Glenda with their luggage. Charlotte came over and gave Kate a hand in the kitchen. They were soon seated around a small table on the balcony munching on some cheese, crackers and fruit, sipping a glass of red wine.

She had supper with Courtney and Glenda in the dining room adjoining the kitchen. It was a simple pasta meal with chicken based on a recipe that she had learned from her neighbor Charlotte. The girls from Nebraska were delighted to be in Texas. Courtney and Glenda knew their way around the island and were looking forward to catching up with some of the people they had met on their previous visit. The conversation at dinner was typical of good friends meeting after a long time. Courtney had had one of her knees operated on recently. As a result, she had gained a little more weight than the year before. She was hoping to get back to her earlier weight by taking long walks along Shipwreck Beach with Glenda.

After Courtney and Glenda retired for the evening, Kate went over to Charlotte and Jerry's house and borrowed Milo for the night once again. She simply did not feel safe without Ray sleeping next to her. Milo wagged his tail cheerfully as he followed her to her house and to the upstairs bedroom, with the balcony from which one could see all the way out into the ocean. Milo liked sleeping in the upstairs balcony. At first, Kate had been afraid that he would simply jump off the balcony in order to go chasing after squirrels. However, even though he had dashed madly across the balcony from one end to the other any number of times, he had always stopped just short of the edge. Kate was satisfied that he was smart enough to know what would happen if he jumped off the edge.

Kate had not made the bed since she had shared it with Ray the night before. There was still an impression in the pillow where he had rested his head. She closed her eyes and tried to pretend that he was sleeping next to her. When she finally went to sleep it was with the wind whispering in her ear the secrets it had carried from Ray's bedroom in Odessa as he lay alone thinking about her. Like the legendary Irish queen Brigid, or any self-respecting female pirate, she had nothing on except the ring he had given her on their anniversary earlier that year. The third anniversary of the day they had met for the first time.

*   *   *

With Troy's help, Kate made a few discreet inquiries and confirmed that the trunk she had purchased had been recovered by the police following the automobile crash that had killed Zachary and Nicole Dubois. The trunk had become public property because no one had stepped forth to claim it even after the Nueces County Sheriff's department had notified the next of kin.

Kate suspected that it was highly probable that their notice had just gotten lost in the shuffle. Even if Lucy had received it, she probably spent more time painting on the beach than she did at home. In addition, dealing with the death of her parents and taking care of all their funeral arrangements must have been a tremendous ordeal. Lucy had enough on her hands between running her business in Galveston and taking care of the details involved in settling her parent's estate in Rockport. She may not have had time to respond to the notice to stop by the Nueces County office to collect an unspecified piece of property.

Kate still had Lucy's contact information and decided that it was only fair that she advise Lucy about her acquisition. She picked up the phone and dialed Lucy's number reluctantly. She was not sure how to respond if Lucy insisted on having the trunk returned to her. How do you tell someone you have something that you know belongs to them, but that since you purchased it at auction it is now legally yours?

Kate knew that the real question is how do you choose not to inform someone you know that you have something that once belonged to them? What do you tell them when they see it displayed prominently in your living room? She would just have to see what Lucy wanted to do with the trunk and try to work out a mutually satisfactory arrangement.

"Hello Lucy," Kate said when Lucy answered the telephone. "It's Kate Houlihan from Goose Island."

"Why hello Kate, how are you. I was just thinking about you the other day," Lucy replied. "I'd like to come and stay at your bed and breakfast again someday. Let me know if that hunk of a college professor you had staying with you last fall is going to be visiting Goose Island again this year. I might just come down myself and show him some of my paintings."

"I sure will, Lucy," Kate replied. "Say, I was reading the newspaper the other day and wonder if you are related to Zachary and Nicole Dubois"

"Yes I am," Lucy said in a somber tone. "You do know what happened to them, right?"

"Yes, I just heard about it. I'm really sorry about your parents," Kate said.

"Yes it was a shock," Lucy replied. "Even though they were getting older I thought they were doing fairly well. I was hoping they would be around for a few more years. Besides, it was such a terrible accident."

"I agree," Kate said.

"All I can say is that my parents led a good, full life and I've come to accept that they are both in a better place," Lucy replied.

"I think I might have purchased something at an auction recently that may have once belonged to your parents," Kate said. "It's a wooden sailor's trunk with a bunch of carvings on it."

"I remember that trunk," Lucy replied. "My mother always kept it in her closet. She said it was a gift from her grandma. We were never really allowed to play with it because she kept it locked up most of the time."

"I see," Kate replied. That explained a few things about the condition that the trunk had been when Kate had examined it. Kate told

Lucy about how she had purchased the trunk at an auction.

Lucy advised her that she was welcome to keep the trunk because she had acquired it legally and therefore she was in fact its rightful owner. "It's yours if you want it," Lucy said. "I am so grateful to you for all the kindness you have shown me over the years, Kate. It's the least that I can do."

"Thanks," Kate said. She knew that Lucy was referring to Kate's role in preserving Lucy's confidentiality as it pertained to the death of her husband many years earlier. Kate was not sure if Lucy realized what she was giving up. However, this was not the time to go into detailed explanations. Besides, Kate wanted to keep the trunk for the moment. "I think it's a beautiful piece of work. I'll probably display it in the lobby of my Bed and Breakfast next to one of your paintings."

Lucy voiced no objections to Kate's plans for the antique trunk. It held as much interest for her as might a piece of unwanted furniture. "It's horribly old," she said. "I think Grandma got it from her mother." She suggested donating it to a museum if it had any historical value and if Kate had no use for it. Kate agreed to do so. With all the recent interest in the trunk, it really did not make sense to return it to Lucy who would be ill equipped to deal with the ruffigans who wanted to possess it at any cost. Just as soon as she had solved the mystery that the trunk contained, she could put the matter to rest.

As a gesture of her friendship, Kate offered to stop by Zachary and Nicole's house from time to time and make sure everything was okay. Lucy was delighted. There was a key hidden in the back yard and Lucy told her how to locate it so that Kate could let herself into the house. "Just let me know if there is anything that needs to be attended to," Lucy said. "I have a yard service to come out and mow the front lawn every other week, but it will be nice to know if there is anything else that needs immediate attention."

"I sure will, Lucy. It's the least I can do," Kate replied as they ended their conversation.

*　　*　　*

Kate stopped by to check up on Zachary and Nicole's house in Rockport the following day. She went around to the side of the house and let herself into the back yard. It was a beautiful house with several tall banana plants along one side of the yard. They gave the house a very relaxing, tropical feeling. She found the key hidden in the back yard and let herself in through the back door. It had not been very difficult to locate the key. It was hidden underneath an oval rock upon which a small brass frog was seated, squirting a jet of water into a perpetual fountain. In fact, if someone had wanted to enter their house in their absence it was in one of the first few places they would have checked for a spare key.

Everything in the house seemed to be in order. She did not find any other pirate memorabilia in the house. The only thing unusual is that when Kate had checked the list of caller id's on the telephone, she saw a telephone number with a New Orleans area code. The call had occurred over the Christmas holidays, right before they had died.

"How very interesting," Kate thought. The telephone number was identical to the one she had received a call from recently, inquiring about the trunk. She jotted down the number on the answering machine for reference. Evidently, the same person had tried to acquire the trunk from Lucy's parents before their death. Perhaps their death had not been a simple accident. It was possible that Zachary and Nicole had died because their assailants may have been trying to prevent them from reaching home at exactly the same time that someone was searching through their house looking for the trunk.

There was a photograph album of Zachary and Nicole's family and Kate thumbed through the pictures recognizing a few places in

Rockport and even some seaside pictures that had been taken on Shipwreck Beach in Goose Island. There was an eye popping photograph of Nicole in a lightly colored one-piece form fitting swimsuit, standing with Lucy on the beach next to a piece of driftwood. Nicole was holding Lucy's hand, her long hair streaming back behind her in the breeze, looking like the answer to Robinson Crusoe's prayers. The swimsuit was just slightly darker than her skin color. She could have been wearing body paint for all that Kate could discern. "Now there's an idea," Kate thought to herself. "Body paint that looks as if you are wearing a swimsuit. With polka dots all stretched out in exactly the right places."

There was another photograph of Lucy sitting on the rocks at Shipwreck Beach. She wondered how many family albums in Goose Island had almost the exact same picture with their children. In so many ways, Shipwreck Beach, the palm trees, sand dunes and the rocks on the beach embodied the spirit of Goose Island.

After returning home, she compared the phone number from Zachary and Nicole's answering machine against the number on her call records. There was no denying that same individual had contacted her shortly after she had been the victim of an attempted burglary.

She considered various options for trying to determine the identity of the individual who had called her after she had taken possession of the trunk. It was a little disturbing to think there was a maniac in the area who would try to run her off the road each time she got on Highway 35.

Kate did an internet search and found a service that provided a reverse number lookup. She was surprised to find that for a small service charge she could obtain the name and address of the owner of the telephone number. The phone number was registered to a company called the New Orleans Traders. Clearly, they were just as interested in the trunk as were Ken and his buddies from France. Was it simply a coincidence that the fellows from France had appeared in Goose Island at about the same time that the trunk had been offered for sale at the Police Auction? Could they be in cahoots with each other?

Kate spoke with Lucy the day after she had gone to check up on Zachary and Nicole's house. They had a long talk about any number of things. Lucy really missed Goose Island more than she cared to admit. Speaking with Kate allowed her to open a door to her past that had remained shut since she had left over a year ago.

Lucy could trace her lineage back for almost five or six generations. However, that did not go back nearly as far as Kate wanted to go. All Lucy could tell her about the wooden chest was that it had been stored in her mother, Nicole's closet. Nicole had received it from her maternal grandmother, Pauline. Lucy explained that Pauline's family were descendants of the LaPierre family tree. According to Lucy, Nicole had told her on more than one occasion that she could trace her family tree to Jacques and Eloise LaPierre, a pair of extremely wealthy landowners who had once owned almost ten thousand acres of farmland in Nueces County.

"My grandma told me that Eloise knew she was special because she was the only kid in the neighborhood who had her own horse when she was a teenager. Stories about Eloise had been passed down in my family for generations. She had a lot of moxie," Lucy told Kate. "She was allowed to go wherever she wanted. They had so much land that she could ride her horse all day in any direction and never leave the family farm. Grandma Pauline said that Eloise loved to go riding with her girl friends' on the beach. She loved hanging out by the Gulf. That's where she met Jacques."

Lucy still had an immense fortune that was managed by a trust fund that had been established a long time ago by her grandparents. Her recollection was that all the money she had inherited had come from the LaPierre side of the family – and had probably belonged to Eloise's Daddy at one time or another.

*   *   *

Kate sat down on her back porch with a glass of red wine. The fountain that Ray had installed for her several years ago bubbled cheerfully and the sounds of birds chirping in the trees filled the air. She went back inside the house to get some birdseed for the bird feeder hanging from the oak tree in the far corner of her yard. Then she settled back down again in her favorite chair, an old wooden Adirondack chair that the previous owner of the house, Frank, had left behind.

She had only met Frank briefly when she had purchased the house. She had spoken with him once again a few years later to let him know he was welcome to visit the Goose Island Bed and Breakfast anytime. Frank had left Goose Island to be closer to his family after his wife had passed away, but his carpentry skills were legendary on the island. He had personally constructed many of the picnic benches placed in strategic locations throughout Goose Island. He had spent many an evening watching the surf come in with his wife seated beside him in her wheel chair.

Kate sipped her wine and ran down her mental checklist of all she had learned about Jean Lafitte. Sometimes Kate did her best thinking just sitting in her porch watching a migrant bird stopping at her bird feeder on his way across the island.

Kate recalled a conversation with Coach Ryan, the football coach of Rockport High School. He had described having Lucy removed from the cheerleading squad because his players could not keep their eye on the ball with her on the sidelines. Coach Ryan and the other teachers had persuaded Lucy to become a drum major for the Rockport High School marching band instead.

Kate could only imagine what Lucy's maternal ancestors had been like. Assuming that Eloise had been as drop-dead gorgeous as Lucy was, Kate imagined her as having been the beauty who had met Jean Lafitte on Shipwreck Beach. Was it possible that Jean Lafitte had become Jacques LaPierre?

Kate tried to picture Eloise meeting Jean Lafitte for the first time. Eloise, the rebel of course, had probably been out riding her horse on the beach, naked from the waist up. This was in the era before swimsuits had been invented. Eloise must have been swimming in one of the sheltered coves in the area in her bloomers, or possibly even in the nude. What would a pirate

King like Jean Lafitte do if he had stumbled on a naked mermaid in the Gulf? Regardless, he had probably snapped to attention and saluted when he had seen Eloise. The only thing he would have needed to win Eloise's heart had been his love of the sea. Something that he had in abundance. His knowledge of the Gulf Coast would surely have made a lasting impression on Eloise. When he left Galveston in flames Jean Lafitte must have disappeared into the wheat fields of Nueces County forever.

There are those who believe that Jean Lafitte was killed at sea, but in Kate's version of the story the gentleman pirate had married the most beautiful girl in Texas. A handsome sea captain who had settled down with the greatest treasure of all, the prettiest maiden this side of New Orleans. A woman so beautiful that Jacques could hear the echo of the sea in her laughter, the undulation of the waves when she walked and the reflections of the stars of the Southern Cross within her eyes when she looked at him. Even more beautiful were the torrid nights when they rolled over and over each other in Eloise's bed, taking turns to see exactly who was the pirate and who was going to be vanquished with love. Each conquest becoming more memorable than the one they had shared the night before.

Kate could see it all so clearly. Having married the prettiest and the richest girl in Nueces County, Jean Lafitte had no use for his pirate treasure. Breaking all ties with the past, he had quietly left behind the map to the treasure hidden beneath the secret compartment of the wooden steamer trunk that now lay before Kate. It was just a little something to pass along to his children, a rainy day fund to keep them going through a rough patch or two. There was no way he could explain to Eloise where the money had come from or how it had been obtained, so he didn't even try. He had all the riches he ever needed with her. The pirate treasure was just a little gift to help ensure the survival of future generations of his family, the sons and daughters whom he took sailing in the Gulf whenever he could, showing them how to navigate by the light of the moon and the position of the stars in the sky. Jacques and Eloise LaPierre's little pirate children had grown up to be big pirate children and he had finally bequeathed his pirate trunk to his daughter before he died. The trunk had then been passed down from generation to generation as a family heirloom to be admired for its workmanship. However, none of his kin had realized the true meaning behind the trunk thanks to the fine upstanding view they had of Jacques' transition to civilian life.

*   *   *

The telephone number Kate had found on Zachary and Nicole's answering machine gnawed at Kate until she knew she would have to do something about it. In many ways, Kate was like a dog with a bone. Once something got under her skin she simply could not let it go until she had followed through on it to her own personal satisfaction.

Kate picked up the telephone and dialed her ex-husband, James' number from memory. She waited for several rings and then hung up the phone. She did not want to leave a message. The minute she put the phone down her telephone started to ring. She picked up the receiver. It was James on the line. It was something of a surprise to hear his voice because she was expecting to get his answering machine.

"Hi Kate," said James. "Did you miss me?"

"More than I thought I would James," Kate replied.

"Why don't you come down to Houston sometime and look me up?" James said.

"I might just do that," Kate replied. "I've been thinking of going down to Galveston to meet Lucy."

"Lucy Matthews?" James asked.

"Yes" Kate replied.

"What's she mixed up in this time?"

"Nothing," Kate said. "Nothing at all. I just thought it would be a good idea to go look her up," she added innocently. "Would you like to come along?"

There was a long pause at the other end of the line. Kate was not given to inviting James to accompany her to go visit her friends and acquaintances. You could sense the wheels turning over slowly in James's head as he realized that he was being roped into something he may not want to be involved with.

"What are you mixed up in this time?" James asked finally.

"It's quite complicated," Kate replied.

"Try me," James said. "Perhaps you'd like to see the legal brief I've prepared on one of the oil companies that was involved in the Deep Water Horizon oil spill where more than 10 million gallons of crude oil were released into a fragile eco-system just 100 miles south east of New Orleans not long ago?"

"I was actually calling about a company in New Orleans," Kate said before James could get going. She really didn't want to re-live the Gulf oil spill.

Then, it all came out in a rush. Kate knew that eventually she was going to require James's help, in the unlikely case that she was able to succeed in finding Jean Lafitte's treasure. She told him all about the pirate's trunk, the robberies that had occurred, the telephone calls from New Orleans and all that she knew about Jean Lafitte.

That is to say that she told James everything except the parts that she had made up in her mind. She did not mention any of her crazy thoughts about Jean Lafitte changing his name to Jacques, getting married to Eloise LaPierre and becoming a farmer and settling down somewhere in Nueces County. Even though it all seemed very real to her in her mind, she knew that she had made that part up and that it would be a mistake to share it with someone like James who like cold hard facts better than sleeping with a willing woman in a soft warm bed. James would have thought she had gone mad, that she had been mentally unstable for decades. She knew that was another reason why she had divorced him a long time ago. She felt that he simply did not believe in her as a person, as he once had.

When Kate was finished communicating all the facts she had gathered, James agreed to find out what he could about the New Orleans Traders.

"Look me up if you do go to Galveston," he said. "I'd love to see you again."

Kate promised to do so. She missed James too. However, as much as she missed James, she knew he had not changed one bit since leaving her behind in Goose Island.

James wanted her back the same way that he would stop to pick up a penny that had fallen out of his pocket. She was not now, nor had she ever been valued as much as the 1933 Saint-Gaudens Gold Double Eagle coin that he kept tucked away close to his heart. It was always in a securely zippered breast pocket of the jacket she had given him for Christmas (the zipper had been custom tailored specially for his jacket).

James continued to be a good friend to her and she did value his friendship very much for old times' sake. However, once she had realized how little she meant to him it had hurt less to part ways, than to try to stay together as they had agreed to on their wedding day. The void in her heart that he had left behind had not really diminished until she met Ray.

It was going to be another week until she saw Ray again. She missed him terribly, so much it made her heart ache. No one knew her better than he did. The moments that they had shared always seemed to go by far too quickly. An entire weekend with Ray could go by in a rush, like a wave that continues to build momentum until it crashes upon the shore.

GOOSE ISLAND BLACK JACK

While waiting for Ray to return to Goose Island, Kate felt like a surfer waiting to catch the next wave on a day when the sea was as calm as a sheet of glass.

≈≈≈≈≈≈

Dry Dock

Louis licked the cream filling out of the éclairs at the Goose Island Bakery, before eating what remained of the pastry. He took an eternity to get through this delicate operation with each of the two éclairs he had purchased for breakfast. Shirley watched his tongue dart into one end of the éclair while he supported it carefully between the thumb and forefinger of his right hand. He was a noisy eater and made disgusting, slurping, sucking sounds in the process. Shirley listened to all of the disgusting noises that emanated from him with fascination.

All sorts of wild imaginations and flights of fancy whirled through Shirley's head. What a charmer she thought as she sucked in her stomach and pulled her T shirt down just a bit to get the fabric to accentuate her figure more closely. She could not wait to get naked with him.

He had been hanging around the Goose Island Bakery from the moment that she had first opened that day and she did not mind at all. She liked looking at his bony ass, or no-ass-at-all, she thought. At least that's how she had described him to Kate. She was secretly hoping that he would come on over behind the store counter and give her a kiss. She wanted to take him home with her, shave the stubble on his face that was his beard and run her fingers through his unkempt hair. Butt naked, of course. "Nekkid," as she liked to say. Shirley had exchanged notes with Olga at the courthouse and learned many urban myths about French sexual preferences. Olga was a virtual encyclopedia of information and Shirley's imagination had done the rest. If Louis had decided to steal first base, he would not have been met with a great deal of resistance. Shirley would just as easily have let him steal a home run.

For his part, Louis was simply following the instructions he had received the night before from his father. To try to learn as much as he could from Shirley about her friend Kate and the location of the trunk she had purchased at auction the previous day. However, Shirley was confused about his references to "zee trunk". Shirley wondered if he was trying to compare his anatomy with that of an elephant. The sexual innuendo was a huge turn-on and she wanted very much to see his elephant moves. However, as hard as he tried to pry and probe he had not been able to obtain this information from

Shirley. The only reason that Shirley had not already told him exactly where it was located is because Kate had not yet entrusted her best friend with this information.

When he finally left the bakery, Shirley disappeared into the kitchen singing "Under the bridges of Paris with you". Louis had introduced Shirley to Eartha Kitt. She found that she liked Eartha Kitt's music almost as much as the musical genius of Ray Price.

He did not stay away for long. In fact, Louis reappeared almost immediately a few minutes time later with a disheveled look on his face. Shirley could tell something was wrong. She wanted to give him a hug and bury his face in her bosom. There was no ailment her twins could not cure with their miraculous healing properties.

"My auto," Louis exclaimed. "Au revior. She gone!"

Shirley could not decipher what Louis was trying to tell her. She just did not understand his accent. It was worse that the bakery chap she had known from West Texas. At least he had a Texas twang to his words. Louis seemed to swallow half of everything he was saying. It was so frustrating. The way he said "gown" for example made her think about women's lingerie.

"My auto. She gone!" reiterated Louis, more vehemently. "Au revoir! Vanished!"

"I'll Rev Ya," Shirley repeated blankly. She blushed when she thought about what Louis must have said. It wasn't much, but it was a start. She beamed with the joy of having conversed with him in French. "Back-atcha-falaya," she added with a radiant smile.

Shirley had just started listening to a French language course. She could only imagine what "Ill Rev Ya" must mean. Perhaps it was one of the words that she had missed when the timer had gone off on her muffins that morning. She would have to listen to that section of the course from the beginning. Now if he had used some of the lines from the production of Mama Mia, like "Voulez-vous coucher avec moi ce soir?"or ""je t'aime" she would have known exactly what he wanted. Kate had told Shirley that listening to Abba was a great way to learn French.

"My car. She gone," Louis said again. "First she flat and when I come back, she not there."

Shirley had no idea what the he was saying, but she finally figured out that it had something to do with his car. "I wish this boy could learn how to talk like a Texan," she thought to herself. "And I know just the person who can teach him how to do that." She beamed.

"Now if we can just get him to say "Howdy" that would be a start.

"You mean to say that your car's been stolen, don't you?" Shirley said as she realized what Louis had been trying to tell her. "You probably need to call in a police report," she added helpfully dialing Troy's mobile telephone number.

When Troy answered, Shirley explained the situation to him.

"I know," Troy replied. "I called in the tow truck. He needs to contact Island Towing".

Shirley could not believe her ears. "You had him towed?" she exclaimed.

"No, I didn't," said Troy. "He was towed by Peter Scully of Island Towing, not me"

"I'll bet you are sitting on your fat ass at a bar somewhere right now with that car thief Pete Scully, sucking on a beer."

"No, I'm not," said Troy. "I'm busy working". He didn't add that it was only because he was waiting for Pete to get off work. Then the two of them were planning to go to the Swamp Shack across the causeway because Pete had offered to buy him a beer when he got off duty. "Please be sure to tell your 'friend' to be sure and stay inside the fire lane next time he parks at the Square," he added.

Shirley 'harrumphed' and hung up the phone. She proceeded to explain the situation to

Louis, slowly realizing that she had just received a surprise gift. She now had Louis all to herself for the rest of the day, while they set about getting his car back from Island Towing. She would have had him towed herself if she had known how things were going to work out.

"Let's go find your car," she said with a smile, as she took off her apron and hung it up for the day. The twins jiggled with excitement. Shirley closed the door to the Goose Island Bakery behind her, and held Louis' hand in hers as they crossed the street. They entered city hall and located Olga at the counter behind one of the courtesy windows. Louis proceeded to describe the situation to her.

"My auto," Louis exclaimed, repeating what he had just told Shirley. "Au revior. She gone!"

Olga could not help noticing how handsome Louis was. All he needed was a shave and a nice Russian military uniform and she would not be able to keep her hands off him. However, she was just as confused with his remark as Shirley had been. "What kind of gown was it?" she asked trying to understand the situation. "Was it black? Was it a night gown?" She had one just like that.

"No, no, no," said Louis. "Not night time gone. Just now car gone into sunshine"

"Why was his car wearing a night gown in the day time?" Olga inquired. "Do you think he was trying to protect it from the seagulls?" she asked, turning her head slightly towards Shirley. "Perhaps it was a convertible with a car bra, like a Lamborghini or something," she added.

"He wasn't driving a convertible and it wasn't a night gown at all," Shirley explained. "It was towed".

Olga looked at them carefully through her glasses. She was on the verge of asking why he was a toad. Shirley looked like a witch sometimes. Could she really do that to a fellow?

Shirley held Louis's hand to shush him because he was not helping the situation. It was nice and warm and she clasped it firmly in hers. Then she put her finger to his lips. She didn't know the French word for "Shut up, dude".

"His car was towed, Olga," Shirley said.

Olga had not seen a toad on the island in decades. This was getting crazy. She could not help noticing Louis' athletic appearance and was a little distracted because one side of his shirt was hanging out of his trousers that appeared to be a little tight for him. The specimen in front of her was definitely a prince, not a frog from the northern latitudes.

As Shirley finally descrambled the situation, Olga reached behind the counter and handed her a copy of a sheet with the contact information for Island Towing.

"We should have a photograph of the parking violation," Olga said. "The towing company sends us a record of each parking violation and here it comes now," she added, looking at the incoming messages on her computer screen. "Hang on while I print a copy for you"

Shirley smiled. She had not let go of Louis's hand since leaving the bakery and it was starting to bead up with sweat. She tightened her grip on his hand. It felt nice and snug against hers.

Louis became really animated when he saw the photograph of his car. It was a grainy looking photograph of a sporty looking sedan. The most visible feature in the photograph was the license plate. There was no evidence of an improperly parked vehicle. However, it did look as if he had not pulled all the way into his parking space.

Shirley had to admit that it was not a bad looking car, even though she would have preferred riding around Goose Island with him in a convertible. Shirley felt a little uncomfortable when she saw the image of Louis's SUV because there was a certain class of men who drove tricked out SUVs with grilles attached to the front of their bumpers and fog lamps on the roof which made the car looked a lot like a mouse. It bothered her that Louis might be one of these human degenerates. She was not interested in someone who was more flash than dash, who cared more about his appearance than his accomplishments. Where Louis was concerned, she had to stop and wonder because he had been in her shop for the entire morning without once sneaking behind the counter for a kiss. She let go of his hand.

"It says here that you were parked more than three feet from the curb, Mr. Louis."

"How much more?" Louis asked. Inquiring minds want to know.

"Mush more than tree feet," replied Olga helpfully. "Mush, mush more." She liked the sound of her words and the way they rolled off her tongue as she imitated Louis's Russian accent. She didn't know he was from France and he looked Russian to her. Some day she was going to have to get a team together and prepare for the Iditarod. "Mush!" she said, with a smile. Her words cut through the air like a whip.

"Oh," said Louis with a blank expression. He was holding his wallet in his hands and reaching inside to see how much money he had inside.

Olga thought that the boy with the bad accent seemed a little dense. "Maybe his mother dropped him on his head a few times when he was a baby," she thought to herself. Not a very bright spark. But he did have an athletic build and looked like he could be useful around a pool. That Shirley sure was as lucky as she could get. First, she had Troy wanting to marry her and now this over-sexed krasavchik of a man was standing next to her with his shirt hanging out his rear end. She wanted to reach across and tuck it in.

"How mush please?" Louis asked again.

Something clicked into place in Olga's brain. Maybe it was the wallet in Louis' hands, or Shirley asking her how much it would cost to get his car back from the towing company.

"I'll be happy to help pay," Shirley said. Her brain was turning to mush.

"Why don't you tuck his shirt in," Olga suggested helpfully looking at Shirley.

"Ooo, yes. Good idea," said Shirley. Her brain was a bit addled with the possibility of doing exactly what Olga had recommended.

"You'll have to call Peter Scully to find out what it will cost," Olga continued. "We don't set the rates and they keep changing them all the time, anyway. You have to pay them directly when you pick up your car."

It must have been the power of suggestion because Louis had just reached back and tucked his shirt in himself just as Shirley started to do the same. Not to be deprived

Shirley put her hand on his skinny waist, yanked his shirt out from behind and tucked it in again. She had to be sure it had been done properly. Then she quickly ran her hand along his bony rear end for good measure. Boy, did he have a firm rear end or what? She patted his behind for good measure. Louis did not complain. He seemed to be used to being waited on hand and foot.

They had to pick up Papa Henri and his brother Sebastian to help with the payment. Pete Scully informed them that he would only accept a cashier's check or a money order and that they had to get it to him by 5:00 pm or else he was going to have to charge a holding fee for the night.

It was definitely a scam and it shamed her that the city resorted to such shady practices to raise revenues. The banks were closed and they packed into her trusty Honda Accord and drove over to the Island Magic – the only grocery store on the island. They paid $193.64 and an extra two dollar handling fee for a cashier's check at the customer window.

Shirley didn't get to hold Louis' hand again since Papa Henri and Sebastian were around. It bothered her that he hadn't tried to bump into her or squeeze her hand the entire time that she had held it at city hall. Perhaps it had been the stress of losing his car. They drove across the causeway to Pete's Island Towing storage facility and retrieved the black Chevy Avalanche a few minutes before 5:00 pm.

Papa Henri and his brother Sebastian spoke in French the entire time. Their conversation was punctuated with questions for Louis who almost always answered in monosyllables. Shirley had no idea what they were talking about. From time to time, they threw in a question or two about Kate. Shirley found herself telling them what a wonderful person Kate was. They seemed to be having some difficulty understanding Kate's relationship to Ray, and were most interested in his whereabouts. "They sure are pretty ignorant," Shirley thought to herself. "To think that Ray is married to a girl called Odessa, and that Kate is his mistress. For a group of international businessmen their understanding of Texas is very limited."

Pete was apologetic and tried to explain that he had had to tow Louis' car in order to comply with the fire code. "It isn't a matter of trying to decide if other cars can get by an improperly parked car, but whether there is enough room for a fire engine. Maybe you should park on the other side of the street where the parking spaces are bigger," he suggested helpfully. "I think part of the problem was that you had a big hulking SUV parked in a space designed for a compact car. And I don't think the flat tire helped much either."

"He has a flat tire?" Shirley interjected. "Can you fix it for him?"

"Sure," Pete said. "I'll take care of that right now."

There was no extra charge for repairing the flat tire. Louis handed Peter the cashier's check and picked up his car. He drove away with Henri and Sebastian. Shirley left to go home to her apartment. She was a little disappointed with Louis. He could at least have invited her to dinner to thank her for her helping him retrieve his car. Not that she would have accepted a dinner invitation from someone she hardly knew. However, it would have been a nice gesture if he had asked for a date. She was confused and mad at herself for finding herself attracted to Louis. There was a plaque in her bakery that read: "It's not what you do, or where you are, but whom you are with that matters". Shirley wanted very much to be with the right someone for the rest of her life. Was that really Troy?

*   *   *

Kate and Shirley were hanging out at the Swamp Shack that evening. There was a bearded musician playing some blues tunes.

Shirley could hear "Sitting on the Dock of the Bay" a zillion times and never get tired of the immensely satisfying feeling of watching the tide roll in. Kate listened to "Ain't no Sunshine," thinking that there was darkness all around her when Ray wasn't around.

Over crab cakes and a glass of red wine, Shirley told Kate all about the manner in which Peter Scully had towed Louis's car from the Goose Island Town Square. "Peter's a pirate," she said. "He's just in it for the money and I think Troy set him up to it."

"Yes, I can see that," Kate replied. She had little or no interest in Louis or his car.

Kate was convinced that Jean Lafitte's treasure was buried somewhere in the area of Rockport or Port Aransas. The discovery of the pirate chest had provided her with the affirmation that she needed for the existence of the treasure.

"Do you know what these fellows from France want?" Kate asked. "I'm still trying to get used to seeing them here on the island every day."

"Louis says he likes my banana nut muffins," Shirley replied. "I think it's because I add grated carrots, raisins, and walnuts to it."

"Yes, you do make good muffins," Kate replied. Clearly, Shirley felt that her muffins were the perfect reason to move across the

Atlantic. In Kate's estimation, the only person who felt that way about Shirley's muffins was Troy. "However, I think those fellows are after something completely different," Kate added. She pondered the best way to get Shirley to understand what might be at stake without offending her.

In 1821, Goose Island was virtually uninhabited, a comfortable distance away from the nearest Spanish missions, far from prying eyes and away from urban areas to minimize the risk of detection by the local population. It would have been a good hiding place for Jean Lafitte. One that was close enough to Galveston so that he could return at a moment's notice and still be far enough to be out of sight from his friends, business associates, and the Federal authorities. Kate felt sure that he would probably hide the treasure near the coast. It seemed unlikely that he would venture too far inland since that would make it harder to access.

The area around Goose Island has so many inlets, coves and outlets that it is a natural setting where a pirate could remain hidden for weeks on end. Copano Bay, Aransas Bay and San Antonio Bay are inter-connected with several points of access to the Gulf. Jean Lafitte could have stayed on Goose Island in 1821 for a long time without fear of detection by the Spanish Authorities and the American forces in the area. A pirate ship could sail north from Aransas Bay towards Port Lavaca and slip back out to the Gulf through Matagorda Bay. Anyone navigating through the sand bars and shoals near Goose Island would have to have taken the time to familiarize himself with its geography. The captain of La Belle, a French ship that ran aground in Matagorda Bay in 1685 had not been so fortunate. However, for Jean Lafitte this would be no different from what he had accomplished first in Barataria, and later in Galveston.

Further south from Port Aransas lay Mustang Island and the Padre Island Seashore. Padre Island is a relatively continuous strip of land almost all the way from Corpus Christi to Port Isabel, a distance of almost 113 miles. South Padre Island includes over seventy miles of beaches, but unlike the area near Port Aransas, it has fewer outlets leading between the Laguna Madre to its west and the Gulf of Mexico to the east. A hideout in the Laguna Madre could easily turn into a dead end, and Kate knew that Jean Lafitte would never allow himself to be trapped in Baffin Bay. She was convinced that the treasure was hidden near Port Aransas with its easy access to the Gulf of Mexico. Corpus Christi and Port Isabel seemed less desirable since these areas were more densely populated than the area near Copano Bay.

Kate knew that she would have to learn her way around the coast in order to have any chance of finding Jean Lafitte's treasure trove. Her neighbor Jerry was an avid angler who was intimately familiar with the coastal area around Copano Bay. Perhaps she would have to enlist his support in order to get to know the coastal marshland that surrounded Goose Island as well as he did. It was all so complicated. However, she had to start somewhere.

"How would you like to go on a picnic to one of the islands nearby?" she finally asked Shirley.

"Sounds like fun," Shirley replied. "Maybe we can borrow some kayaks and go fishing sometime."

"That sounds like a really good idea," Kate said. "How did you know that is something I've always wanted to do?"

Shirley just smiled. "Maybe we need to go down to the mall sometime and get new swimsuits," Shirley said. "Something a little more European with a more translucent fabric and with a higher cut, perhaps."

"Sounds like a plan," Kate replied. She needed a new swimsuit with a better chlorine resistant fabric. The one she had been wearing in her spa had started to thin out in certain places.

The bearded musician who had been entertaining the customers at the Swamp Shack was taking a break. He stopped at the bar for a longneck and then walked over to the table by the window where the girls were seated. "You girls aren't from around here are you?" he asked.

"Have we met?" Kate asked.

"We just did," the musician replied. He was not deterred by Kate's response. "I knew you were from out of town because heaven is a long way from here."

"Hate to disappoint you," Shirley said.

"Well then we should go get a coffee together, because I like you a latte," he continued.

"Excuse me," Kate said. "We have to be leaving now." She grabbed Shirley's hand and the girls quickly waved goodbye before Shirley could volunteer any personal information to their new friend.

*　　*　　*

Kate had trouble getting to bed without Ray beside her. Ever since she had acquired the trunk, she had difficulty sleeping by herself. Not quite sure what to do with herself at two in the morning she was quickly becoming addicted to waking up in the middle of the night and using her computer to browse the internet. She had downloaded and printed dozens of detailed geographical maps of the Texas Gulf Coast. So much so, that she could wallpaper her room with them. The maps showing all the inlets and outlets to the Gulf Coast for miles and miles from the vicinity of Goose Island lay strewn across her bedroom floor. Jean Lafitte would have been impressed. This was the information he had carried around in his head. She compared the geographical contours of the myriad small islands, bays and peninsulas with an image of the pirate flag. She was hoping to locate an island or a body of water along the Gulf Coast near Port Aransas that resembled the shape of the pirates' eye.

The fact that both eyes were mirror images of each other seemed significant. It was as if Jean Lafitte was trying to tell his descendants exactly where to look for his treasure. Kate was convinced that the shape of the eye socket represented a geographical contour such as a body of water, like Copano Bay. When she found one that matched then she supposed that the diamond eyeball in the middle of the pirate's eye identified the spot where the treasure lay buried. She was looking for an island or a rock in the middle of the bay that was at the proper position within the bay. To meet these criteria she had to find an island within the bay located just west of dead center so that it would align itself with the diamond eyeball in the pirate flag.

On the other hand, the pirate's eye could also represent an island in the shape of the pirate's eye. The diamond eyeball in the pirate flag could represent the location of the buried treasure. However, up to now Kate had not found any islands that matched the contour of the eye.

Her eyes were starting to glaze over from the effort of studying the screen so intently. She looked at a tiny speck of dust on her screen and tried to clean it the old-fashioned way by moistening her forefinger with her tongue and gently dabbing at the screen. It wasn't working. It refused to budge. She increased the zoom on the page in front of her and immediately realized that she had just located a small island in the middle of Mesquite Bay. The bay itself had a circular outline so that it did in fact resemble the shape of the eye socket on the pirate flag.

Kate stared at the small island on the screen in front of her with awe. The island was located slightly off center within the bay, almost exactly where the diamond had been in the middle of the eye on the pirate flag. There was just one problem. The island in the middle of Mesquite Bay was located east of center, i.e. it was on the wrong side of the bay. To be in the precise location of the iris within the eye of the flag, 'Treasure Island' should have been located slightly west of the center of the bay, not the other way around.

Kate concluded that the pirate flag had intentionally inverted the image of the location of the treasure trove. The location of the treasure could only be determined from the context of the pirate himself, not from the position of someone seated across the table from the pirate. This made perfect sense because pirates live in the shadow of the recognized world, typically on the wrong side of the law. By reversing the location of the island on the pirate flag, Jean had accomplished two objectives. Firstly, he had obfuscated the location of the treasure from casual observed in the 'real' world. Secondly, he was making a statement about himself, that he was indeed a real pirate and buccaneer. The map could only be interpreted by someone who shared the same mindset that he did. Now all she needed was a way to get to the island and go exploring.

*　　*　　*

Kate had always thought it would be fun to learn how to kayak, just to get a short distance away from the shore in order to get a better position from which to watch the sunset. Since the initial outlay associated with purchasing an ocean kayak was very modest, she decided to fund the cost of a couple of kayaks to go exploring the area with Shirley. She could always plant flowers in it if she got tired of paddling around Goose Island.

Shirley and Kate pulled into the parking lot of a sporting goods outlet near Port Aransas that had opened its doors less than a year ago. The number of vehicles in the parking lot outside the store was evidence of its immense popularity with anglers of all ages in the area. It seemed that everyone in Rockport was out looking for sporting equipment after getting off from work. After circling around the parking lot looking unsuccessfully for an open space, they finally parked at a small pharmacy across the street.

Kate was unprepared for the vast array of canoes, kayaks and other small recreational fishing boats that lined the walls and hung from the rafters inside the store. It took more than an hour to sort through the available choices. There were orange, yellow, red, blue and green kayaks, sit-in kayaks and sit-on kayaks. After pondering the choices displayed on the wall, Kate surmised that the type she needed was the sit-on type, also referred to as 'ocean kayaks'.

"Sit-in kayaks look more comfortable and are probably better if you plan to be out in the hot sun for a long time because they protect your legs," Kate said to Shirley, as they tried to analyze the options.

"I guess the sit-on kind are more practical for kayaking around Copano Bay because the other type would just fill up with water on a rough day," Shirley replied.

"That would be my guess," Kate said.

A friendly looking member of the sales staff called Mike came by to help them decide whether to get a one-person, or a two-person kayak. The two person kayak looked like it would be more fun, but Kate reasoned that it would be more difficult to transport, because it was several feet longer than the one-person kayak. The girls decided to purchase a pair of one-person kayaks.

There were a lot of admiring looks from the other shoppers as the sales staff helped carry the kayaks to the checkout stand. There were even a few low whistles from some gray wolves in the next aisle, wanting to know when and where the girls were planning to go kayaking.

"I guess we'll have plenty of help getting these in and out of the water," Kate said to Shirley, as they followed behind Mike, one of the sales staff who helped strap the kayaks to the top of their car.

"I'm sure we'll get plenty of help," Shirley replied. "Especially if I'm with you. What self-respecting Texan can resist two helpless women with a pair of kayaks that match the color of their swimsuits?"

Each kayak was balanced precariously on top of a shopping cart and was wheeled out the front entrance to the store. Kate drove her station wagon around to the front and they proceeded to hoist the kayaks on top of the carrier on the roof of the station wagon. Hoisting the kayaks onto the top of the station wagon and strapping them down turned out to be a laborious process. They were all perspiring by the time it was finished. Even Kate and Shirley who contributed very little to the process were exhausted from watching Mike do all the work. The muscles on his arms rippled in the sunshine and Kate gave Shirley the 'please don't stare' look to no avail.

Mike didn't mind. He was busy loading up the kayaks and wanted to make sure they did not fly off the top of the station wagon before his customers got home. "Next time you do this make sure your kayak is tied down in at least two places, or else it will fly off the top of your station wagon and you'll be lucky if it doesn't injure somebody," the sales clerk advised the girls. Then he attached a small red flag to the end of each kayak and patted it lovingly as if he would a small puppy.

"You're going to love these," he added. "Did you need anything else?" he inquired.

Kate kicked Shirley on the shin to shut her up just before she started to speak up. "Is that enough to hold it in place?" Kate asked quickly. "Don't you need to tie it to the front bumper or something?"

"You can if you want," said Mike. "I think it should be okay if you aren't going to drive over fifty five. "If you plan to drive on the interstate you should probably buy an aftermarket carrier to hold the kayaks down securely"

"Ouch," said Shirley, after Mike had returned to the store. "What was that all about?"

"You had that foot massage look in your eye, and don't you deny it," Kate replied.

About an hour after walking out of the store with their purchase, the girls finally made their way out of the parking lot. It was getting dark. The first of what they hoped were going to be many unforgettable kayaking expeditions would have to wait until the next day. Kate turned on the radio as they approached Highway 35 with their brightly colored kayaks perched precariously on top of her station wagon. Kate was careful not to drive above fifty-five m.p.h. The last thing she wanted was for the kayaks to go flying off the top of her station wagon.

Shirley was still complaining that they should have bought the red kayak instead of the orange one and Kate had to remind her that the red kayak was a 'sit-in' product whereas the orange one was a 'sit-on' type of kayak that was better suited for their purposes.

"I should sit on you!" Shirley said.

"Just try it sister" Kate replied as they both laughed at the thought.

They made good progress along the highway and were rapidly approaching the Copano Bay Bridge. They were driving with the windows rolled down and the tires on Kate's station wagon made a staccato sound as she traversed each section of the bridge. Kate slowed as they rounded the top of the bridge, wondering if she was going to be buffeted by the wind. She need not have worried. There was just a pleasant breeze in the air and from the top of Copano Bay Bridge the water below seemed to be as still as a sheet of glass. The thought of a leisurely kayak trip to one of the islands on the Texas Gulf Coast resonated in her mind as the car rolled effortlessly down the other side of the bridge and turned down Main Street towards the Goose Island Township.

Shirley waved at Ken Porter as he ambled across Main Street. Ken did a double take when he saw the girls with their brightly colored kayaks. However, he was not too surprised to wave back and blow them a kiss. The girls turned on Shore Drive and slowly made their way past Shipwreck Beach. They got a big smile from Charlotte and Jerry as they pulled into Kate's driveway. It was a beautiful day and everyone on the island was outdoors enjoying the weather. Courtney and Glenda came outside to inspect their new purchase. Glenda whispered something to Courtney about looking for buried treasure. Kate was sure that she would have plenty of volunteers if she needed any help looking for the treasure.

As they surveyed the kayaks on top of the station wagon after they were parked in Kate's driveway, the girls decided that it was too much trouble to unload them right away. They agreed to go on a christening voyage the following Sunday. Ray was not due to visit Goose Island again for another week and Troy was working a weekend shift. Both Kate and Shirley had nothing else planned for the weekend. Kate dropped Shirley at her apartment with the kayaks anchored securely to the top of her station wagon. That was where they remained for several days where they received many admiring looks and more than a little attention from the folks on Goose Island.

When someone asked her about the kayaks, Kate explained how she wanted to explore the islands and coastal marshes around Goose Island to get to know the area better. However, no one was buying her story because

GOOSE ISLAND BLACK JACK

Shirley had already told several people that they were looking for buried treasure. That included Troy and Louis.

≈≈≈≈≈≈

Mesquite Bay

For their first expedition, Kate had selected Mesquite Bay, which lies between Matagorda Island and the Aransas National Wildlife Refuge. At its widest point Mesquite Bay is about five miles across. The Gulf Intra-Coastal Water Way runs along the western edge of Mesquite Bay. Since the area tends to have more water traffic throughout the afternoon, they decided to make an early morning run to the island.

Shirley spent Saturday night in one of the vacant guest rooms at the Golden Goose Bed and Breakfast. They had a wonderful dinner at home the night before with Troy, Glenda, Courtney and Kate's neighbors Charlotte and Jerry. Kate was trying out a new recipe for mango cashew chicken and everyone agreed it was wonderful. The spices were just right. Sweet, tangy and delicious, without being overpowering.

Troy and Jerry gave the girls a lot of advice and insisted they take life jackets with them. Jerry offered to go looking for them if they did not return home by early in the afternoon. However, he knew better than to try to dissuade them. Goose Island women have an Amazonian streak and can be pretty tough and hard headed once they have made up their minds.

Kate and Shirley woke up at first light. They gathered their gear and got in the car to drive north in the direction of the township of Austwell near the Aransas National Wildlife Refuge. There was a light mist in the air when they set off from Goose Island. The mist in the air that fogged Kate's windshield, making it difficult to see the road. However, they did not pass a single car on the way. There was hardly another soul on the road. Before long they were making their way past the Austwell city limits sign. Population 519. They reached the entrance to the Aransas National Wildlife Refuge just before sunrise. It did not take long to get their kayaks out on the water and begin traversing the expanse of water between them and the island in the middle of the bay.

They planned to paddle south through Mustang Lake and go across the Intracoastal Water Way at Ayres Bay. That would take them to Mesquite Bay. From there they planned to paddle along the eastern edge of Mesquite Bay that bordered Matagorda Island until it was time make their way across the bay and head for Treasure Island. Just a hop, skip, and jump to where the pirate treasure lay in the glint of the eye on the pirate flag.

It was a very pleasant April day and a cool breeze wafted over the ocean. In the morning sky that lay in front of them, they saw groups of birds, ducks and wild geese, flying in formation across the water. Kate's plan was to follow the coastline on the west side of Mesquite Bay for several miles, then cut across through to the center of the bay, and hope that she could locate Treasure Island.

They began the trip along the coastline at a leisurely pace. The girls may have assumed that they were the only ones up so bright and early, but they could not have been more wrong. There was a small group of bird watchers on the observation deck at the Wildlife Refuge looking intently in their direction with a telescope. The girls looked back to see the oversized frame of a familiar individual standing on the deck. It seemed safe to assume that Kenneth Porter and his henchmen had followed them from Austwell. He was in the company of several smaller figures peering at them through their binoculars. Shirley was quite flattered by the attention she was receiving from Louis. She paused to brush her hair, letting her hand trail seductively in the water like a mermaid caressing the waves with the palm of her hand. It was comforting to think that he had taken the trouble to wake up early and follow her all the way from Goose Island to Austwell. She blew him a kiss when she was sure Kate was not looking. She knew Kate did not approve of her interest in Louis.

A new flock of geese passed them and they could hear the birds honking at each other far above. The people on the observation deck at the Wildlife Refuge were starting to look like little ant people. However, Kate could sense the binoculars on the observation deck following their every movement. It made her uncomfortable and she could not wait to get further away. She started to paddle with renewed vigor. The kayaks sliced through the water effortlessly. It was almost time to make a turn to the east and travel past Mustang Lake to Ayers Bay, which stretched out in front of them looking about as large as the entire Pacific Ocean.

"Wait for me," yelled Shirley who was not used to the extended physical exertion that this entailed. Kate eased up on the paddle in her kayak until she was floating effortlessly in the water. She opened a couple of cans of beer as she slowed down to allow Shirley to catch up. In the distance behind them, she could see the flashing lights of a police cruiser. It did not take much imagination to conclude that the Frenchmen might have just received another traffic violation.

"Way to go Troy," she thought. Her spirits lifted instantly as she realized that Troy was more than able to handle the competition. She handed Shirley a beer as she caught up with her and watched her gulp it down thirstily.

"Thanks," Shirley said. "I needed that."

There is nothing better than sucking down a cold beer on a kayak, except maybe two cold beers. Kayaking was fun and they were growing more coordinated with each stroke of their oars. They made rapid progress as their craft moved smoothly along the water. However, they were still about an hour away from their destination. They paused briefly to open a second can of beer, enjoying the sunrise.

"I sure hope we don't run into any alligators or crocodiles around here," said Shirley.

"That's a comforting thought," Kate replied.

They hugged the coastline of the Aransas National Wildlife Refuge, just a short distance from the shore just to be sure that they did not disturb any of the wildlife. They saw several blue heron and egrets foraging for food in the shallow water of the marshland near the shore. They made a hard left once they reached Ayers Bay. At the rate they were going they would be on Matagorda Island before long.

They paddled along steadily. The birds that had been darting around them near the Wildlife Refuge disappeared as they made their way across a thin swirl of fog. Kate assumed the fog would dissipate quickly and peered into the distance to see how far they were from Matagorda Island. She was appalled at what she saw next. In the distance was the hulking profile of an oncoming barge making its way lazily across the Gulf Intracoastal Water Way.

Shirley looked at Kate with dismay as they watched the approaching barge close the gap between them. The barge was moving more rapidly than it had appeared to be going from a distance. It was huge. They had probably miscalculated its speed due to the large size of the barge. Unless it slowed down immediately, it was on a collision course with their puny kayaks.

The girls knew that they were going to have a hard time negotiating the backwash in the barge's wake. They were in a no-man's land zone where it was difficult trying to decide whether to paddle on and hope the barge would see them and slow down, or to turn around and take a chance on repeating the maneuver with another seagoing vehicle on their next attempt to cross the waterway.

However, Kate had come prepared for such an eventuality. She reached in her backpack and took out an air-horn, a small canister of compressed air with a horn at one end. A few short blasts later, she had the attention of the captain on the barge. He slowed the barge sufficiently, just in time to let the girls pass in front of him.

"Good thinking, Kate," Shirley said.

"Thanks," Kate replied. "It was either that, or we would have had to take off our T-shirts and waved them over our heads to get their attention!"

"That would definitely have done the job," Shirley replied. "Is that Matagorda Island in the distance?"

"I think so," Kate said.

They closed in on the island, covering the remaining distance within a few minutes. Once they reached the relative safety of the island, they started to relax and paddle a little more easily. The paddled around the south western side of the island in a silence interrupted only by the sound of water lapping against their kayaks, the slow swish of the paddles hitting the water and a plethora of bird calls, warbles and twitters. They were now in Mesquite Bay. It was a virtual oasis of nature, away from the sounds of human civilization. The serenity and absence of urban civilization was beautiful. It was just shortly after dawn and they could see any number of small birds, a few egrets and waterfowl.

"Did you know that most birds have toes with a muscular formation that tightens up like a little clamp when they relax?" Kate asked.

"Really," Shirley replied. "What does that do?"

"For one thing it helps them sleep perched on a tree branch at night," Kate replied.

"That's amazing," Shirley replied. "I always wondered how they did that."

They paddled on for a while as they circumnavigated around the island. The sun was up and sunlight streamed across the ripples they were making in the water. From time to time, they could make out an occasional shadowy outline of a fish in the water. Kate spotted a flock of birds hovering over a small land mass in the distance. It had to be Treasure Island since it was in the middle of Mesquite Bay and the girls paddled across towards it without difficulty.

"Jerry told me this is the best place to fish in the USA," Kate said.

"I agree," Shirley, remarked. "I love the feel of the Texas Gulf Coast. If I was Jean Lafitte, I'd be here every day with my bride."

"It is absolutely beautiful here," said Kate. "Can you imagine coming here and watching the mating dance of a pair of whooping cranes?"

"That would be awesome," Shirley replied.

"I'll bet Jeanne proposed to Eloise somewhere in this very bay," Kate said.

"Who's that?" Shirley inquired.

"Oh just someone from this area," Kate replied.

"That sounds so romantic," Shirley said dreamily.

They reached Matagorda Island a short while later. Treasure Island was actually a small group of islands in the middle of Mesquite Bay. They were actually quite easy to find because of the birds flying overhead and the herons fishing in ankle deep water near the islands. The girls worked their way around until they found a small sheltered lagoon where they could stop. They pulled their kayaks out of the water and dragged them up the beach to make sure they could not float away.

They had brought a picnic lunch with them and so they walked over to a shaded spot underneath some palm trees. They settled down to catch their breath. Kayaking can be hard work. The girls opened up their picnic lunches and proceeded to refuel.

"This is a great place to spend a lazy afternoon," Kate said.

"Yep," replied Shirley. "That was easily the best sandwich I've ever eaten."

"Funny how things taste better when you are outdoors," Kate said.

"I agree. It was delicious. We should do this more often," Shirley said.

The island they were on was extremely small and they could travel from one end of the island to the other in a few short minutes. There was hardly any vegetation, just a few occasional palm trees. The island had a sandy beach on all sides and the highest point was probably no more than ten feet above sea level. The other islands near them did not seem to be much larger.

"It looks like a good fishing spot," Shirley said. "I'm surprised the island is even here at all. It would not take much for it to disappear into the bay after a good-sized hurricane. It's a pleasant spot but there's just one problem. It doesn't have any restrooms."

"Oui Madame," said Kate.

"Yep, I've gotta wee," said Shirley. "Cold beer will do that to you every time. I'll be right back." She hurried around to the other side of the small cluster of trees. "I'm hot!" she exclaimed when she returned. She took off her T-shirt and waded into the rippling water for a dip. The water in the bay seemed clean enough and when she got to where it was waist deep Shirley dove in head first for a swim. It was a warm sunny day. The water felt heavenly from the moment it touched her skin. "Come on in, Kate," Shirley said. "The water's great. It feels just right, not too warm, not too cool, just dead solid perfect."

Kate hesitated for a minute. The death of Nicole and Zachary, the break-in at her B&B, all the interest in the sailor's trunk had given her a lot to think about. She took a careful look all around to make sure there were no strangers lurking in the shadows. She paused for a minute to put on some suntan lotion and then the spirit of pirate adventure caught up with her and she followed Shirley into the bay. The suntan lotion on her body glistened in the sunlight as she waded into the clear blue water in Copano Bay. Shirley was right. The water did feel great. They frolicked in the water and swam in the bay like a pair of mermaids. Then they walked out on the beach and sat down in the shade of the cluster of trees. They put on some more sun tan lotion and spread their towels out on the sand for a generous helping of Vitamin D. After some time they took another dip and walked along the beach looking for buried treasure and seashells. They could have been a pair of schoolchildren on a field trip collecting calcium carbonate specimens for a class project.

"This place is great. I'm going to have to come back here with Ray sometime," Kate said.

"Let me know when you plan to come here," Shirley said. "I don't want to run into you having sex on the beach. That would take scar me emotionally for the rest of my life."

"Oh please," Kate replied. "You know people do it all the time."

"I guess so," Shirley said. "It's only been once for me, when I was graduating from high school. It wasn't very good."

"You should bring Troy out here sometime," Kate said.

"I might," replied Shirley, unconvincingly.

"What about that Frenchman?" Kate asked, trying not to be too inquisitive. "What's going on with you two?"

"I haven't been able to figure him out," Shirley replied. "He spends a lot of time in the bakery but I'm not sure if he's really interested in me or just my muffins. He hasn't even tried to get to first base. Louis is either waiting for a fast ball on the outside corner of the plate that he can hit out of the ball park, or maybe I'm just not his type."

"I wonder if Jean Lafitte used to bring his girl friends here," Kate mused.

"I'll bet he did," Shirley replied. "This is a perfect spot for a luau. All you need out here is some rum, a ukulele, some palm trees, banana leaves, river rocks, firewood and a roasted pig."

Kate looked around. It was a beautiful spot. A great place for a small grass shack built with palm tree fronds. However, clearly it was not ideal for hiding pirate treasure. Anything that had been hidden here could easily end up as a casualty to the hurricanes that roared through the Gulf each year. It could disappear completely with the shifting sands of time and end up as a shallow sandbar beneath the waves of the ocean by the time one returned to retrieve it.

The sound of waves lapping gently along the shore was broken by the dull sputter of a motor boat in the distance. They waited for it to go away. However, the sound of the motor boat grew louder and suddenly came into view. The motor boat stopped and had gone silent, bobbing up and down in the distance as if to say "Don't mind me; I'm just part of the scenery". They could see some movement in the distance.

"Uh oh," said Kate. "That's got to be Troy driving by just to keep an eye on you," Kate remarked. The girls had strayed a little further than they had planned from the shelter of the trees and it was obvious they had already been spotted.

Shirley looked around her nervously. Troy was certainly capable of doing just that. The girls turned to walk back towards the grove of trees where they had left their T-shirts. There seemed to be more than one person on the boat. If it was not Troy then it was possible the Frenchmen had followed them. Kate was very conscious of them tracking her movements. She had not appreciated the fact that they had spied upon them from the fishing pier in Austwell with their field glasses.

"Here's a really cool shell," Kate said, bending down as she picked it up. She paused to get a better look at the boat. The letters on the boat were hard to read from this distance. "Does that look like a Blue Horizon Charter?" she asked Shirley. Blue Horizon was a fishing charter that operated out of Port Aransas.

"Yes it is," said Shirley as she walked toward Kate. "I doubt that it's Troy. By my count there are at least four people on the boat."

"I agree," said Kate. "It's probably not Troy. I suspect it's the Frenchmen who have been hanging around with Ken. Although, I don't see Ken anywhere on deck."

"He must be below the deck," Shirley said. "Probably getting seasick!" At that, the girls broke out in laughter.

Shirley heaved a sigh of relief. She really did not like Troy following her movements as much as he did. Sometimes she felt as if he was stalking her. Who knew what surveillance equipment he had in his police cruiser. Now Louis was a completely different matter. He seemed like such a lost, sick puppy that she couldn't help her desire to possess him and help him become organized. She knew that Kate thought he was a loser, and in all fairness, she had only known him for a few short weeks. However, as far as she was concerned he could put his shoes under her bed anytime. Frenchmen were renowned for being excellent lovers, men who knew all about the secret arts of making love and how to do all kinds of special stuff with their hands, fingers, tongue and toes! Why should she have to settle for less? Shirley had felt very deprived in this area from the time that her first boyfriend had practically raped her in his urgent need to satisfy himself at her expense. That was never going to happen again.

Kate and Shirley could not make out who was on the boat. It could be anybody. Kate knew that it would take a few visits to the Swamp Shack to find out who had been on the charter that day. If the three Frenchman had rented the fishing charter, then the boys from France got a free picture postcard from Texas.

The Goose Island girls walked slowly along the shore, as if the fishing boat were invisible. They stopped every now and then to pick up a few more seashells. They were not about to let the fishing charter know it bothered them in the least. In any case, the boys from France were probably quite used to nudity in public beaches. It was not anything they had not seen a hundred times before in Biscarosse. The only person who would be inconvenienced with their nudity was Ken Porter. If he was with them, Kate knew that he would not be able to sleep without wetting himself for months afterwards.

"I think that's Louis on the boat," Shirley said. "I get hot just thinking about him," she added.

"I know," said Kate. "I don't trust him." Shirley did not know about the New Orleans Traders. Kate hoped that they were not watching her from the fishing boat.

Shirley giggled. She placed the palms of her hands underneath her breasts in a seductive gesture. "Choux à la crème" she said with a reference to a delightful cream filled French pastry she had just learned to make. She relished the thought that Louis may be watching her through his field glasses.

Kate smiled. "You better put your muffins away girl, before someone comes here looking for honey BBQ ribs to sink their teeth into," she said.

When Kate and Shirley reached the grove of palm trees, they put on their T-shirts. Life seemed to return to normal as soon as they were dressed once again. They hauled their kayaks down to the water and began to paddle back home. The fishing boat seemed to have disappeared to the other side of Treasure Island. Shirley's heart was racing nineteen to the dozen as she thought of Louis checking her out from the fishing boat.

"That was fun," said Shirley. "I hope we gave those pirates from France their money's worth."

"Any self-respecting Texan would need to hold his ten gallon hat in front of him for a month after seeing you on the beach," Kate replied. "Troy is in for the treat of a lifetime when he finally gets you alone for an evening."

Shirley smiled, "So that's where the expression 'hats off' comes from, don't you think?" She basked in the pleasure of knowing that she had crossed an imaginary line in the sand. It was fun to be a bad girl every now and then.

"I just don't see where Jean Lafitte would have hidden his treasure out on that beach," Kate said.

"I agree. I think the treasure was the beach," Shirley replied.

*   *   *

As they wound their way back to Matagorda Island, they heard a roar in the distance. The sound engulfed them and suddenly a division of four military jets flew screaming through the air above them.

"Wow!" said Shirley. "What was that?"

"Probably a group of flying Mustangs," replied Kate who had spent many a late night watching WWII movies with her Dad as a child. As far as she was concerned, all military airplanes were Mustangs.

"There's an Air Force base not far from here," Shirley said.

"There must be something," replied Kate as she suddenly noticed a dot on the water moving rapidly towards them on the horizon. "I believe we have just met our escort home."

The tiny black dot had grown bigger as a Coast Guard Cutter approached them. It closed the distance between itself and the kayaks within a few minutes. A smartly dressed man in a white shirt, white shorts and seaman's cap stood at the bow of the ship.

"Hello," boomed a male voice from the cutter.

The girls waved back. Shirley kept waving even after Kate had stopped. She blew a kiss towards the handsome figure of the uniformed Coast Guard Officer.

Kate glared at her. The Coast Guard Cutter drew up next to them and stopped a short distance away to keep from capsizing their kayaks. They exchanged pleasantries and explained that they were just out on a birding expedition. After a few minutes, the Coast Guard Officer directed their attention to the opening that led to Mustang Lake and allowed them to continue their trip back to the Wildlife Refuge. As they paddled back the same way they had come the Coast Guard Cutter disappeared from view.

"It's good to see our tax dollars at work, helping keep the area safe from suspicious individuals," Shirley said.

"Just keep your shirt on and you'll be okay," Kate replied.

Kate thought that it seemed a little unusual to have attracted the Coast Guard's attention in an area that essentially comprised public land. Perhaps they had strayed too close to the military's nuclear arsenal.

The trip back took twice as long as their journey to Matagorda Island earlier that morning. They were tired and hungry and forced themselves to paddle back steadily, ignoring the heat and the glare of the mid-day sunshine. It was almost noon before they returned to the Wildlife Refuge. Throwing kayaks into the water was a lot easier than hauling them back out again and they struggled to free the red ice chest that contained their remaining beer. There was no sign of Kenneth Porter or the Frenchmen anywhere.

It took their combined efforts to carry the red cooler with the beer over to Kate's station wagon. Then they strapped their kayaks to a wheeled contraption to haul then from the edge of the water to the station wagon. Then they struggled to load their kayaks back on top of Kate's station wagon before starting their return trip back to Goose Island. Strapping the kayaks to the top of the wagon was a lot more difficult than they had expected, but eventually they got it done.

"It's not great but think it'll hold till we get home," Kate remarked as she added a final slipknot to the rope holding the kayaks in place. She attached a small red flag to the kayak to warn others on the highway of their precariously balanced cargo.

They drove along the road from the Wildlife Refuge to the Tivoli turn-off and headed south on Highway 35 towards Goose Island. Kate was driving well below the posted speed limit when a large SUV appeared behind her an in her rear view mirror. She could not make out the driver of the SUV. All she could see was that the fellow had a beard.

"Hey that looks like the musician who was pestering us at the Swamp Shack the other day," Kate said.

"Where?" asked Shirley.

"I think he's following us," Kate said. She pointed behind them while she peered into the reflection her rear view mirror.

"Really!" Shirley exclaimed. "Isn't that a little strange?"

"It's weird, is what I think," Kate replied. "Just what you get for living in Texas. Just a mix of He made a quick list of the folks who were still on the pier and Cowboys with prickly pears and Karankawa Indians."

"Is that like adding chocolate to a blueberry muffin," Shirley inquired.

Kate did not have time to respond. The car behind her was following so close that it was practically touching her rear bumper. Kate slowed and edged over in her lane to give the SUV behind them room to pass. For all practical purposes, she was now driving on the shoulder of the highway. However, the SUV stayed right on her rear bumper. It was a little creepy because there was no traffic from the opposite direction and plenty of room to pass her at any time. Not wanting to admit that she was being intimidated, Kate returned to the middle of her lane. As soon as she did so, Kate felt her station wagon lurch forward as she was bumped from behind. This was not funny.

"Shirley," Kate said urgently as she tried to size up the situation. "Call Troy and ask for help."

Shirley took her cell phone out of her purse. She was just about to press the buttons to dial Troy's number when the bearded fellow in the SUV rammed their station wagon again.

The cars collided with a loud WHACK! Kate's station wagon veered to one side as she fought to regain control. The cell phone fell out of Shirley's hands and fell to the floor.

"Rats!" Shirley screamed. "I've dropped the phone!"

"Here! Take mine," Kate said as she pushed her handbag towards Shirley.

SMACK! Kate's station wagon was bumped from behind once again. All she could see was the front bumper of the SUV in her rear view mirror.

Shirley dialed Troy's personal telephone and advised him of the situation. As she hung up the phone, the SUV was closing in on them again. The driver of the SUV seemed determined to run her off the road.

"Shirley," Kate yelled. "Do something".

Shirley took off her seat belt and climbed over to the back seat. She found the cooler and took out a can of beer. She squeezed her frame through the sunroof on top of the station wagon. It was not easy because the kayaks were in her way, but she was able to push them aside. Her hair was blowing past her ears the wrong way. She waited until the SUV was right behind them again. Then she zinged the beer can past the precariously balanced kayaks over the top of the station wagon.

"Woo Hoo!" Shirley screamed as the beer can hit its target. "Step on it sister!" she said looking down at Kate.

"Are you okay?" Kate screamed. She stepped on the gas and her station wagon lurched forward, rocketing down Highway 35. The fellows in Detroit sure knew how to build an engine.

The beer can exploded when it hit the driver's window. The SUV slowed just a fraction. It was enough to buy them another thirty seconds before the driver put on his windshield wipers and came after them again.

Shirley took aim with another beer can and lobbed it back. It missed and exploded on the pavement. So did her next beer and the one after that bounced harmlessly off the hood of the SUV. He was right behind her once again when she pitched another strike that whistled past the kayaks and exploded in a fury of foam on the windshield once again. It was an excellent pitch. The beer can took out one of the windshield wipers of the SUV. The captain of the Goose Island Softball League had just found her groove. She reloaded her perfectly shaped hand. She placed her index finger against the beer tab of the next can and waited for the SUV to close the gap before her next strike.

"Yee-haaa! Take that Sucker" Shirley yelled. A jagged line appeared in the windshield and Shirley knew the beer was having its desired effect on the occupant of the SUV. However, they were running low on beer and the next thing she found in her hand when she reached in the cooler was a small softball sized jar of mayonnaise.

The next time the SUV closed the gap, Shirley waited until it was almost touching the rear bumper of Kate's station wagon. The bottle of mayo left Shirley's hand like a ninety mile an hour fastball. It flew through the air and shattered the windshield. Despite the shattered windshield the SUV was still accelerating and it smacked into Kates wagon again with an alarming thud. Shirley had to hold on to keep from falling over backwards. Kate reached into the storage compartment to the left of her seat and removed a small utility knife. She handed Shirley the knife and motioned her to cut the cord holding the kayaks in place. Shirley grasped one of the kayaks with her free hand while Kate gunned the accelerator. With the SUV just a few inches away from Kate's station wagon, Shirley sliced through the cord holding the red kayak in place. The red kayak hung in the air for a moment, suspended like an acrobat at the circus, and then it flipped over as it broke loose of its remaining restraints and crashed through the front of the SUV's windshield for another strike. It all happened in a flash.

The SUV slowed down almost immediately. Kate heaved a sigh of relief as the SUV came to a halt behind her. She continued driving home well above the speed limit. She only slowed down when she was sure they had successfully repelled the attack from the SUV. They continued on to Goose Island without further incident. Kate was convinced that the driver of the SUV had to be one of the Frenchmen or someone working for the New Orleans Traders.

"That was fun," Shirley said as they finally turned off Highway 35 and headed down the road that led into their town ship. "You know what they say about beer, it's not just for breakfast anymore."

"I hope we didn't hurt anybody," Kate said.

"Well it jolly well serves him right, if we did," Shirley said. Her heart was still beating twice as fast as it normally did. "Is it my imagination, or did that fellow remind you of the musician who tried to chat us up at the Swamp Shack the other day?" Kate asked.

"Yep," said Shirley. "He sure did! The next time I see him I'm going to knock him off the stage with some watermelon seeds!"

"Too bad we used up all our beer," Kate said.

"There's still one somewhere in the car," Shirley replied. "I was so nervous, I dropped one before I could throw it out the window."

Kate pulled into her driveway and looked at the smashed rear end of her car. The rear bumper was a mess. A few more French kisses from the SUV and her station wagon would look more like a sub-compact automobile. Shirley helped Kate unload the remaining kayak from the station wagon and they placed it beside the garage. Her heart was still pounding at twice its normal rate.

"Thanks for saving my life," Kate said.

"Sure," Shirley said. "Good thing we had lots of beer."

Kate nodded quietly. The whole incident had left her speechless. It didn't make any sense. Why would someone try to run her off the road on a lonely country road between Goose Island and Tivoli? Did the attacker think that the cooler full of beer was actually full of pirate gold and silver? Had someone observed them loading the station wagon at the Wildlife Refuge and assumed that the girls were trying to make off with Jean Lafitte's treasure trove? Had that person decided to move in for the kill after they had done all the detective work involved in deciphering the clues and finding the treasure?

"Did you get a look at the fellow in the SUV?" Kate asked

"No, not really. He had a beard, but did not look like anyone I know," Shirley replied.

Troy drove up to Kate's house a short while later. He had driven all the way to the Tivoli turn off on Highway 35 without finding any sign of a red kayak or a damaged SUV.

"All I found were some warm beer cans along the side of the highway," he said as he popped open a can. He was off duty now. "I couldn't help noticing it because it's my favorite kind of beer. I had to stop and pick it up."

"So does that beer go into evidence room at the Sherriff's office?" Shirley asked smiling broadly.

Troy didn't answer right away. "I'm not supposed to drink on duty Miss Shirley, so you're welcome to it," he said handing the can over to her.

"Thanks," Shirley said. She reached over and took the beer over from him. She opened it carefully, expecting it to explode but it had had plenty of time to settle. She took a long swallow and passed the can to Kate who did the same. It felt good to be home, safe and sound.

"Anyone who stops to pick up an unopened beer lying along the side of the road has got to be a true Texan," Kate said, turning towards Shirley.

"Either that or he's a prickly pear," Shirley replied.

"I guess the driver of the SUV must have driven home with the kayak sticking out the front of his windshield," Kate said.

"I think he was trying to throw a scare into you, Miss Kate," Troy said. "Outside of that I'm not sure what he could possibly have hoped to gain by attacking you the way he did."

"That maniac was trying to run us off the road!" Shirley exclaimed. "We could have ended up dead!"

"Just like Zachary and Nicole," Kate said softly, almost as if she was talking to herself.

."Who?" Shirley and Troy asked in unison.

"The couple who owned the wooden trunk before I bought it at auction," Kate added.

"I suppose it is possible that it was the same person," said Troy.

What was really frustrating about the entire incident was that they were no closer to solving the mystery of the wooden trunk. The group dispersed. Everyone was exhausted. What had started out as a picnic had ended as a violent reminder of the reality that they faced every day after finding the pirates trunk. Kate rummaged in her car until she found the beer that Shirley had dropped under the front seat. She sipped it slowly as she went into the house.

"What a day," Kate thought to herself as she started to check her messages when her phone rang. It was Shirley on the line.

≈≈≈≈≈≈

Fool's Gold

"Kate," began Shirley. "I've been robbed."

"What?" Kate said. "Are you okay?"

"Yes, I think so," said Shirley. "The door was open and the apartment had been broken into when I returned home a short while ago. I'm not sure if they took anything. This doesn't make sense because I'm sure I don't have anything of much value. Why would someone think it was work the time an effort to try and rob me?"

"Just hang on Shirley. Go outside your apartment and wait near the apartment manager's office. Please get out of the apartment in case someone is still there. I'll be right over" Kate said.

Kate hopped on her bicycle and was at the Breakers Apartments in less than two minutes. She got there just as Troy was pulling up with his lights flashing and his siren blaring.

The break-in was very similar to the one that had been orchestrated at Kate's house.

There was definitely a pattern to the robber's motives. However, Kate could not help wondering how many people were involved. The fellow who had broken into Shirley's apartment could not have been the same person who had driven them off the road. There were definitely at least two separate individuals involved in the highway incident and the break-in. Perhaps they were working together. The bearded attacker on the highway may have been trying to given the robber at Shirley's apartment time to complete his break-in. If the blues musician from the Swamp Shack had been responsible for the highway incident then who had broken into Shirley's apartment? Who was the fellow on the fishing boat spying on them in Mesquite Bay? Was there a whole army of deviates hell bent on making their lives miserable?

"I'm just glad you are okay," Kate said.

They followed Troy through the apartment as he went through each room meticulously. After all this was his fiancée whose home had been broken into and vandalized.

"Do you really have to go through my underwear, Troy?" Shirley asked as Troy went through the apartment with a fine toothcomb. At the rate he was going it would take all year before he was done.

"Sorry," Troy said sheepishly. "I must have gotten a little distracted, that's all. I'm almost done here."

Troy finished his report while seated at the kitchen table while Kate and Shirley waited in the living room.

"You'll have to get the door repaired," said Kate. "Perhaps the apartment complex will help you with that.

"I should think they will," Shirley said. "I guess this is pretty similar to what happened over at your place not too long ago, is it?"

"I'm pretty sure it's the same person or persons doing this," said Troy from the dining room. "I can't wait to wring their necks."

*   *   *

After Troy left, Kate insisted that Shirley spend the night at the B&B. She had plenty of room and they could tidy up Shirley's apartment together the next day. Shirley did not protest. They returned to the B&B in Kate's station wagon. It was still driving reasonably well.

Kate went into the kitchen to prepare dinner, a green salad and a casserole dish. Courtney and Glenda were seated by the window, playing a word game. They greeted Kate warmly. Shirley watched the news with Courtney and Glenda while Kate was baking the caserole. They shared a bottle of red wine with dinner. Kate and Shirley shared some of the highlights of the day with Courtney and Glenda. Kate shared just enough information to explain the damage to her station wagon. Even though Courtney and Glenda were quite capable of whacking an intruder with their walking sticks, it would not be good for her houseguests to feel concerned for their safety.

The rear fender on her station wagon was damaged, and the license plate would need a little duct tape to hold it in place. However, at least it was still drivable. She needed the vehicle to operate the B&B. Ray was due in on Friday and she was really looking forward to seeing him again.

Courtney complimented her on how fresh and radiant she looked whenever Ray came to visit.

"Thanks," Kate nodded. There were no secrets in this house.

"I think you make a lovely couple, dear," Glenda added.

Kate thanked them both. Sometimes she felt closer to Courtney and Glenda than she did to her own mother who was more prone to find fault with her friends than to approve of them. After Courtney and Glenda had retired to their rooms, Kate and Shirley Kate cleared away the dishes after dinner. Kate shared her suspicions about the three Frenchmen with Shirley. It was an uphill sell, because Shirley had her mind made up that Louis was one of the good guys. If she had known he was going to break into her apartment she would probably have left the key under the doormat.

"If Louis broke into my apartment while we were out kayaking, then who were the men watching us from the boat at Matagorda Island?" Shirley said.

"I don't know," Kate said slowly. She had not really been able to see who was on the boat.

"I'm sure he didn't do it," Shirley replied. "He's not like that."

*   *   *

Kate woke early the next morning. She brewed a fresh pot of coffee and got busy in in the kitchen to prepare breakfast for her guests. She placed some freshly squeezed orange juice in a small carafe resting on a bed of ice cubes. Then, she sliced some fresh strawberries and served these with blueberries and some mildly sweetened sour cream. She poured herself a cup of coffee and waited for her guests to wake up and enter the dining area in the kitchen. She surveyed her kitchen table with the satisfaction of knowing that she had just served another perfect meal for her guests.

While she was waiting for Shirley, Courtney and Glenda to wake, Kate dialed the telephone number of her insurance company to report the damage to her station wagon. No, she did not know who had bumped into her car on Highway 35. Yes, she had filed a police report. After taking down the information about the accident, the insurance company assured her the use of a loaner vehicle while her car was being repaired at one of their approved repair facilities. Kate insisted that the loaner vehicle had to be either a full size car in order to allow her to continue to operate her B&B. The insurance company advised her to send some pictures of the damage to them vial email. An insurance adjuster would stop by to look at her vehicle the next day.

Kate knew it was only a matter of time before the hoodlums who had broken into Shirley's apartment would make another attempt to steal the trunk. She had owned the chest for a few short weeks and both her house and Shirley's apartment had been burglarized. She really did not like putting her friends at risk of a break-in.

After breakfast, Kate picked up the phone and dialed Troy's telephone number. She approached Troy for assistance in finding a place to store the trunk for a while. Troy was equally concerned and already given the matter considerable thought. He was convinced that the three Frenchmen were the root cause of the recent break-ins. He did not like them hanging around on 'his' island. He advised Kate that he would be more than happy to take possession of the trunk on her behalf. He was secretly hoping they would try to break into his house. When they did, he planned to gather the evidence that he needed to put them safely behind bars for a long time.

Jerry came over to help. They retrieved the trunk from the attic. Troy and Jerry helped load it into her station wagon.

"That's an awesome trunk, Kate" Troy said after they had carried it into his apartment. "The fire breathing dragon on one side of the trunk looks like it's about to blow some serious smoke."

"Thanks Troy," Kate said. "You know it used to belong to Lucy Dubois's parents at one time."

"Lucy Dubois!" Troy exclaimed. "I remember her. She moved out of town last year, didn't she? She sure has had a difficult life. Was that her Mom and Dad that were killed in the hit and run on Highway 35 right after Christmas?" Troy asked. "The one where the driver lost control and ran off the road?" he added. "I happened to be in the area that day and helped direct traffic right after the crash. We had to close both sides of the highway for some time to let the emergency vehicles through to the crash site. It seemed as though traffic was backed up all the way to Tivoli."

"Yes," Kate replied. "My guess is that Zachary and Nicole were returning from Corpus Christi after having the trunk evaluated," Kate replied. "The individuals responsible for the accident were probably not aware that the trunk was in the vehicle, or else they would have stolen it immediately after the accident. There was a break-in at Zachary and Nicole's house at the time of the crash. I think the break-in and the crash were related. The crash prevented Zachary and Nicole from returning home and interrupting the burglars who were searching for the trunk at that very time! After the crash, the trunk ended up in police custody until I purchased it at auction last week."

"Wow!" Troy's eyes narrowed. If the Frenchmen were responsible for the death of an elderly, retired couple from Goose Island, then they were going to have to pay for their crime. "So their house was being burgled at about the same time that the crash took place. I guess the crooks were trying to keep them from getting home so that they could rob their place while they were out."

"Exactly," Kate replied. "The burglary was never reported because Zachary and Nicole never made it home that night." She breathed a sigh of relief. Troy was finally getting around to seeing it her way.

Meanwhile Troy's police training kicked into high gear. "That makes sense," he said. "How do you know about this?"

"Lucy had me check up on her parents' house for her," Kate said. "When I was there I happened to notice that there was a New Orleans telephone number on their answering machine. I recognized it because it was the exact same number as someone who called me up asking to buy the trunk recently. It's hard to miss a 504 New Orleans area code. The message had been left on their answering machine the morning of the crash. It had to be related because both Zachary and Nicole were dead by the evening."

"And you saw some evidence of a break-in?" Troy asked.

"Yep!" Kate replied. "The back door had been broken into. The burglars probably used a credit card to wedge the door open. It's not that hard to do."

"That's very interesting," Troy said. "So this crazy trunk might be indirectly responsible for the death of two innocent people at

Christmas and two burglaries in the last month. How very interesting."

"I'll admit it's circumstantial," Kate replied. "However, there is one more detail. Zachary and Nicole's dog Bentley was picked up by animal control that evening. My guess is that Bentley chased the burglars away and then ended up outside the house after they left. One of the neighbors went to the front door to contact Zachary and Nicole to let them know that Bentley was stuck outside the house. When they did not answer, they called Lucy. In the meantime, Animal Control picked up Bentley. Lucy had a friend rescue Bentley from Animal Control the next day."

"How much do you know about this trunk anyway?" he asked

"Not a whole lot," Kate replied.

"I know it's none of my business, Kate, but if you don't mind I'd like to make a few discreet inquiries if that is okay with you."

"That sounds better than okay Troy," Kate said. "I'm very grateful for any help you can provide." Since the accident had occurred near Goose Island Kate knew that Troy planned to make it his business. Still, it never hurts to thank someone for their efforts, even if they are only trying to do their job.

*   *   *

Her new kitchen counters were installed later that day. True to their word, the installers from the hardware store were in and out of her kitchen in less than two hours.

"I think I'm in love with Amarillo Bamboo Quartz" Kate remarked as she gazed at the new counters after the installers had left. She wiped down her new granite counters with a polishing compound until they gleamed. Glenda and Courtney nodded with approval.

"Welcome to the twenty first century," Courtney said.

"Yes dear," Glenda added. "The plastic counters you had before were probably as old as me, a relic of the fifties and sixties".

"You mean forties, don't you?" Courtney said.

"They didn't make synthetic counters in the forties," Glenda retorted. "All we had then was ceramic tile on concrete. I think you're starting to lose your memory, dear."

"I had plastic counters in the forties," Courtney insisted.

Glenda chose to ignore Courtney's remark. "All I'm saying dear is that the new counters look absolutely wonderful," Glenda replied.

Shirley and Troy stopped by the house later that day to admire the counters as well.

"Awesome," said Shirley.

"Very nice," Troy added.

"If I didn't know any better, I'd say there were real specks of gold in the granite," Shirley said.

"Fool's gold," Troy replied. "Looks just like the real thing."

*   *   *

Still glowing with satisfaction from having had her kitchen counters replaced, and the anticipation of meeting Ray again Kate left Goose Island and drover to Corpus Christi to meet Ray at the airport. They stopped to eat at the Swamp Shack on the way to Goose Island. Even though he had been away for four paltry days, it had seemed like an eternity. So much had happened.

The bearded guitarist who had approached Kate the last time she had been at the Swamp Shack with Shirley was nowhere in sight. Instead, there were three older guys playing some familiar Country and Western tunes. Kate asked the bartender, a shapely girl named Tish, if she had seen him and learned that he was not scheduled to return anytime soon. He was from New Orleans and as far as Tish knew, he had returned to play at a bar near Jackson Square. Kate raised her eyebrows. Was it simply a coincidence that the bearded guitarist had returned to New Orleans right after someone with a beard had tried to run her off the road?

"What's that all about?" Ray inquired.

"Oh nothing," Kate said. "Fellow with a beard. He was just playing some Delta Blues here the other day. Pretty good musician."

"Oh! Okay," Ray said.

Kate filled Ray in on all the adventures she had just had. She had so much to tell him. Ray was amazed that she had actually purchased a pair of kayaks and spent the day with Shirley looking for buried treasure on a small island in Mesquite Bay. Kate skipped over the part where the Blue Dolphin Charter had surprised Shirley and herself while they were swimming in the water near Matagorda. She continued her account with the insane drive home. "Who were these people?" she wondered, even as she filled Ray in on the events that had transpired since his last visit.

"Do you think the fellow behind the wheel of that SUV was that bearded musician," Ray asked.

"Hard to say," Kate replied. "It's not a crime to have a beard."

"I guess it comes in handy to have a beard when you don't want to be recognized," Ray said.

Kate was convinced that the break-in at Shirley's apartment had been orchestrated by the New Orleans Traders at the precise moment that their station wagon was being attacked on Highway 35. Just like Nicole and Zachary. The only difference is that she had survived, thanks to Shirley's softball skills. It was too much of a coincidence.

"Wow!" Ray said, as Kate had just paused to catch her breath. "This is so unbelievable. I'm so glad you're okay".

"It's been a really crazy week," Kate replied. "I feel as though I stepped into the twilight zone."

They left the restaurant and returned home. The sun was just going down as they crossed the Copano Bay Causeway.

"I love going over this bridge," Kate remarked. "I especially love the feeling of floating momentarily on a cloud of air when going over the top of the bridge. It's the moment when you can see all of Goose Island surrounded by water as far as the eye can see. It feels as if I'm getting a warm hug and welcome back from Goose Island each time I return home."

Ray held her hand and kissed it gently. As they passed Shipwreck Beach, he pulled off the road. There was a full moon out that evening. The light from the moon danced upon the water and they watched the waves roll towards the shore. He could smell the aroma of the perfume Kate was wearing. She wrapped her fingers around his hand, and gave him a little squeeze. And just like that everything was right with the world once again. Ray turned towards her and gave her three little kisses – the third kiss was their secret handshake. They drove silently to her house. Kate always felt as though she was on fire whenever she was with Ray. She couldn't wait to be alone with him.

"I always feel warm and loved when I'm next to you Kate," Ray said as they walked into the living room.

"Me too," she said, giving him a hug in the kitchen as she paused to pick up a bottle of wine from the kitchen counter. "Here, hold this," she said handing him the bottle while reaching in the kitchen drawer for a bottle opener.

"I love you Kate," Ray said as he took the bottle of wine from her. He recognized the label. It was the same wine they always shared when they were together. He opened the bottle. The familiar spice, cherry and oak flavor was smooth and refreshing. He took another sip. "I don't think I could ever see enough of you," he confessed earnestly as he caressed her hands. He meant every word he was saying. He liked nothing better than when he was alone with

Kate, the most beautiful girl in the world. He never tired of looking into her hazel brown eyes or listening to her musical voice as she described the routine events in her everyday life. Every word she spoke made the most mundane things come alive in a magical way. Everything that Kate did was wonderful and exciting. The time they spent together seemed to disappear quickly, making entire days feel like minutes.

"Well in that case, there's a lot more to look at," she said. There was no sign of Courtney and Glenda. Kate unzipped the zipper on her jeans very deliberately and started towards the stairs. She took off her T-shirt in a single movement, turning back briefly to see if he was behind her, going up the stairs two at a time to her room.

"Slow down," Ray said. "I wanted to do that," he added as he tried to keep up with her. "With my teeth!"

"Too late," she replied, as she entered the room. She tossed her T-shirt on the chair by the window.

True to form, Kate wasn't wearing any bloomers. Ray's eyeballs popped a wheelie. They did a double turn in their sockets as he gazed at the dessert menu, trying to decide where to start.

"You look just like a slice of apple pie with two scoops of vanilla ice cream," he said.

GOOSE ISLAND BLACK JACK

"I'm not sure about this," Kate replied with a laugh. "You look like you haven't eaten in weeks. Are you sure you can handle all these calories!"

≈≈≈≈≈

Ferdies

Peter Scully showed up early the next morning just as Kate was getting the coffee started. She was not expecting to find his tow truck in the driveway at the crack of dawn. She hurried outside to ask him whatever in the world he thought he was doing.

"Well, hello, Miss Kate," Peter said. "Top of the morning to you."

"Don't you ever sleep?" Kate asked. She liked Peter. He had an honest face and an open, easy smile. He never kept his customers waiting. Anyone who had called to request his services for a tow could count on him to make an appearance within minutes. Quite unlike Bill Smithers, the fellow who had helped Kate with repairs to her spa and who practically had to be goaded into action.

"I can't sleep a wink, since I got hitched last year," Pete replied with a wink. "You know how it is once you do that, Miss Kate. Miss Betty is not like any other pick-up truck I've known."

Kate smiled. Obviously, Pete was referring to his new wife, Betty, and not some run-down old F150.

"So I take it Miss Betty's got a nice engine does she?" Kate inquired. "I hear she came with a lifetime warranty."

"That she did, Miss Kate. I plan to keep her until death do us part. She is a real beauty, Miss Kate. Very sleek. Nice profile. Great features. You should see the controls on the dashboard. It'll astound you just to look at all the features she has. You name it. She's got it. Zero to sixty in less than three seconds. Betty is better than a top of the line V8 –Hemi. I'm in love with her," Pete replied. "Anyhow, I'm here to pick up your station wagon and take it down to Port Aransas for repairs," Pete added, coming back down to earth. "The fellow from the insurance company should be here any minute with your loaner."

Sure enough a black sedan pulled into the driveway even as Pete was getting Kate's station wagon hitched up to his tow truck. A well-dressed fellow stepped out of the sedan. He handed Kate a set of keys. She signed the documents he placed before her on his clipboard, and took some pictures of the damage to her station wagon.

"I am impressed, Peter," Kate remarked. "You seem to have branched out well beyond the tow truck business"

"Well, you know how it is, Miss Kate," Peter replied. "A fellow has to do what a fellow must do. . Miss Betty thought that it might be good to get into the Insurance business, in addition to what I was doing before. She has a computer in the house and knows how to fill out all the forms and such. I could never do it without her."

The fellow who had driven the black sedan to Kate's house hopped into the tow truck with Peter. Before long, both Peter and the insurance man pulled out of Kate's driveway with her wagon. Miss Betty seemed to have a good head on her shoulders.

*   *   *

Shirley and Troy stopped by the B&B later the next day. The girls were in no mood to cook. They decided to eat at a popular local Italian restaurant, Giordano's, a landmark institution located at one end of the Goose Island Square. Giordano's always had excellent food and an outstanding house wine that was imported directly from Italy. The tomatoes and peppers that were used in many of the dishes on the restaurant's menu often came directly from

Francesca Giordano's green house. The plants loved the temperate Texas climate and flourished under the love and attention that Francesca lavished on them.

"Do you ever get any customers who try to pay you in silver?" Shirley asked Kate, moving her arm away from the table as Donatello Giordano, the proprietor of the restaurant, opened a bottle of Chianti and leaned forward to serve them.

"Not that I recall," Kate replied. "Why do you ask?"

"Louis asked me if anyone had ever tried to pay me in silver," Shirley said. "Apparently people in Bordeaux use it all the time. I told him that we quit using silver coins back in the sixties. Occasionally, I find a silver JFK dime in my change drawer at the bakery at the end of the day, but it's so rare that I honestly don't recall the last time I found one. "

Kate and Ray exchanged glances across the table. Donatello had finished pouring the wine but it seemed that he too wanted to listen to this conversation.

"Louis' dad, Henri is the owner of an antique store in France," Shirley said by way of explanation. She looked around the table expectantly for further questions, suddenly aware that everyone around the table was looking at her.

"So that's in addition to the Goose Island Antiques?" Kate said.

"Yes," Shirley replied. "His brother Sebastian teaches history at a university near Paris," she added.

"How nice," Kate replied.

There seemed to be a pattern to the madness after all. Someone who taught history probably knew more than a little bit about Jean Lafitte. Someone like Sebastian who was familiar with the locale where Jean had been raised probably knew all about Jean's legacy. Kate wondered if Henri and Sebastian were related to Jean Lafitte through common ancestry.

"Did Louis tell you what these silver coins look like?" Kate asked Shirley.

"I think they are the same shape and size as the ones we have in America," Shirley said. "But they don't have a picture of a lady or a president on them. From what I understand they are called Ferdies," she said distractedly. "Perhaps Louis said they are Freddies? I'm not sure. I think he said they have pictures of lions on them. I told him I'd be sure to let him know if I ever found one in my change drawer."

"He's probably talking about Spanish silver coins from the 1850's," Ray said. "They had a picture of King Ferdinand of Spain on them."

"His Uncle Sebastian did say something about Spain," Shirley said. "Is that part of France?"

"No," Kate replied. "It's a separate country in Europe that's just south of France."

"Oh I get it. You mean like Mexico," Shirley said.

Kate nodded. She was not sure what Shirley got and didn't get, or whether it even mattered, so long as she kept making the best muffins, kolaches and éclairs in town.

"Spanish silver dollars used to be widely used in America and in the new world before we had our own currency," Ray said. "In fact you could break a silver coin into eight bits. Two bits were a quarter and four bits were a half dollar."

The others at the table looked at Ray in amazement. He was a walking encyclopedia.

"King Ferdinand and Queen Isabella of Spain were actually responsible for encouraging Christopher Columbus in his search for the 'new' world," Ray continued. "One of the oldest cities in Texas is Port Isabel, which is named after Queen Isabella."

"Is that what this trunk business is all about?" Troy asked. "Does someone think that thing is full of old Spanish silver coins?"

"We are still trying to figure that out, ourselves," Kate replied.

Donatello stood by the table, waiting to take their order. "I grew up looking for treasure," he said, his deep voice resonating as he reminisced about his childhood. "I used to love going to the beach when I was a kid. I used to think it was only a matter of time before I found a hoard of old coins and helped my parents buy their own house."

"Spanish silver was used all over the world at one time," Donatello continued. "Don't forget that Spain ruled the world in the fifteenth century. I used to go swimming in the bay when I was a boy looking for Spanish silver coins. I even found one or two, but you had to dive deep into the ocean to find them. My brother and I used to go swimming naked in the ocean. Sometimes my girlfriend used to come along." He turned to see if his wife, Francesca was listening.

Kate turned to look at Francesca. It was hard to imagine Donatello, a portly middle-aged man, and heavy-set Francesca, swimming naked in the Bay of Sicily.

"Not me," Francesca said, shaking her head. "Must have been someone else. We are going to have to talk about this tonight, mio caro," she said, turning to Donatello.

"Si tesoro mio," he replied.

"We had a lot of fun," he continued. "It is very liberating to be free in every possible way." Donatello was looking directly at Kate and Shirley with a wistful expression on his face.

Kate looked at Shirley and her eyes registered the raised eyebrow look that told her Shirley had had the exact same thought. Was it possible that the man in the boat who had witnessed their brazen adventure on the sandy isle in Copano Bay had probably been no other than Donatello? If so, the girls knew that their secret was safe with him.

I could hold my breath for almost two minutes when I was sixteen," Donatello continued. "I would have found more silver coins if I had not started smoking when I turned eighteen. I was only trying to impress Francesca. Thank goodness she made me stop smoking before she would marry me."

Donatello explained how the Spanish dollar coins had milled edges to prevent the practice of shaving the edges of the coins between transactions.

"Those men from France were asking me about silver coins, not long ago," he continued. "I told them that I know all about silver coins. I told them that for one Spanish silver dollar with a picture of King Charles of Spain, you could have all the pizza you want for a month. After some time they stopped asking me about silver."

"Spanish dollars were the main currency of the new world for several hundred years, until

America began minting its own dollars in 1857," Ray explained. "In fact the word 'dollar' comes from the Bohemian 'taler' which is named after the valley or 'tal' where silver was mined to make coins for the Holy Roman Empire."

"How cool," Kate said. "Since Spain ruled Mexico, which included Texas, for over three hundred years, ending in 1821, I suppose it is possible that there could be some Spanish Talers buried in our very own back yard."

"Yes indeed," replied Donatello. "Be careful, Kate. There is a rumor on the island that you may have found a secret treasure map. You know how people talk! Please do be careful. I love you like a daughter and I am concerned about your safety". Then he turned to attend to some of the other customers in the restaurant.

Donatello's cautionary remarks stopped Kate dead in her tracks. Suddenly Goose Island seemed to have shrunk in size as she felt that she was being observed by everyone in the restaurant. Besides her friends and neighbors, everyone except Shirley, she did not know whom she could trust. Kate knew Shirley so well that she knew that she would never intentionally reveal confidential information to anyone. It would happen purely by accident. Ever since Shirley had befriended Louis, Kate knew that anything she shared with Shirley would automatically reach Louis and probably the rest of the island as well. It was a good thing that Shirley did not know the precise location of the trunk at that time. It would have to be moved somewhere safe before long, preferably off the island.

"Spain ruled the world for hundreds of years until they were conquered by Napoleon," Ray added, not realizing Kate's predicament. This was just another problem to be solved, and he was more than up to the challenge. "Everything changed after Napoleon was defeated by the British in 1814. It was a very difficult time for all their colonies around the world. "

*   *   *

Kate studied maps of many of the islands in the world and compared each one to the shape of the hollowed out eye within the skull on the pirate flag. There were several close matches. One of the matches resembled Indian Key, a small island in the midst of the Florida Keys. This seemed possible given the role that the Keys had played in the early days of the Confederate States of America. In the early 1800's the keys were called the Wrecking Islands due to the number of ships that had run aground in the Keys as they rounded the Dry Tortugas on their way to the Atlantic from New Orleans. Pirates roamed up and down the Florida Keys, and Jean Lafitte would have known the Florida coastline as well as he knew Texas. However, Kate's first thought was that Jean would not have selected the Florida Keys to hide his treasure. There were so many ruffigans loitering around the Florida Keys at any given time. He could not have felt comfortable about being observed while he was actively attempting to hide his fortune. Any one of a hundred other pirates would surely have helped themselves to his treasure before he was out of sight of Indian Key. He would have returned years later to retrieve a handful of sand instead of the gold and silver he expected to find.

The shape and contour of the right eye of the pirate skull was also a close match for the island of Kauai, in Hawaii. The placement of the diamond just to the west of the center of the eye suggested that the treasure was located somewhere near the central region on the West Coast of Kauai. Kate's imagination ran wild as she concluded that the treasure was behind a waterfall in Kauai. The relative distance of Kauai from Texas was simply a minor detail. An expert sailor like Jean Lafitte could easily have circumnavigated the globe at any time in his career to visit the Sandwich Isles.

As Kate studied the digital photograph of the pirate flag that she had transferred to her computer she noticed the number 1821 carved into the cross guard, directly below the hilt of the sword to the right of the waterfall. 1821 was the year that Mexico gained its independence from Spain. It was also the year when Jean Lafitte left Galveston, never to be seen again. Why was this number present on the flag? It must have had a special significance for Jean. When he had left Galveston in 1821, after setting fire to his garrison, perhaps it was not a random act of desperation but one that had been planned secretly for many years.

The number could also represent something entirely different such as the distance from the treasure trove from a landmark. It might not be a calendar year at all. When Kate discussed this with Ray, he listened intently to her analysis. He was most intrigued with the suggestion that the shape of the pirate's eye looked like an island. As far as Raymond was concerned, islands were synonymous with adventure. As a child, Raymond Looney had spent several vacations visiting his grandparents in Sarasota, Florida. Grandpa and Grandma Looney had retired to live just a short distance from Siesta Key. Raymond was a welcome visitor who kept Grandma Looney entertained with his incessant chatter on many long walks along the sandy beaches nearby. His earliest childhood memories were of walking on the beach with Grandma Looney, wading through the breakers, swimming in the ocean, and building sandcastles. Grandma Looney had created a Pirate Adventure game that she played with him. She would draw a treasure map in the sand, and they would pretend that a piece of driftwood, a seashell, or even a coconut was buried treasure. He had grown up dreaming of finding a trove of pirate booty and sharing it with Grandma.

Ray's grandparents had taken him along on several camping trips in Florida. He was a more than willing tag-a-long who loved hanging out with Grandma Looney as she traipsed through some of the less strenuous hiking trails in the area. Ray was an intellectual sponge who soaked in all the biological diversity of Florida Everglades as Grandma Looney proceeded to take him under her wing and describe the flora and fauna of the plants in the region in detail. He also loved the beach. There had been several days in his life when nothing could have been better than to catch a few waves on South Beach.

Kate explained that she thought the treasure map on the Popeye the sailor's trunk suggested that the treasure was located on an island with a circular shape such as Kauai, or Indian Key in the Florida Keys. The location of the diamond in the eye socket on the map suggested the location of the treasure. The water flowing out of the pirate mouth suggested a relationship to a body of water such as a river or a waterfall 1821 paces from the beach.

"Why do you think the gold is hidden behind a waterfall?" Ray inquired, as he struggled to catch up with Kate's analysis of the pirate map. He was having some difficulty understanding the abstractions that the map represented.

"It's just a guess," replied Kate. "The map on the pirate flag has three diamonds sewn into the fabric, one in each eye and a third one on the pirates tooth which has lots of water flowing out of the mouth. The diamonds in the eye sockets tell you where to look for the treasure. The water flowing out of the pirate's mouth looks like it could be a waterfall or river of some kind. The diamond on the pirates tooth suggests that it is hidden behind a rock or boulder behind a body of water."

Kate hesitated to say much more because she wanted to get Ray's point of view uncluttered by her own personal bias. She had already decided that the treasure couldn't be in Texas because Texans had been looking for Jean Lafitte's treasure for decades. If the treasure had been buried in Texas, Kate was sure that someone would have found it by now.

"If you're looking for an island with a circular shape having lots of rivers and waterfalls, then it might just as well be in Kauai," Ray remarked.

"It does seem to be the perfect hiding place," Kate replied. "But it is such a long way from Texas that I just don't see how Jean Lafitte could have managed to sail all the way to Kauai when he left Galveston in 1821," Kate said. "Do you know if Hawaii had even been discovered by 1821?"

"Sure. Captain Cook died in Hawaii in 1779," Ray explained. "He had visited the Sandwich Islands once before on an earlier voyage. The first time he was perceived as a mythical God returning from across the sea. When he returned the second time, he was killed by the natives. According to the legend, God was only supposed to make one trip to the island. There was nothing in the legend about his return trip and some of the natives thought he was a phony when he returned."

"They were probably just trying to protect their women," Kate replied.

"That too," Ray said. "Most men get pretty upset when their wives run off with strangers, instead of staying home and taking care of their domestic needs."

"You mean like cooking and cleaning?" Kate asked. Her voice turned up one octave but Ray missed this subtle shift in their conversation.

"Exactly," Ray replied.

"Right!" Kate said. "Well around here the men don't eat unless they wash the dishes, take out the trash, and sweep the kitchen floor after supper. And there are a few weekly chores as well."

Ray didn't like the direction this was headed. "All I'm saying Kate is that if Captain Cook could travel to Hawaii twice by 1779, then maybe Jean Lafitte could have gone there and hidden his treasure there forty two years later."

"Well, yes. I suspect that Jean Lafitte was every bit a sailor as Captain Cook," Kate said in agreement.

"His pirate ship was much more modern and he certainly had the skills to go there if he chose to do so," Ray continued. "It does seem like a pretty good hiding place," he added, trying to build upon his theory.

"It does seem a little far," Kate said. "To travel to Kauai from Galveston he would have had to travel all the way around the tip of South America. The Panama Canal didn't appear on the map for another hundred years."

"Yes he would have to travel past Cape Horn, or 'Tierra Del Fuego' as it is called because of the mist that covers the islands at the southern tip of South America," Ray said. "A lot of gold and silver traveled to Spain from the New World making Spain one of the richest countries in Europe for some time," Ray continued. "Any self-respecting pirate would have seen it as his sworn duty to relieve the Spanish galleons of some of the treasure they were carrying back to Spain from the New World. He must have been familiar with the trip from Texas to Cape Horn."

"It is such a long journey," Kate replied. "It's over six thousand miles from Galveston to Cape Horn. Add on seven and a half thousand miles from there to Hawaii. Then there's the return journey. It is a bit of a hike. It would have taken at least a year to go there and back."

"How do you know he came back?" Ray inquired.

As Kate paused to reflect on Ray's question, she knew intuitively that the treasure was not in Kauai. Jean Lafitte had not spent a year travelling back and forth to Kauai, leaving his sweetheart, Eloise, behind in Corpus Christi. Kate also knew that Eloise had not left her family to live thousands of miles away from them. Jean Lafitte must have stashed his treasure in a safe place long before he had torched his garrison in Galveston in 1821. The treasure had to be in an area that he knew well and one he could easily have travelled to prior to his retirement. Indian Key was a far more likely spot for the treasure despite the popularity of the Florida Keys with all the other pirates in the region.

"The notion that Jean buried his treasure in Hawaii is so far-fetched that I hardly believe it could be true," Kate said. "If he had hidden his treasure chest on an island so far away that very few Europeans had ever traveled to it, the natives would probably dig up whatever he had left behind the minute he sailed away from the island. From what I understand, the natives were delighted to have bits of sea glass. Can you imagine how ecstatic they would be if they had found gold, silver, real rubies and diamonds? I think the chief would use those to decorate his New Year's Eve party dress."

"Well you do have a point there, Kate," Ray said. "Perhaps Kauai would make a terrible hiding place. However, you must admit the right eye looks remarkably similar to the island of Kauai. Hey, I wonder if we could somehow convince the trio from France that the treasure is somewhere else, other than in Goose Island. Do you think we could get Henri, Sebastian, and Louis off our backs and go searching for the treasure in Europe or in the Sandwich Islands?"

"Boy wouldn't that be sweet," Kate said. "It sure would be nice if we could get them to go somewhere far away and give us a chance to live in peace for a while."

"I wouldn't mind going to the Florida Keys for a vacation if you're up to it," Ray suggested. "The Keys are every bit as beautiful as Hawaii, and a lot closer to get to. There's a lot higher chance that Jean Lafitte spent some time in Florida after leaving Galveston. The Florida Keys and the Panhandle coastline is simply beautiful. I'll bet I can get you to fall in love with me all over again if we go there. It could be a most unforgettable experience."

"You are such a sweet boy," Kate said, giving him a hug. "I'm already in love with you and don't ever forget it. I'd go anywhere with you."

She closed her eyes and kissed him just as they cast off in a sudden rush of desire and rode the trade winds to a tropical destination. A place with white sandy beaches, palm trees, and rainbows. Sea water so clear and blue that you could look down and see schools of fish swimming in the ocean.

"Every moment I spend with you is unforgettable," Kate said.

≈≈≈≈≈≈

Batten Hatches

Kate had just returned home from a trip to the store. She knew something was wrong the moment she pulled into her driveway and got out of her car. Instead of coming up to the fence with his ball, Milo was pawing furiously at the back door to his house. He was determined to get inside even if he had to shred the door with his toenails. She paused when he saw Kate in her driveway.

"Woof!" he said, looking intently at Kate from across the yard. "Woof!" There was a sense of urgency in his bark that got Kate's attention. It sounded as though he had swallowed a dragonfly.

"Hey there, Milo," Kate said. "What's up buddy?"

"Woof!" replied Milo hoarsely and pawed at the screen door that led to his kitchen

Kate walked around to the front of Charlotte and Jerry's house and rang the doorbell. There was no response. In the distance, she could hear Milo bark once more.

She tried the handle on the door and found that it was locked. There was no one home.

She walked back to her station wagon and was about to go into her house when Milo barked again and pawed frantically at his screen door. That was unusual.

"Here Milo," Kate said. "Come here boy."

However, Milo steadfastly refused to come to the fence. He interspersed his barks with a soulful whine as if he was trying to tell Kate something.

Kate knew that she was going to have to go across the fence to find out why Milo was acting so strange. She went into her garage for a minute and returned with two small folding metal chairs. She placed one chair on either side of the chain link fence that separated them and fashioned an impromptu ladder that allowed her to make her way across to the other side of the back yard.

As soon as she was in his back yard Milo raced towards her and stopped on a dime. She patted him on the head. He barked and ran around her several times in a complete circle. Then he barked again, ran back to the house and pawed frantically at the screen door. It was torn in a few places and would have been in shreds before long. The back entrance that led into the house immediately beyond the screen door was ajar. Kate opened the screen door a few inches and peered inside.

"Hello," she said. "Hello Charlotte. Hello Jerry. Is anybody there?"

There was no answer.

"Woof!" said Milo gruffly as he nosed his way past the open door and rushed into the kitchen. He went into the dining room and barked again. Kate followed him into the house. It was quiet, except for Milo's barking and there did not seem to be anyone home. Kate looked around the kitchen without seeing anything significant. Then she made her way into the dining area and gasped. Jerry's lifeless body lay on the floor in a pool of blood.

Kate felt all the air leave the room in an instant.

"Holy Mackerel!" she exclaimed under her breath along with a few choice words that cannot be repeated. She ran into the kitchen, grabbed the telephone and dialed 911 for help. She gave them her address and a brief description of the situation. As she placed the telephone back in its cradle an ugly thought ran through her head as she realized that Charlotte could be lying in a similar condition elsewhere in the house. It was possible that the assailants who wanted to get their hands on the wooden chest so desperately could still be in the house.

Milo was sitting by Jerry, licking his cheek. Kate approached them tentatively not quite sure what to do. In the distance, she could hear the sound of a police siren and she decided the best course of action was to wait for the emergency response team to arrive. She felt Jerry's pulse and it seemed okay.

Kate took off her belt and fashioned a leash that she attached to Milo's collar. If she was going to do a thorough search through the house she wanted some protection with her and having Milo by her side seemed like a good idea. He could look very menacing when he bared his teeth at somebody. She picked up a metal saucepan from the kitchen. Thus armed, she proceeded to search the house.

Kate's room-to-room search through the entire house seemed to last an eternity. She made a conscious decision that her goal was to determine if Charlotte needed help and not to ferret out an intruder hiding behind the bedroom door. If someone was still in the house, then he could remain hidden wherever he wanted to until help arrived.

"Hello Charlotte," she said as she opened the door to the master bedroom. "Are you there?" There was no answer and she took a quick look around and quickly moved on. It was like walking on pins and needles but she forced herself to go through each room, look inside the master bath and to open the closets and glance inside. She was certain that Milo would alert her if there were any strangers hiding behind the shower, or underneath the bed.

"Good boy," she said patting Milo on the head from time to time.

Milo smiled back at her in return. He drooled saliva on the floor. He was starting to calm down and be less agitated.

A cursory examination through each room assured her that Charlotte was not in the house. Kate recalled having passed Charlotte in the greeting cards section of the grocery store, earlier that day. She could not be sure. In any case, she was not home. Charlotte had either been taken hostage or she was out shopping, or looking for seashells on the beach. Kate was aware that Troy was going to be all over her case for disturbing the scene of the crime. She tried not to touch anything, gingerly opening the handles of the doors to the bedrooms with her knee and then pushing them open with her foot. She could hear the wail of the sirens just as she completed her search. She returned to the kitchen and sat down on a chair next to Jerry.

*   *   *

The paramedics showed up within a minute and took over the situation. Ray had come over to help almost at the same time, just as soon as Kate had called him. He held Kate's hand and tried to assure her that everything was going to be fine. Jerry was strapped into a stretcher next to her.

Kate and Ray rode to the hospital in the ambulance with Jerry, who had not regained consciousness or said a single word from the time she had found him bleeding to death in his dining room.

"Is he going to be okay?" she asked the paramedic seated next to her.

"I think he'll be okay, Miss," he replied. He seemed to know what he was doing. "He's lost a lot of blood but he still has a strong pulse. Of course, we won't know for sure until we get to the hospital, but I think he should make it. All because you called us up in time. Another thirty minutes or so and it could have been a different story."

Despite his assurances, Kate could not help feeling terrified, as she sat in the ambulance holding Jerry's hand. She was mortified that her trunk had been the cause of the attack on him. If anything happened to him, she could not live with herself. She really needed to do something about the trunk.

When they reached the hospital, the medical staff wheeled him into the ER immediately. Kate sat in the waiting room outside the ER while they examined him. She was still there when Charlotte and Shirley came charging in looking for Jerry. They allowed Charlotte to go back into one of the private rooms in the ER where Jerry was recuperating. After some time she reappeared and motioned to them to follow her into a small private recovery area. Jerry lay motionless on the bed looking quite exhausted. He smiled at them and barely lifted his hand to acknowledge them when they came in.

He had a nasty bruise on his forehead. Charlotte mentioned that he had a mild concussion and that he was going to be moved to one of the regular patient rooms shortly. He was going to stay in the hospital for a few days for a period of observation. The prognosis was that he was going to be fine and that there did not appear to be any serious long-term effects. All his motor functions were fine.

"Thanks Kate," he said weakly. "Thanks for your help in getting me to the hospital. If you hadn't come over when you did, I'm not sure what would have happened.

"I'm so sorry Jerry," Kate replied. "I know this all happened because of the trunk."

"I don't know Kate," Jerry said. "It could have been anything."

Charlotte told them that Jerry had just returned home from a trip to the store when a big burly fellow in an orange T-shirt had rushed past him in the hallway leading to the dining room. The burglar had shoved Jerry against the wall. Jerry had fallen backwards and had banged his head on the floor. He had passed out almost immediately. He had no idea who the burglar was. It was not someone whom he recognized.

Jerry protested that his injury was just a scratch, but that didn't explain the stitches on his forehead. He had been very fortunate that it had not been any worse. Kate could not help wondering about the potential outcome if the burglar had had a gun, or if Charlotte had been there when it had happened.

Troy agreed with Kate that there was definitely a pattern and that the robbery attempt was an attempt to locate the pirate trunk.

"I can't wait for them to come to my house next," he said. "They definitely seem to want it badly enough. I'm going to nail them if they do."

Kate and Troy were convinced that Louis had orchestrated the burglary attempt. However, Jerry was certain that none of the Frenchmen had been involved in the attack. He was sure he would have recognized them if they had been involved.

Troy proceeded to install a security system in his apartment. It was a relatively simple project since the link from the security camera to the control station in his bedroom was a wireless connection. All he had to do was install the camera and then go through the setup on his computer. In less than an hour, he was able to view and record the images that were transmitted by the camera several times each second. The images were also available wirelessly on his cell phone so that he could monitor his apartment remotely. He wanted to go on the offensive and set a trap that would allow him to smoke out the villains. Something that would allow him to arrest the villains and put them away for good.

*   *   *

Kate had just stepped out of the shower that evening when her ex-husband James called. She heard the phone ring and ran across the upstairs bedroom to answer it without stopping to dry off or pick up a towel. There had been so much going on lately that she was determined not to miss getting an update from someone. She was hoping that Troy had some news of an arrest or some other important development.

Leaving a trail of wet foot prints on the tiled floor she stood behind the modest protection of a large arm chair keeping an eye on the door in case one of her houseguests decided to come upstairs. It would not be good if someone walked into her room and found her completely naked. Kate looked down at the cushions on the armchair, trying to decide if she could hide behind one of the cushions if necessary.

"Hey there, Kate," said James cheerfully. "How are you?"

"Wet," Kate replied. "I just got out of the shower."

"I see," James said. "How wet are you exactly?"

"Very". Kate knew exactly what was going through his mind. She should have let his phone call go to voice mail. "Do we have to talk now or can I call you back in a few minutes?"

James ignored her request for additional time. "You better get your big girl panties on," he said. "I've done some research on the company you mentioned the last time we spoke. An outfit called the New Orleans Traders. I've been able to find out as much about this company as the clothes you have on right now."

"Oh," said Kate with a smile. That did not sound good. James had always had a way with words. Kate smiled at the comparison. It was how he had gotten to her in the first place."

"It's some kind of shell organization – one shell group that owns another shell group," James added. New Orleans Traders is incorporated in the Bahamas. It is privately owned by Bahama Shipping, which in turn is owned by The Caribbean Cargo Company. I have no idea what they do, but any time someone goes to so much trouble to obfuscate their identity you can pretty much bet that they are up to no good."

"Maybe I should write my Congressman," Kate offered. "I haven't written to him for so long he probably thinks I have forgotten about him."

"You should do probably do that," James replied. "You need to be careful, Kate," he said. "I wouldn't do business with the New Orleans Traders if I were you."

"I agree," Kate said. She was dry by now and checking herself out in the full-length mirror in her bedroom. She sucked in her stomach as she studied herself in the mirror. There, that was better. Exactly as she remembered the voluptuous curves of her hourglass waist the day she had turned forty.

"Anything else I can do for you?" he asked.

"No," Kate replied. "Thanks for asking."

"Did you find the sunken treasure, yet?" he asked.

"Not yet," Kate replied truthfully. "I'm still trying to figure out where it might be".

"I'm sure you will get it figured out before long Kate," he said. "No one knows you quite as well as I do. You do know that it belongs to the State of Texas if you find it, don't you?" he said.

Kate stiffened. "You mean to say that I don't get to keep anything I find?" she asked.

"That's the law," he replied.

"Wow!" Kate exclaimed as she realized that she was going to have to suffer being robbed and attacked in her attempt to uncover the legacy of Jean Lafitte, only to have the State of Texas step in at the end and take over anything of value that she might find.

"Of course if it's on dry land the rules could be different," he added. "It seems to make a difference whether it is. I've been trying to read up on the law regarding this".

"Thanks James." Kate replied.

"Well, it was good talking with you," he said. "Come buy me dinner some time."

"I might just do that someday," she said. "Goodbye James." The telephone line clicked as she disconnected the call.

The break-in at Charlotte and Jerry's had left Kate with an enormous feeling of guilt for having involved her dear friend and neighbor in an extremely dangerous situation. Meanwhile Troy was very concerned that Shirley could be the next target and Ray was concerned for Kate's safety.

GOOSE ISLAND BLACK JACK

The next few days went by without incident. There were no further burglary attempts involving the trunk. The robbers had either decided that the trunk was not in Jerry's house, or they lacked the gumption to attempt another robbery. It would not have surprised Kate if Shirley had tipped Louis off regarding the installation of the security system at Troy's apartment.

~~~~~~

Cast Off

Ray wondered if he could get Kate away from Goose Island for a few weeks to let things cool down a little. They were having dinner at Giordano's, a local Italian restaurant, when Ray had suggested going on vacation and before long several residents of the island had stopped by their table to offer their travel experiences. The proprietor of the restaurant, Donatello Giordano and his wife Francesca stopped by their table to recommend a vacation to Italy, comparing it to "heaven on earth," the most beautiful place in the world. Donatello had grown up near Macari, not far from San Vito Lo Capo. Francesca also admonished Kate to be sure to visit her native island of Sicily. She leaned towards Kate and whispered conspiratorially that the beach of San Vito Lo Capo had the best-looking fish in the sea.

"But there is darkness even in the most beautiful places on earth and some vacation destinations are well known for their problems with drugs, prostitution and all sorts of vices,"

Francesca had warned her. "Be careful when you go off the beaten track. You are much safer in areas frequented by tourists. If you wander into areas where tourists are not expected to go, you need to know about the dangers that exist." Francesca paused. Her eyes softened. "A beautiful girl like you, I'm sure you will be welcome anywhere," she added. "And I know you can take care of yourself."

"Thanks Francesca," Kate had replied.

The prospect of going to an exotic destination for a vacation was an exciting one. Kate had not had a real vacation since opening the Golden Goose Bread and Breakfast in 2011. Spending a few days with Ray as her cabana boy seemed perfectly wonderful. She would like nothing better than to have Ray standing next to her and holding up her towel.

"Let's go visit the Florida Keys," Ray said.

"Sounds like you have a plan," Kate said.

"A plan that involves being alone on an island with the most beautiful girl in the world sleeping beside me under the stars and making love to her in the moonlight," Ray replied.

"I think you're dreaming," Kate replied. However, it did get her thinking that perhaps they would visit the Florida Keys after all. Jean Lafitte had to hide his treasure somewhere, and the area around Indian Key and Shell Island was about as good as any other place that he could have selected.

"No I'm not," Ray said. "She is too, the most beautiful girl in the world."

Kate smiled with pleasure and leaned over to give him a kiss. One more that demanded his complete attention so that he would remember her for the rest of his life.

* * *

The telephone was ringing off the hook when Kate walked into the lobby of the Golden Goose. It was a call from Lucy Matthews in Galveston. She was in tears. Her art studio had just been robbed.

"It was strange, Kate," Lucy said. "I'm not sure if they actually took anything with them. However, they slash all my canvasses. They shredded all the paintings that I have worked on. All my best art has been ruined."

"What exactly do you mean about not being sure if they took anything?" Kate asked. This was starting to become a familiar pattern, with one exception. They had turned the break-in into a destructive rampage. When your house is broken into and nothing is missing, it means that the robbers did not find what they were looking for. The destruction suggested that the robbers were more than a little disappointed with their failure to find what they had wanted. Kate was certain that the trunk robbers were up to no good once again.

"Well the front door had been forced open," Lucy said. "I say that it had been forced open, but in all likelihood it had been kicked open because the wood around the door had been shattered. There was nothing missing from the studio, but everything else is ruined."

Lucy went on to describe the damage. In addition to the damage to her artwork, several pieces of crystal and pottery had been broken. It looked as if they had started throwing things around in a rage.

"I'm sorry Lucy," Kate said finally. "We have had a few robberies at Goose Island as well." Kate discreetly avoided mentioning the connection between the break-ins and the trunk. After all, she was the next of kin for Nicole and Zachary. After the break-in at Kate's B&B, Shirley's apartment, and Charlotte and Jerry's hose, the robbers had turned their attention to Lucy's studio in Galveston. Perhaps that was a good sign for the folks on Goose Island.

"I'm not sure how to describe how I feel," Lucy said. "I just feel so violated. The knowledge that someone who wants to enter my studio can do so with impunity at any time is very disturbing."

"Have you contacted the local authorities?" Kate asked. She really did not know how to respond to Lucy's comments. She had felt the same way when her house had been burglarized. It was a shame that the Irish Guard were not around to put a stop to the string of break-ins.

"Did they check for fingerprints?" continued Kate. If they had checked for prints, Kate was certain they would match the prints that had been found in the Goose Island break-ins.

"Yes," Lucy replied. "I honestly don't think the authorities can do very much about it. I'm not convinced that they can protect me very well. I feel as though I need to get away for a few days. I'm thinking of coming back to Goose Island for a short while. Do you have any vacancies at the Golden Goose?"

"Why, sure," Kate replied. "You are most welcome to stay with me. I have plenty of room for you to stay as long as you would like. There are two other ladies staying with me at present. Courtney and Glenda, who are some of the nicest people I know. They are here from Nebraska and I expect they will be here through Easter. I think you'll enjoy meeting them."

"Thanks Kate', said Lucy. "I'll come as soon as I can get away from here."

GOOSE ISLAND BLACK JACK

When Lucy arrived the following day, Kate was amazed at the transformation she had undergone since leaving Goose Island. She seemed very relaxed and easy going, with a cheerful smile. She had also put on a little more weight. It made her personality seem warmer.

Lucy shared her experiences about living in Galveston with Kate, Courtney and Glenda. It was a fun place with lots of visitors and Cruise ships leaving each week for exotic destinations in the Caribbean. Galveston had lots of restaurants, a historic shopping district, a water park and even an indoor botanical garden. Free from the demons that had haunted her at Goose Island, Lucy had become a successful artist with a thriving art studio in the historic Strand district in Galveston.

Kate loved hearing about Galveston, but she knew that she could never leave the simplicity and natural beauty of Goose Island. Not everyone on the island knew that Lucy had moved to Galveston. They greeted her as if she had never left Goose Island. The death of her parents earlier in the year had been yet another tragedy for Lucy to overcome. Kate had the sense that Lucy attributed their death to an unfortunate, but random traffic accident, brought on by physical impairments attributable to old age. She did not seem to suspect that the accident could have been an act of foul play.

Lucy seemed content to recall her childhood memories while growing up at Goose Island and the places that her parents had taken her to visit along the Texas Gulf Coast. It was these memories that had been responsible for her love of the ocean. Memories that came to life in each of the numerous seascapes she had painted over the years. Lucy was one of those rare individuals who could spend the entire day on the beach painting a sand dune. Kate was convinced that somewhere within her subconscious, Lucy's mind held the key to the location of Jean Lafitte's treasure. It had to be a secret that had been passed down from one generation to the next within her family, even if it had not been spelled out in financial terms.

The break-in at Lucy's art studio was the last straw, as far as Ray was concerned. It was clear that whoever wanted to get the wooden trunk was determined to possess it, at all costs. Ray had a long talk with Kate. Between them, they decided that the best course of action was to make the trunk disappear completely.

Ray was determined to get Kate away from Goose Island even if it was only for a few days. He turned the pages of the Goose Island News slowly, as he tried to develop a plan of action. The local stories in the newspaper really did not tell him much more about Goose Island than he already knew. Main Street was going to be closed for an afternoon for the annual Goose Island July Fourth celebration. There was going to be a brass band in the Goose Island Square and fireworks over Copano Bay after dark. Local artists were invited to reserve a table to display their artwork. Ray made a mental note to let Lucy know about the Arts Festival..

As he turned the newspaper to the Metro News Section there was an unusual photograph of a tow truck face down in the water with its rear end sticking up above the surface. It was unusual in the sense that the tow truck was actually being pulled out of the water by a second tow truck. The news story next to the photograph stated that the local tow truck operator, Peter Scully had suffered an unfortunate accident at the north end of the Copano Bay Causeway. The accident had occurred when an SUV he was towing had unexpectedly had a flat tire. The SUV had pulled sharply to the right, going suddenly over the edge of the guardrail into Copano Bay. Peter's tow truck had been pulled sideways into the water by the weight of the SUV. He had died instantly.

Ray did not know Peter Scully very well, but he knew Kate had used his services a few times and thought of him as a decent chap. He found her making a sandwich on the new granite counter in her kitchen and informed her of the news. Kate stopped what she was doing to look at the story in the newspaper. The shattered windshield on the SUV being pulled out of the water looked familiar. She turned white as a sheet as the color drained from her face. She wondered if the SUV that Peter had been towing when he had driven off the bridge was the same one that had tried to push her and Shirley off the road when they were returning from their kayak expedition to Austwell.

The thought that had flashed through her mind was that were not what they seemed to be. There was something disconcertingly familiar about the SUV and its broken windshield. Kate looked at the photograph for several minutes. It would not have surprised her if she had seen a beer can lodged in the radiator grille, but there was none in sight. This was no accidental tire blow out.

"Why would they kill Pete?" she asked Ray.

Ray looked at her with surprise, not following her train of thought. "But it was an accident," he protested.

"Right!" Kate exclaimed. Sometimes Ray could be so vary simple-minded and naive. "And my grandmother was born under a rhubarb tree smoking a cigar," she replied, as she stormed back into the kitchen to resume making her sandwiches. She was convinced there had been some foul play in Peter's death, but had no idea how or why it had been done, or by whom.

Kate had never met Peter's wife Betty Scully. However, she knew she was going to have to attend the funeral service and offer her condolences. She had to learn something more about Peter's unfortunate death and the reason why it may have occurred. Perhaps she could even find out who had rented his services to tow the battered SUV to the bottom of Copano Bay.

*   *   *

Shirley and Kate were out shopping for some new swimsuits at the mall at Corpus Christi, when Kate happened to mention her upcoming trip to Florida. She should have known better. Shirley could never keep a secret. It was the quickest way to tell everyone at Goose Island about her plans. In a belated attempt at damage control, Kate added the suggestion that she would probably fly into Pensacola, rent a vehicle at the airport and then drive to Fort Walton for some R&R. Before long, everyone who stopped by the Goose Island Bakery knew more about Kate's plans to visit Florida than she did herself.

"I'm so happy for you, Kate," Shirley said. "You simply must visit Panama City. I've been to Panama City just once in my life and I would love to go back some day. The water is so clear in Panama City and the sand is almost completely white. It's just so beautiful and romantic."

"Thanks," Kate replied. "I think it will be a lot of fun." She neglected to tell Shirley that she really was not planning to go anywhere near Panama City. With any luck, this would be enough to provide her with a little peace and quiet while she visited the Florida Keys.

Shirley was delighted for her friend, Kate. Why couldn't her fiancée, Troy be more like Ray? She had still not decided if she was going to accept his marriage proposal. If he had asked her to go to Panama City, she would have accepted immediately. The problem was that his idea of a good time was going to the rodeo in Fort Worth, munching on BBQ Ribs at the Cattleman's Restaurant in the Stockyards for dinner, and listening to Jerry Jeff Walker sing songs about redneck mothers and sangria wine.

The girls concluded their swimsuit purchases. Kate selected an astonishing one-piece suit that she knew the twins would love. It had bright red and white polka dots all over. Shirley purchased one that had a zipper in front in a blue and green aquatic pattern. As they walked through the shopping mall in Corpus Christi, they both agreed with Ray's suggestion that it was time for the wooden chest to disappear from Goose Island. There were several people with the last name of Houlihan in Limerick. Between the two of them, they decided that a replica of the chest would have to be shipped to Kate's fictitious aunt in Limerick, Ireland. Meanwhile the real trunk would continue to stay hidden in Troy's apartment.

They purchased an appropriately sized steamer trunk from one of the specialty stores at the mall and stopped at a discount-clothing store to buy more than a dozen western shirts, the ones with sugar snap buttons. They packed these in the trunk with a note explaining that it was a gift from the Houlihan's in Texas.

On the way home, Kate and Shirley stopped at the Goose Island Post Office to ship the trunk her fictitious aunt Beebe Houlihan, using the address of a pub in Limerick. There was a note on the envelope that the contents were time dated and were to be opened immediately upon receipt. They did not put a return address.

Everyone in the Post Office got a look at the trunk as the girls were wrapping it up with brown paper and cardboard on the floor of the Post Office. They practically had to step over and around it on the floor. The girls made sure that everyone saw where the package was being shipped to. The girls were counting on the

Goose Island Chatterbox Network to get the word out that the trunk was now in Ireland.

After leaving the Post Office, they stopped at Kate's house on Marlin and turned on the spa. They put on their new swimsuits, poured a glass of red wine into a plastic cup, and hopped into the hot tub just as it was getting nice and warm. The trunk was now officially in Ireland. Kate and Shirley knew that the Goose Island Women would be sure to get to talking about the trunk. Before long, Olga or someone else on the island would help spread the word that the trunk was no longer on Goose Island.

"If the Garda Síochána police in Ireland catch a fellow going around breaking into people's homes, looking for a trunk in Limerick, it takes them less than half an hour to find out whom he is working for and why the trunk was so bloody important". Kate said.

"How do they do that?" Shirley asked. We might need some help from them on Goose Island.

"They pour a quart of Tullamore Dew down the burglar's throat," Kate said. "That's to loosen his tongue until he names all his accomplices and the favorite bar where they can be found."

"I see," Shirley said with a laugh. "Is that how they do it in Ireland?"

"While they stare at him wearing their dark sunglasses," Kate added.

"Then they'll probably toss them into a wee loch somewhere and let Nessie take care of them," Shirley replied. "However, only after they've been soaked in a fresh batch of Irish whisky. Just enough of a soaking to get Nessie's attention. You wouldn't want to waste anything that had been aged for any length of time on someone like that."

"Yes," Kate agreed. "It would be cruel and unusual punishment to Nessie to give her someone who is still sober. She might take it as an insult if you throw someone into the Loch with a blood alcohol level is below the legal limit."

"I'm not sure there is a limit in Ireland," Shirley replied. They raised their glasses in a toast to each other.

"Here's mud in your eye," said Kate.

"Sláinte," Shirley replied. The water in the spa bubbled effortlessly around them.

"Hello Ladies," said Courtney. "Do you have room for two more?" she inquired as Glenda followed her to the spa.

Before long, all four girls were seated in the spa. Courtney and Glenda promised to help spread the word.

"I used to know a Beebe Houlihan from Limerick a long time ago," Courtney said. "Didn't you go to school with her, Glenda?"

"Why yes I sure did," Glenda replied with a twinkle in her eyes.

Kate and Shirley practically jumped when they heard this. They had not intended to transfer their problems with the trunk on some unsuspecting, dear old woman in Ireland.

"Good Grief!" Kate said.

"Oh don't worry about a thing dearie," Courtney replied. "Beebe Houlihan is built like a steam shovel. She'll run over anyone who bothers her with her Hino".

"I'm sorry, dear, did you say Hine?" Glenda inquired.

"You misheard, darling," Courtney replied. "We'll have to get your hearing aid checked. I said Hino, which is an Irish truck that has nothing in common with Texas wine or the rear end of a barn."

It did not take Kate and Shirley very long to realize the ladies were simply having some fun at their expense.

*   *   *

The first thing Kate noticed when she pulled into the parking lot of the Goose Island Funeral Home was the number of cars in the parking lot. The police cruiser was parked next to the hearse and it was clear that Troy would be leading the funeral procession to the graveyard. It seemed as though the whole town had come to pay their final respects to Peter Scully. His wife Betty was seated inside the first row of pews with their two-year-old daughter. Kate and Shirley joined the procession of mourners that streamed tearfully past the coffin and then stopped briefly to offer their condolences to Betty.

Peter's pastor delivered a eulogy that moved the crowd. Afterwards there was a small reception where Kate had a few minutes alone with Betty.

"I'm so sorry Betty. Peter was a wonderful man. He is going to be missed by us all."

"I know," said Betty wiping away a tear.

"If you ever need anything, don't hesitate to give me a call," Kate added. "You know we'll always be there for you and for your daughter."

"Thanks," said Betty, wiping away a few more tears.

"Yes please," Shirley added. "Please let us know if there is anything we can do to help out."

"Okay, thanks. You are too kind," said Betty.

"By the way," Kate continued, "Lucy Dubois asked me to convey her regrets. Lucy tells me Bill helped tow her parent's car earlier this year."

"You're welcome," said Betty tearfully. "I wish he had never towed that car. Maybe he would still be here with me." Her expression changed suddenly, from sadness to anger. "It's not your fault," she said. "You didn't know."

"Know what?" Kate asked.

"Nothing," said Betty as she turned away from Kate.

Betty's comments confirmed Kate's suspicion that it had been Peter who had towed the vehicle that Nicole and Zachary had been driving after the crash that had taken their lives. Kate was sure that Betty knew more about Peter's death than she was ever going to admit. In any case, this was not the time or place to make any further inquiries. Kate and Shirley continued paused beside a table within the reception room as they waited for the funeral procession to leave for the graveyard.

The Goose Island Chatterbox Network had already started to spread the word about the trunk. Donatello and Francesca stopped by to speak with Kate and Shirley. "I'm glad you sent the trunk away, Kate," said Donatello. "Perhaps if you had done it sooner, this poor boy would not have died. It is very wise of you to dispose of it before more people on the island get hurt."

"Thanks Don," Kate replied. "I'm sorry I did not think to do it sooner." Kate shivered. She had no idea that people on the island were holding her responsible for Peter's death. It really wasn't fair.

"It was a beautiful chest," Shirley said turning to Francesca. "It even had a carving of the Loch Ness monster on one side and a Viking ship on the other. So it was almost like a piece of Irish maritime history."

"That is such a nice thing to do Kate," said Francesca. "To give the Irish people back a little bit of their history."

"Thanks Francesca," Kate replied.

The knowledge that Goose Island had been blessed with a pirate chest seemed to come as no surprise to anyone. However, the fact that it now resided in Ireland seemed to get everyone's attention. The stories grew more fanciful as many of the other townspeople stopped by their table to chat. Within a short while the chest had been decorated with Sumo wrestlers, a Chinese dragon and a fleet of nuclear submarines.

Several people came up to Kate to inquire about her upcoming vacation. Kenneth Porter and the Frenchmen were among the most curious about her plans. Kate replied that she would only be gone for about ten days and that she was leaving Shirley in charge of the Golden Goose until she returned. Shirley added that her parents Bridget and Sean were planning to come down to give her a hand while Kate was away. Kate made a mental note to advise Bridget not to accept any additional houseguests at the Golden Goose Bed and Breakfast in her absence. All she needed was one or more unfettered Frenchmen staying in her B&B establishment in her absence.

Finally, it was time for everyone to leave for the burial. They filed out of the funeral home and walked solemnly to their cars. Troy led the procession out of the parking lot with the lights flashing on his police cruiser. The hearse followed close behind and everyone followed with their car lights on.

*   *   *

Kate was down at city hall a few days later to pay her water bill. Since she lived within walking distance from city hall, it didn't seem worth the cost of postage to mail it in. As she walked down the hallway to the cashier's station at city hall Kate had the distinct impression that everybody who lived on Goose Island was looking at her. For reasons that Kate could never understand it was impossible to keep anything a secret from all of the nosy, prying, busy bodies on the island. Sometimes it seemed that folks on the island knew what you were planning to do even before you knew about it yourself.

There was a small breakfast café in Rockport where the hostess stood outside the entrance and waited for customers to walk up to her to be seated. Kate stopped by for a sandwich after paying her water bill. The hostess looked at her intently with a snarky smile on her face, one that seemed to suggest that she had X-ray vision and could see through Kate's clothing. It was none of her business if Kate chose not to wear any underwear. The hostess with the X-ray vision always made Kate uncomfortable and she would have stopped eating there a long time ago if the food had not been so good. Now it seemed as if everyone on Goose Island had a snarky smile and X-ray vision. Kate felt as if she had worn her clothes inside out, or worse as if she was completely naked as she went about her business on the island. Goose Island seemed to have been re-ignited with a fresh round of speculation about Jean Lafitte's treasure. The notion that the treasure was in Panama City had caught on like wildfire. Theories about the treasure became wilder and more fanciful with every passing minute.

"I heard you were going to Hawaii," said Olga, when Kate happened to run into her at city hall. "Best of luck. I wish I could come along."

"Thanks Olga," Kate had replied. "I wish I were going to Hawaii. Actually we are going to Panama City in Florida. It's located just past Destin and Fort Walton Beach in the Florida Panhandle. You're welcome to come with us any time."

"Hawaii is so beautiful," Olga continued, as if she had not heard Kate. "However, Panama sounds like fun too. I wish I could do that, but I don't have any more vacation left this year," said Olga. "Besides, someone has to stay here and make sure the ruffians don't do anything foolish to our little piece of heaven here on the island."

"Maybe we can have luau on Goose Island when I get back," Kate replied. "I'm sure I'll need a lot of help from everyone on the island finishing all the oranges that I plan to bring back with me from Florida."

"Would those be something like golden delicious pineapples?" Olga asked lowering her voice conspiratorially.

"Absolutely. Golden delicious oranges. " Kate replied.

Olga chuckled as if it was her very own private joke. The conversation exchange fueled the talk amongst the town-folk of Kate's plans to go on an adventure trip to look for the golden delicious apples, oranges, and pineapples. You know! The ones that Jean Lafitte planted almost two hundred years ago. Bigger, brighter and sweeter than any other kind of fruit. They were so big, bright and beautiful that they practically glowed in the dark.

*   *   *

Bridget and Sean pulled up to the Golden Goose in a weathered red pickup towing a small travel trailer behind them. They arrived the week before Memorial Day. The weather was perfect and Kate's garden was in full bloom. However, summer was not far away and Bridget knew that a few weeks of air-conditioned comfort at the Goose Island Bed and Breakfast would be a welcome change from the travel trailer.

Bridget and Sean had spent most of the year touring across the Southwest United States. Camping out together brought them closer to nature and to each other. Bridget loved to bump into Sean and squeeze past him about fifty times each day in the narrow hallway that led from the entrance of the trailer, past the kitchen area, to the dinette with windows all around at the end of the trailer. The dinette collapsed to make room for a full size bed and Bridget could recall in vivid detail, many memorable moments looking out the windows at the stars in the sky, or herons near a lake, or simply looking up at the roof of the trailer in a trance – thinking that it doesn't get much better than this!. However, there was no denying that she secretly longed for a hot bath and a comfortable bed to sleep in even if it was only for a few days. She was looking forward to being the Assistant Manager of the Goose Island Bread and Breakfast in Kate's absence. She would not mind staying on a little longer if Kate needed additional help after she returned from vacation.

Bridget made herself at home in one of the rooms downstairs next to Courtney and Glenda. She was a wonderful cook and the kitchen at the Golden Goose seemed to come alive with strange and wonderful aromas while she cooked. In the few short days that remained before Kate left for her vacation Bridget became a familiar sight as she bustled into and out of the kitchen in her flamboyant nightgowns. It seemed that she never got fully dressed unless she was actually planning to go out of the house.

Courtney and Glenda loved her cooking and never tired of listening to her adventures. She was having a whale of a time staying at the Golden Goose and her infectious warmth spilled over to everyone around her. As far as Bridget was concerned, the Golden Goose could just as soon have been the Ritz Carlton of Goose Island. Bridget, Courtney and Glenda quickly became spa buddies at the Golden Goose in no time at all. They would soak in the sunset over a glass of wine each evening giggling at each other as Bridget regaled them with her travel experiences. Courtney and Glenda had a few experiences of their own to share involving telephone poles and repair-men.

Bridget regaled everyone with tales from her adventures on the road. She had watched meteor showers in December under the West Texas night sky that were more impressive than the fireworks display over the Brazos River at Waco on the Fourth of July. She had seen hillsides covered in wild bluebonnets and Indian paintbrush near Austin in Spring. She had attended several musical concerts across the State of Texas with Sean. They had attended an Oak Ridge Boys concert at Billy Bob's in Fort Worth. The audience participation had been so loud that you could not hear the musicians past the first three strains of Elvira. The only thing audible sounds after the Oak Ridge Boys said "oom-pa-pa-maow-maow", was the chant of the audience singing along. Bridget couldn't decide what she had enjoyed the most. It was probably a tie between seeing the Marfa lights near Alpine, Texas, and her attendance at an Elvis impersonation event in Lufkin. She had Glenda and Courtney join her in a chorus as she sang the chorus to "Love me tender" as they enjoyed the frothy bubbles over glasses of mimosa in the hot tub in Kate's back yard.

Sean did not know it but they referred to him as their cabana boy. Sean was a very mild mannered individual. He served fresh mimosas when their glasses ran dry, something that happened frequently, and changed the music when necessary. He was not judgmental and Courtney thought he had a nice ass for a senior citizen.

"That's only because I spank him every night," Bridget whispered, conspiratorially as he disappeared inside the kitchen to freshen up their glasses.

Glenda giggled. The mimosas were getting to her.

When he wasn't busy handling his cabana boy responsibilities, he busied himself oiling door hinges, changing light bulbs and rearranging the mulch in the garden. He made himself as useful as possible while staying within earshot and completely out of sight. Courtney and Glenda giggled like little school girls every time they saw him observing them over his bifocals.

"You ladies keep it together, out there," Kate yelled from across the garden where she was watering her day lilies.

They broke into laughter and flashed her in unison. There was a sound of a glass breaking inside the kitchen. That brought more laughter and another flash in the direction of the kitchen.

GOOSE ISLAND BLACK JACK

"I'm not sure if I can leave you in charge while I'm gone," Kate said to Bridget.

"Oh she'll be just fine," Glenda replied. "We'll keep an eye on her". This was something the girls found frightfully amusing. Then they would all burst out laughing again for no apparent reason.

≈≈≈≈≈≈

Key Largo

Kate and Ray began their trip to Florida early Friday morning before Memorial Day. Kate and Ray were taking separate flights to Dallas. Kate was to catch a flight from Corpus Christi to Dallas, while Ray travelled to Dallas from Odessa. Once they reached Dallas, they were to catch a flight together from Dallas to Miami. Shirley offered to drive Kate to the airport. However, Kate knew that Shirley had to open the bakery at 6:00 am each morning and she declined her most generous offer.

Kate left Goose Island bright and early on Friday morning for the long drive from Goose Island to the airport. A few drops of rain fell on her windshield as she crossed the Copano Bay Causeway headed south on Highway 35. She checked her rear view mirror to make sure she wasn't being followed. All she needed was a crazy driver in an SUV inches away from her rear bumper. She wouldn't need Shirley's pitching arm this time. The snub-nosed Beretta in her glove box would do nicely. The wind and rain started to pick up by the time she reached the ferry at Port Aransas. She called Ray on the ferry ride across to Port Aransas.

"Well, are you excited?" Kate asked. "This is our first vacation together."

"Hello Kate," Ray replied. "I'm just getting ready to go to the airport. I had to stay up all night to finish some project deliverables." He sounded really groggy and sleep-deprived.

"You might be in for a surprise when I tell you about your next homework assignment," Kate replied. "You better hope that you can stay up all night when I see you," she added.

"Sure will, Kate. I love you," Ray said. "I'll meet up with you at the airport in Dallas."

Kate hung up only after she was sure that he was awake and on his way to the airport to catch his flight. Having a vacation in Miami by herself was not her idea of a good time. The ferry docked in Port Aransas a few minutes later. Kate breezed down the strip of highway that led past Mustang Island. There was hardly any traffic. The sky turned blue as she was driving and she saw a flock of pelicans flying in formation over the water as she drove over the bridge over Oso Bay on the JFK Causeway. A short while later she pulled into the first available parking space at the remote parking lot at Corpus Christi International Airport. She placed the Beretta in a small gun case and locked it within the trunk of her car. It seemed unnecessary to take it with her on vacation.

As Kate walked up to the gate, she looked at the electronic display behind the counter and noticed with dismay that her flight had been delayed due to the inclement weather. There was nothing to do but wait. She called Ray and left a message letting him know she was probably going to be late getting into Dallas. The first flight delay from Corpus Christi led to a second and before you could say, "I told you so," Kate had missed her connection from Dallas to Miami.

The inclement weather had only affected flight schedules in Corpus Christi. Ray reached Dallas as planned and soon realized that Kate was going to be delayed. He called her on the phone. They agreed that he was to continue on, and meet up with her in Miami.

Ray reached Miami shortly before noon. He retrieved Kate's messages with updated flight information regarding her arrival later in the evening. He picked up a red Jeep from the rental car agency and a short time later, he was on US 1, headed toward Key Largo. He wanted to surprise Kate. He had the whole day to plan a surprise until it was time to pick her up at the airport that evening. He stopped at a General Store on the way to Key Largo and picked up some decorations, including a banner that said 'Welcome' and some flowers. He checked into the hotel at Key Largo. He went up to his room and made an impromptu flower arrangement using a plastic container that he had purchased. He spread the banner out over the dresser along with some confetti. The hotel was a beautiful arrangement of small buildings in a semicircle with a pool and spa in the middle. There was a small archway at one end of the pool along a small path leading to the ocean. The view was spectacular with a sandy white beach and clear blue water. Everything looked perfect.

Later, Ray drove down US-1 to the Bahia Honda. He parked his car and walked up to the picnic area by the beach. The waves rippled noiselessly against the shoreline. Nothing had changed. The abandoned Bahia Honda Bridge was still very much a part of the landscape. It was just as he had remembered it growing up in Florida, and he felt as if he had just found an old childhood friend. He pictured his Grandma in her blue one-piece swimsuit, soaking up rays of liquid sunshine in her beach chair near the water. Grandma was reading her Agatha Christie novel, while her grandson put on his snorkel mask and flippers and said "Hey Grandma look what I found" and held up a piece of driftwood.

The camping area at Bahia Honda had a sheltered grove of native trees with a number of camping areas arranged on either side of the road. Each campsite had a small driveway, a picnic table and a leveled area that was ideal for pitching a tent. The daily camping fee was very modest so he went ahead and paid for the entire two weeks they planned to be in Key Largo. Ray was fortunate enough to get a campsite overlooking the beach. It provided the perfect spot to watch the sunset with Kate. He pitched the tent that he had purchased at the General Store a few hours ago and left behind a bottle of Cabernet wine and a bottle opener in an insulated bag within the tent.

He changed into his swimming briefs within the tent and walked down to the beach. The water was clean and clear blue. Sandy ridges were clearly visible beneath the water and seemed to flicker in the sunlight. There were occasional schools of fish darting around underneath the water from time to time. Their bodies were translucent and the only thing that made them visible was the sunlight reflecting off their bodies as they foraged for food. The waves were very calm and rolled in toward the shore in one large ripple of water after another. Each wave made its way slowly across the bay before unfurling on the shore and spreading along the entire length of the beach before receding quickly to make way for the next wave. The weather was perfect. The beach, the water and the campsite was beautiful. The only thing missing was Kate.

*   *   *

Ray arrived at the airport to meet Kate promptly in time for her flight that evening. He located the baggage claim for the incoming flight from Dallas and settled down to wait. After the plane landed and all the passengers had picked up their bags and dispersed, he started to worry. There was Kate's bag going around and around the baggage carousel but there was no sign of Kate herself. It must have come in on an earlier flight.

The baggage claim area had a lousy cell phone signal. Ray walked over to a small café by the entrance to the gates and got some coffee. He was just taking his first sip of coffee when his telephone rang.

"Hi," she said

"Where are you?" he asked, turning to ride the escalator down one level to the ticket counter to look for her.

"I'm at the airport in Miami!" Kate said breathlessly. Where are you?

"Near the baggage claim escalators," he said.

"Me too," Kate replied.

"Really?" Ray asked. He turned around to look for Kate. There was no one in sight with Kate's long auburn hair, voluptuous curves and great looking legs anywhere in the airport. "Never mind, I'll be right over," he added.

He returned to baggage claim and caught sight of Kate as he was coming down the escalator. She looked fabulous. By far, the prettiest girl in the room. As he approached, he could see Kate with her hands on her hips looking in the opposite direction while he made his way past the maze of baggage suitcases lined up on the floor. She pretended not to notice him as she allowed him to sneak up on her. Kate turned at the last possible minute to snag and envelop him in her arms.

"There you are!" she said as she turned at the last minute and snagged him in her arms. "You are just what I have been waiting for!"

She gave Ray one of her amazing hugs. He loved to feel the touch of her body next to his. The smoothness of the sheer fabric of her dress excited him as soon as he put his arms around her. He nuzzled against her neck for a minute waiting for her to give him a kiss, which she did! It was delicious.

"I should have you arrested for carrying that dangerous weapon around in your pocket," she said, as she brushed up against him discreetly. "How did you get through security?"

"I missed you," Ray replied as he picked up her bags and they started towards the parking garage. "I was worried that you were not going to make it in today."

"I see!" Kate remarked. "Tell me about it," she said, giving his arm a friendly caress.

Ray mumbled something about coffee.

"I knew it," she replied. "I reach Miami just a little bit late and you are already trying to make a move on the coffee shop girl. Well I hope you had lots of coffee because I'm going to keep you up all night."

"It's so good to see you," Ray said with a laugh.

"Is it too late to go to the beach?" Kate asked. "I'm sick of seeing all these fabulously tanned people walking around the airport in flip flops."

"I'm glad you're okay. I was really worried about you," Ray said.

"I called you at least four times after I landed here. I thought you had abandoned me."

"Sorry. I think the reception inside the baggage claim area isn't very good," Ray said. "I had to go upstairs to get your messages."

The loaded up the Jeep and Kate hopped into the passenger seat next to Ray. "I'm not letting you out of my sight for the next two weeks," Kate said, adjusting her seat belt. She gave him a measured look that left no doubt that she meant exactly what she had just said. Then she reached for his hand and held it tightly against her side. Kate could feel the excitement course through her body as she reached over to give him a peck on the cheek.

Kate was amazed at the difference in scenery between Key Largo and Goose Island. They stopped at a scenic lookout near Key Largo and stepped out of the vehicle to look at the view of the Florida Straits past the bougainvillea and the tropical palms.

"What do you think those plants are?" she asked pointing to a small cluster of fruit bearing trees.

"I don't know. Probably Key Limes," replied Ray.

"That sounds delicious," Kate said.

"Yep," Ray answered. "Florida Key Limes are rumored to have magical aphrodisiac properties."

"I'll just have to try it won't I?" Kate said, smiling as they got back into the car. She winked at him over the top of the vehicle. Ray blew her a kiss from the other side and Kate deftly caught it in her hands, smacked her lips, and blew it right back at him. As she got in behind the wheel of the car, her skirt moved up to expose a large expanse of thigh.

"Pervert," she remarked as she turned to see him buckle his seat belt. "Keep your hands to yourself, or there won't be any dessert for you tonight.

"Yes, Ms. President," Ray replied with a laugh as he turned to kiss her. Their lips met once, twice, and then three times in rapid succession before she felt his tongue exploring every inch of her mouth. She gasped as she felt his hand on her thigh and quickly swatted it away.

"Now where is this hotel we are going to be staying at?" she inquired.

"Not far," Ray replied as they exited the airport and started down the highway towards Key Largo. It took over an hour to get there. Kate was asleep by the time they reached. The sun had gone down for the evening but there was plenty of light in the parking lot thanks to a beautiful full moon. Kate stumbled groggily out of the Jeep when they arrived.

"Did you get lost?" she asked. "Or did we have to drive to Texas and back in order to pick up some moonshine?"

"Let's go check out the beach," Ray replied. He knew that was the only thing that would satisfy her at that moment."

The foliage around the hotel was lush and beautifully maintained. There was a sign at the end of the parking lot that pointed the way to the beach. They stowed their gear inside their room, changed into their swimsuits and walked down to the water. It was a short pleasant walk down a trail that led to a beautiful sandy beach.

The sand was almost pure white and the water in the bay was crystal clear. There were a few people swimming in the ocean in the moonlight with snorkeling gear trying to spot the occasional fish. It was beautiful. Kate and Ray swam a short distance from the shore. The taste of the cool salt water felt wonderful. Kate could feel all her cares start to melt away. The beach was on the Gulf side of Key Largo and they watched the moon shine through the puffy white clouds that floated lazily over the water.

The resort at Key Largo was beautiful. If there was anything lacking at all, it was the authenticity of the neatly manicured lawns and immaculately maintained property. "This place seems a little too well maintained to be real," Kate remarked, looking all around her as they walked back to their room. "I think I would be more comfortable in a real neighborhood where people park their cars on the grass and weeds growing in the cracks in the sidewalk." Kate said.

"I know what you mean," Ray replied.

"Next time let's just find a little grass shack by the ocean with a kayak parked outside the front door," Kate added. They walked into their apartment and hung their towels up to dry on the backs of the chairs on the patio. Kate sat down on the sofa and tugged on his hand and motioned him to sit down next to her."

"I know just such a place," Ray replied. "It is about an hour from here. Let's go check it out tomorrow."

"Is there anything you want to check out today?" Kate asked playfully. She unbuttoned his shirt and caressed his chest.

"I'd like a taste some farm fresh golden delicious pineapples," said Ray as he moved closer to where she was sitting on the sofa. The ones that melt in your mouth.

"I was hoping you'd say that," Kate replied. She reached behind her back to loosen the strap on her bikini top. Kate turned towards him pausing provocatively to jiggle her body with a small shimmy just as she lifted her top and it fell noiselessly to the floor.

"Oh my goodness," Ray replied.

"Will there be anything else, Sir?" she inquired.

She leaned forward to kiss him on the head.

Ray was too busy to reply. Kate moaned softly as she slipped out of her bikini. Ray moved silently down to her belly button. Kate placed her hands on his head pushing him lower. The steady hum of the air conditioner could be heard as it clicked on automatically to cool the room.

Kate pulled him close to her. "Dinner is served, Sir," she whispered. "Mahi-Mahi tacos with farm fresh papayas." Ray feasted voraciously on the main course. They tumbled headlong against the back of the sofa, throwing the pillows down on the floor. Kate raised her left leg over the back of the sofa. The sofa springs in the upholstery complained to no avail. She bit his ear each time he leaned forward to tell her how much he loved her. When it was over, they lay motionless in the darkness for several minutes. Neither one of them wanted to make that first physical movement that would destroy the spell of that magic moment. As if they could make the precious moments they had just shared last forever by staying as still as possible.

"You are the most beautiful woman in the world, Kate," Ray said.

Kate smiled, beaming with satisfaction. Then she turned towards him, gave him a kiss and whispered softly. "Are you going to jump that leg, or do I have to?" The springs on the sofa complained vehemently, as if to say "No, not again." However, the couple that lay spread-eagled in the darkness were just getting started.

Kate and Ray went to the Caribbean Grille for dinner. They sat beside a small round, hand-carved, wooden table in the corner of the room. There was a bank of louvered rattan windows behind them. They ordered some mojitos and sipped them slowly using their straws to mix the mint leaves into the drink. The room began to fill up with people. The server took their order for a large sausage pizza with olives. A short while later she went around the room and opened the louvered windows wide, flooding the restaurant with fresh air. The colored lights outside the restaurant twinkled in the darkness. Ray ordered some Sandbar IPA on draft. They sipped on their beer as they waited for their meal, listening to a small group of musicians on a makeshift stage.

The music was a mix of old Jazz tunes and Caribbean Blues standards. Everyone in the room was tapping their feet and from time to time one or two couples would move into the only open area next to the crowded bar for a dance. It was nice to be able to relax like this at the end of the evening. Kate snuggled next to Ray and felt completely at peace. It was one of those magic moments when everything is just right. She linked her arm underneath his and held his hand feeling completely connected to him in every way. When they got up to dance to the next song, she could feel the heat of his body against her own. She placed her head gently against his shoulder as they swayed slowly to the music.

*   *   *

After dinner, Kate and Ray retired to their hotel room. Kate opened the door to the balcony in the living room to catch a whiff of the ocean air that wafted across towards her. The palm trees outside the house swayed in the breeze and Kate could sense their movement in the moonlight. It was the perfect way to end a day of spent kayaking, hiking, swimming in the ocean and basking in the sun. She sensed Ray behind her and turned to give him a peck on the lips. And another one. And finally, one long, unforgettable kiss that she knew she would remember for the rest of her life. They turned out the lights and lay down in a luxuriant bed resplendent with pillows. Their windows were open and the fan whirring overhead circulated the island air around the room with ease.

Ray reached over to hold her hand and caress her arm. She could feel his head against her shoulder. Kate reached across and unbuttoned his shirt. She turned towards him and winked conspiratorially.

"I guess you're not too tired to do some heavy lifting after all," she said.

"Not when I'm next to the most beautiful girl in the world," Ray replied.

"I see," Kate replied. "I like a man who takes his job seriously."

"I love you, Kate," Ray said. "More than anything in the whole world."

Yes, I see," Kate said, as she reached over to kiss him over and over and over again. And then all that she could feel was the warmth of his touch, the smell of his body, and the intense love that she felt for him. Outside they could hear the sound of the surf as the waves crashed on the shore in the distance. Everything around her slowed down to a crawl until she could hear the chop-chop-chop sound of the fan above her and each splash of the waves. The blades of the fan were like frames in a movie that she could pause, fast forward and rewind until time stood still. She stifled a scream as her heart stopped beating for just one moment, before her pulse began ticking once again.

"Here's looking back at you, grasshopper," Ray replied tenderly.

"Tu sei un dono del cielo," she whispered with a smile. She leaned forward to reposition the pillow underneath her head, her hair askew, her lipstick smeared. Her breasts moved with a motion entirely of their own. They seemed to be talking to him all by themselves. Her eyes pierced through Ray with the love and affection that she felt for him.

"You look beautiful," Ray replied as he snuggled his way into the space between the twins.

"It's just the freshly consummated look you like so much," she replied.

He fell asleep almost instantly. Snug as a bug in a rug, thought Kate, as she ran her fingers through his hair. For herself, Kate was drenched with perspiration and lay motionless for several minutes in the half-light of the moon. She looked at the stars in the night sky through the open window while she paused to catch her breath. Eventually the fan caught up with her and matched each beat of her heart with each chop-chop-chop-chop sound that it made in the darkness.

≈≈≈≈≈≈

Indian Key

The next morning Kate and Ray stopped by the Sunrise Supermarket located near the hotel and picked up some supplies. Sunscreen, snacks, bottled water, a nice red Igloo cooler with wheels for portability, sodas, beer, ice, and some detailed maps of the area. They drove down to Islamorada where they stopped at a kayak rental facility and rented a two-person kayak for the rest of the day. This would allow them to travel a short distance up and down the coast.

They walked down a narrow path that led to the water through a residential neighborhood. Ray pulled the kayak behind them, balanced precariously on a wheeled fixture that was attached beneath the kayak with straps going around it to hold it in place. Kate pulled the red Igloo cooler behind her. After crossing a narrow footbridge that spanned a small irrigation canal, they entered a city park that was situated on the edge of the river. The wheeled fixture was unstrapped from the kayak, removed and returned to a holding area near the footbridge.

Kate stepped into the kayak and Ray pushed it off the shore getting his tennis shoes thoroughly soaked in the process. As they floated away from the shore, they quickly learned to match strokes with each other. It didn't take long to get underway and begin a leisurely trip up the coast. The water lapped against their kayak as they moved along slowly. As they traveled, they passed a row of houses that backed up to the shore, some with small watercraft anchored alongside privately owned piers. Some of the houses that they passed had an occasional canine resident that made its presence known, barking at them from a distance.

After some time the houses thinned out and then the only thing that remained was the two of them paddling their ocean kayak up towards Indian Key. The lush green foliage that had surrounded them while they were near the shore was replaced with bright sunshine. It was very relaxing. In the distance, they could see the island with a few small hills and some trees. They made a right turn at one of the channel buoys as instructed by the kayak outfitters and followed the markers down a narrower channel. The water was less than fifteen or twenty feet deep and Kate could see the dappled patterns of sunshine refracting through ripples in the waves upon the ground below. A flock of pelicans was flying overhead. They floated lazily across the sky, and tipped their wings as if to welcome them on their journey.

Kate had packed some fresh oranges and sliced pineapples in a plastic box that lay on a bed of ice in a red Igloo cooler. She opened the container and placed a few pieces of pineapple on the palm of her hand. She offered some to Ray who leaned forward and ate them right off her hand and then proceeded to lick her fingers as well.

"You are such an animal," she said. Kate laughed, feeling a rush of electricity course through her body. He was such a caveman! How could she resist him? She looked at his broad shoulders. Beads of sweat trickled down his back and she knew she would dream about licking them off his body later that night. When they were alone and she was safe in his arms, she would kiss every inch of his body from head to toe. She smiled at the thought of driving him wild. He had no idea what she had in store for him.

Ray did most of the heavy lifting and paddled steadily for some time. After a few miles, the channel became shallower. There was a small beach directly in front of them. "That's probably where we need to park our kayak," Ray suggested.

Kate agreed. They hopped off the kayak and stepped into the water. Kate waded to the shore and Ray pulled the kayak out of the water and anchored it tenuously against a rock. Between the two of them, they hoisted their kayaks out of the water and placed them securely on higher ground. It would not do to let the kayaks float away by accident.

There was a small channel of water flowing out towards the ocean and Kate started to walk along one side of the channel. Was it possible that there was an underground freshwater spring in this remote location in the Keys?

"Let's see where this goes!" Kate exclaimed and then she disappeared from view.

Ray picked up the bag pack that contained their supplies and hauled the cooler along behind him. As soon as he picked it up, he could feel its weight on his shoulders. It was going to be incredibly difficult to travel very far with the cooler.

"This thing weighs a ton," he said. "What have you packed in here?"

"Just some pineapples, sandwiches, water and beer," Kate replied. "Also some rocks so that we could defend ourselves in case we meet any cannibals on the trail," she replied in the sugary sweet tone of voice that made it abundantly clear that she really didn't want to be questioned about the contents of the bright red Igloo, or the ice cream cartons inside it..

"That sounds delicious. I don't believe I've ever tasted anything as sweet as the golden delicious pineapples I had for dessert yesterday," said Ray.

"You might not get another bite if the cannibals get their hands on them," Kate replied. "Good thing I packed the rocks, huh?" said Kate cheerfully. She pouted unconvincingly, sticking her tongue out and pulled her T-shirt up to her chin, blinding him with her twins for an instant.

"You should know better," he said with a laugh. "The cannibals will be down here any minute to kidnap such a tasty morsel. Whatever will I do without you?"

"You'd better not be thinking of doing without me," Kate replied as she turned to continue down the path between the trees on either side of the trail.

"We better lighten this cooler in case we have to make a run for it," he said as he paused to empty some of the melted ice cubes from the cooler. "Much better," he said as he hoisted the cooler up over his shoulder.

The journey along the side of the river was uneventful. They passed a trove of guava trees along the way and paused to pick a few.

They washed the fruit in the melted ice in the bottom of the cooler and ate them as a snack. It was an amazing feeling to find fresh fruit that was yours for the taking right off the land. Ray washed his guava down with a beer that he shared with Kate. After a few miles, the trail widened as they approached a clearing. They could hear the sound of water in the distance and they knew they had to be very close to the other end of the island. They descended carefully towards the sound of the water from the trail by making their way over several large boulders. Once past the boulders they found themselves on the edge of a crystal clear lagoon surrounded by rocks on all sides. The water bubbled up through the rock formation and fell into the pool in a waterfall at one end of the lagoon. Both Kate and Ray had their swimsuits on underneath their T-shirts. They piled their gear on a large rock at one end of the lagoon and quickly entered the pool. The water was much cooler than they had expected. It took a few moments to swim to the waterfall at the end of the lagoon. The rocks beneath their feet were exceedingly slippery. They made their way gingerly along the waterfall until they were directly underneath it. The water cascaded over their bodies in sheets, forcing them away from its direct path. It was an incredible feeling.

"Now where would you hide your treasure if you were a pirate?" Kate asked. Everything she had seen so far seemed to match up with the map to Jean Lafitte's treasure.

"I would hide it inside your swimsuit," Ray replied.

"Maybe I should take it off right now so don't have to waste any time looking for it," she said.

"Good idea," Ray replied. Kate was a treasure all by herself. "You're worth your weight in gold, you know".

"More," said Kate removing the top of her bikini.

"Nice tan," Ray said. "You look like a brick house full of gold with some Titanium in the middle."

"Glad you like it," she replied. Kate blew him a kiss. She splashed Ray with as much water as she could trap in her hands. Then she deftly stepped aside as he lunged towards her. Ray fell helplessly into the lagoon.

"Starting to slow down a bit there, aren't you mate," Kate said.

"Do you still think this is where Jean Lafitte buried his treasure back in 1821?" Ray asked.

"Maybe," Kate replied. "Let's take a look around, shall we".

She swam across the lagoon to the waterfall and looked behind it as carefully as possible. The treasure had to be behind the waterfall. There was no hiding place nearby that was nearly as good as the area immediately behind the falls. All the other rocks and boulders in the area were far too open and exposed to be of use. She checked every crevice in the rocks behind the waterfall to no avail. There were no nooks and crannies large enough to shelter a treasure of any size. More importantly, she did not see anything that she could intuitively connect with Jean Lafitte's treasure map. After standing under the waterfall for a few minutes she made her way back across to the other side.

They swam in the lagoon for a bit. It was heavenly. When it was abundantly clear that there was no treasure hidden behind the waterfall they stepped out of the lagoon to dry off. They made their way carefully to a pleasant spot on a large boulder in the shade of some trees. Ray opened a couple of beers. Kate scoured the area looking for a cave or some other hiding place. Neanderthal man had known a thing or two about nature that his descendants seemed to have forgotten. The warm sunshine, the cool water, birds chirping in the trees, everything was perfect.

"Let's take a look around the rest of this island," Ray said.

The got up and put on their tennis shoes. Kate scrambled awkwardly over the closest rocks with Ray right behind her. It was impossible to travel three yards in any direction without having to negotiate her way over a rocky boulder. "There's no way you could mark off 1821 paces from the waterfall," Kate thought to herself. The best she could hope to accomplish was to travel back down the trail they had used to get to the waterfall. They decided to head back to their kayaks, with Kate counting the paces each step of the way. Conversation was useless, as Kate refused to let herself be distracted lest she lose count.

They continued on, past the lagoon and reached the other side of the island before the designated number of paces had expired. 1821 paces is a lot of paces. Almost a mile, Kate thought. She looked at the water around her as if to visualize the precise location where she would have been after 1821 paces if she had been permitted to continue unimpeded.

"1821 paces from the waterfall has got to be smack-dab in the middle of the Atlantic Ocean!" she said finally, as she turned and looked at Ray despondently. Kate was not sure what she had expected to find on Indian Key. There should have been something on the island. Some hiding place, a cave, a rocky cavern, or perhaps a large misshapen rock that could be moved over to one side to unearth the hidden treasure. If it was in the middle of the ocean, it would take a team of scuba divers to find it. She sat down on the beach looking out over the water. The surf bubbled past her toes. Ray sat down next to her.

There was a moment's silence before Ray responded. "Perhaps the ocean is treasure," Ray said. "The ocean and everything in it. "

"I love you," Kate said. She reached towards him and kissed him tenderly.

They sat by the side of the ocean, consumed the rest of their sandwiches and chased their food down with the beer Kate had packed. They proceeded to walk around the coastline at a leisurely pace to return to their kayaks. Along the way they passed by a small clearing with a few graves. The grave markers comprised a collection of stones in the shape of a cross lying on the ground.

"That makes you wonder what happened to the person buried in the sand. Do you think the treasure could be buried in one of those graves?" Ray asked.

"Not sure if I want to find out," Kate replied. "Besides that's not what is described in the map."

"I agree," Ray replied. It could be a memorial for someone lost at sea in a storm"

"I hope it's not some lost souls who died looking for treasure," Kate added. If the New Orleans Traders and their cohorts had had their way, she would have been six feet under by now. Why was everyone convinced that there was a treasure to be found just because of a crazy map in an old pirate chest. If she couldn't decipher the map maybe she should give it to the Traders and let them figure it out. As it was right now they were simply waiting for her and Ray to find the treasure for them, so they could wrest it away from her at the last minute. This cat and mouse game was getting old.

The walked from one end of the island to the other. There was nothing more to see. Kate helped Ray put their kayak back in the water. Once she had gotten over her reluctance to get her Nikes soaking wet, getting in and out of the kayak had become a piece of cake. She clambered into her spot as the chief navigator in charge of the kayak run back to Islamorada while Ray pushed the kayak along until the water was a little more than knee deep. Then he jumped in as well and they started to paddle back towards the marina where they had started their trip that morning. The sun was setting in the western sky and Kate was convinced that she saw a flash of green over the horizon just before the sun went down over the water.

They pulled their kayaks out of the water at a small park beside the marina. The rolling fixture that they had used to haul the kayaks to the shore was exactly where they had left it earlier that day. They strapped the wheels on to the kayaks and pulled them carefully across the parking lot, over a narrow bridge, and past a cluster of banana trees to return them to the kayak outfitter.

*   *   *

A short walk across the road took them to an open-air shopping mall. They meandered through the mall and Kate purchased a few souvenirs from the general store at the end of the mall. There was a group of high school students performing a set of Jazz Standards in the small amphitheater in the center of the shopping mall. Kate and Ray sat at a picnic table having an alfresco dinner in the patio outside a quaint restaurant at the end of the mall.

Kate's shrimp appetizer was grilled to perfection and served with just the right seasonings. She sipped her generous serving of Cabernet wine contentedly. However, mid-way through her second coconut grilled shrimp Kate practically choked on a bite.

"What's wrong," Ray asked. He was genuinely concerned. Kate looked like she could not breathe. Ray had heard of the Heimlich maneuver he had no idea how to perform it. He got up quickly getting ready to grab her from behind and somehow squeeze the morsel that was choking her. It was supposed to pop right out of her mouth. Thankfully, Kate motioned for him to sit back down. "Are you okay?" he asked her.

"It's him," Kate sputtered, whispering hoarsely and holding up her napkin as if to hide behind it.

"Who?" Ray asked. All he could see was a bulky posterior as another group of customers was being seated at a table across the fake waterfall.

"Ken Porter, with Huey, Dewey and Louie," Kate replied. "I might have guessed that Ken was their partner in crime."

"They must have decided to follow us here," Ray said. "Either that or it's just a huge coincidence. Imagine meeting someone you know from back home in Goose Island on Key Largo. Do you think they picked this precise spot for an island vacation at the same time as us through pure coincidence?"

"I don't see how we can give them the benefit of the doubt," said Kate, as they repositioned their chairs behind a potted plant near the indoor waterfall. "Ken's probably been filling their brains with all sorts of foolish notions about Jean Lafitte's treasure."

Kate kept an eye on the foursome at the other table. When Ken Porter got up to use the washroom she accosted him in the hallway just outside the door to the Men's room. He must have been in a hurry because had started unzipping his pants.

"Why hello there, Kate," Ken said when he saw her approaching him. "How nice to see you! Fancy meeting you here." He struggled with his zipper, trying to get it back up again. It was caught on the fabric of his clothes. Old sneaky snake who was dealing with the immediate problem of shutting down Ken's full bladder stayed well within the confines of Ken's trousers.

"Yes, imagine that," Kate replied.

Despite his surprise at being noticed, Ken could not pass up the opportunity to give Kate a hug and he had his arms around her before she could make an evasive maneuver. Ken had smothered Kate with his arms and had his hands on her behind. Kate struggled to extricate herself from his grasp. "It's nice to see you both again," he said looking down at her cleavage. He gave her another small peck on the cheek and a small squeeze before finally letting go.

"Thanks," Kate said as she wriggled free. "I can't say the same about you. What are you doing here, Ken?" Kate asked pointedly. She had practically had to knee him in the groin to get out of his grip.

"I'm just here on vacation, Kate, that's all. I heard you were coming out here and it seemed like a great idea, so I decided to do the same." He did not mention Huey, Dewey, and Louis, but it was clear that they were in this together. He was either working for them, or they were working for him. It really did not matter.

They were just out on vacation to get a little sand and sun, he explained. Besides, Henri was paying for his trip and he really did not feel like passing up a chance to fuel up at some of the best restaurants in the world at someone else's expense.

"You must try the Veal Tender Loin here, Kate," he remarked. "The beef here is so juicy and succulent it just melts in your mouth." He smacked his lips with a disgusting slurping sound. It was so like Ken to be consumed with thoughts of food even in this, perhaps the most beautiful place on earth.

Kate made it clear to Ken that it would be fine with her if she didn't see him again until they returned to Goose Island. However, it was also clear that Kate and Ray would be seeing a lot more of Ken and his French fries because they were stayed on Key Largo. In fact, they were staying in the same hotel, located directly across the parking lot from where Kate and Ray were situated. Ken and his buddies had adjoining ocean view suites on the corner of the building so they could watch Kate and Ray come and go as they entered and left their apartment. Kate wondered if they had taken the time to install a spy cam to monitor their movements.

≈≈≈≈≈≈

Alligator Reef

The next few days went by in a rush. It was not very comforting to be shadowed everywhere by Ken and the three Frenchmen. Thanks to his size, Ken was easy to spot from a distance. However, the Frenchmen were not so easy to spot, and Kate did not trust them as far as she could throw Ken! Kate found herself looking for Ken and his buddies every time she went anywhere with Ray. The stalkers had ruined more than one meal as far as Kate was concerned. On one occasion, Kate walked around an Oleander bush in the parking lot and found Henri and Louis were spying on her through a pair of field glasses. Another time that Kate spotted Louis in the distance and waved genially in his direction. He ignored her, pretending to be invisible. Kate continued on her way knowing that she had let him know she was on to his shenanigans. It was a delicate balance between the hunter and the hunted.

"He seems to be one brick short of a full load, doesn't he?" replied Ray.

"The good thing about him being here is that he's not on Goose Island to prey on Shirley's good natured personality and affections." Kate shuddered at the thought of Louis and Shirley in a sexually compromising position.

"I agree," Ray said. "If he hangs around Shirley long enough she might jump his bony ass whether he wants to or not. I think she likes him more than she would be willing to admit."

Kate grimaced. The image of Shirley with her legs wrapped around Louis was more than she could handle. "Most women are attracted to rogues and villainous characters with low IQs," she replied.

"I knew there was a reason why you picked me," Ray said.

"I especially like the fact that you are blind in one eye," Kate said. "We'll have to stop somewhere and pick up a patch for the other eye before I knock it out as well." Then she undid the topmost button on her blouse to let him know that was not an idle threat.

* * *

Kate navigated the Jeep carefully down the one lane Overseas Highway South from Islamorada towards Long Key. As they crossed the bridge near Lower Matecumbe Key she marveled at the engineering complexity of linking all the islands in the Florida Keys together. Kate was enjoying the scenery with one eye on the horizon and the other on the road before her to make sure she stayed well within her portion of the road. It was all too easy to veer off to one side with each new bend in the road. "Just like life," Kate thought. "You just have to hit the reset button sometimes, think about what you are doing and consider where you are going to end up if you don't make some changes." Beside her, Ray was soaking up the view outside the passenger's window.

Kate wanted to visit the Alligator Reef Lighthouse near Islamorada. Ray had no idea why anyone would enjoy visiting an area frequented by alligators. Kate explained that there were no alligators near Alligator Reef. The lighthouse is named after the USS Alligator which was shipwrecked there in 1822. It was fifty years later when the lighthouse was built in 1873. The lighthouse stands 136 feet tall, and has survived several major hurricanes thanks to its design which allows much of the wind to pass through its iron frame structure. However, the lighthouse was closed to the public, as are all the other lighthouses along the Keys. The only way to get to Alligator Reef is via kayak.

They loaded up their kayak rental with the supplies they had brought. The Igloo cooler was coming in really handy. Alligator Reef was about four miles off shore and it would probably take them over an hour to get to the lighthouse and another hour to get back. Their plan was to kayak to Alligator Reef and do some snorkeling at the Cheeca Rocks near the lighthouse.

They anchored their kayak to one of the supports at the lighthouse and snorkeled right underneath the structure, marveling at the manner in which it was anchored to the sea floor. The snorkeling at the Cheeca Rocks was amazing. Kate saw several French Angelfish, and a few Sea-Monkeys.

Sea-Monkeys are a type of brine crustacean shrimp whose tails resemble monkeys. They are unique in the sense that they can enter a state of suspended animation in times of adverse environmental conditions, and stay in that state indefinitely, until conditions improve. This phenomenon is called "cryptobiosis". It allows these creatures to be purchased as packets of lifeless dust from a pet store. The dust is actually brine shrimp eggs. Pour the dust in a tank of purified water, and the Sea-Monkeys spring to life. They grow steadily over the next few weeks, feeding on a diet of yeast and spirulina.

When they returned to Islamorada they paused to rearrange the contents of their cooler. Kate popped open some beer and handed a can to Ray.

"There is a string of at least six surviving lighthouses along the Florida Keys," Ray noted as they leaned back in their seats under the shade of a palm tree. "The lighthouses served to warn sailors of the rocks near the Florida coast line. Sea captains liked to sail close to the shore to avoid the current from the Gulf Stream as they sailed past the Keys. The reward for doing so was that it took several days off an arduous trip from Europe. The risk was that you could end up wrecking your boat on the rocks."

"That must have been hard to do when the weather was bad," Kate remarked. "Especially during hurricanes."

"Yes it was," Ray said. "Hurricanes were hard to predict and seemed to come out of nowhere."

"Didn't Columbus run into a hurricane one his way to America?" Kate asked. She recalled that he had been separated from the other ships in his convoy during a storm.

"Yes," Ray replied. "It was on his last voyage. He did not have a barometer as it had not yet been invented. When he anchored for the night, the sea was as smooth as glass. There was a lot of marine activity around him. However, he had seen this phenomenon on an earlier trip and took it as a sign of an approaching storm. He told his captains where to meet if that event should occur. The storm that night was unlike anything they had seen before. Each of the four ships in the convoy were blown four different directions. However, they all survived and regrouped within a few days. "

"It had to be pretty scary to experience something like that," Kate said.

"Yes it was," Ray replied. "Ninety percent of the sailors on the early expeditions did not know how to swim. Columbus was the exception. He once jumped off a burning ship and swam several miles to safety."

"I'd sign up to go sailing with him," Kate remarked. "Wouldn't you?"

"Possibly," Ray said. "Let's stop at Sombrero Beach when we get to Marathon," Ray said. "It should be right after the seven mile bridge. I'd like to check out the Sombrero Key Lighthouse if we have time."

"Sure," Kate said. "We have all day to get to Key West. We could even see the lighthouse at Key Biscayne"

Despite the indisputable beauty of the sheer blue expanse of water that lay spread out on either side of the highway Kate longed to be back in her own home at Goose Island. There was no denying that Lower Matecumbe Key and Long Key were beautiful. However Goose Island was 'her' island, and she missed walking along Shipwreck Beach and looking up at the

Copano Bay bridge in the distance. She missed everybody on Goose Island.

There was a steady stream of cars approaching her from the opposite direction and Kate appreciated the ones that had the foresight to turn on their headlights. It helped make them more visible and the last thing Kate wanted was to be involved in an accident with another vehicle in this remote place. She observed a large cargo van approaching rapidly from the opposite direction with disapproval. The driver seemed intent on passing just about every other car on the road as he darted in and out of traffic.

"Watch out," said Ray as he braced himself against the dashboard. The cargo van was headed directly towards her, as if he was intent on a collision. Kate was not sure if he would continue towards her, or move to her right to avoid a collision by driving on the shoulder on the Gulf side of the highway.

"I am watching," Kate replied tersely.

A head-on collision seemed inevitable. At the last possible minute, Kate swerved hard to the left, kicking up a cloud of dust as she drove across the median. In a few short seconds, the Jeep lurched over the patch of dirt in the middle of the road, across the lane of the oncoming traffic and onto the shoulder on the Atlantic side of the highway. Horns blaring! Lights flashing! The Jeep chomped over the road, its tires complaining as they went bumpity, bump, bump. thump over the paved edge of the highway onto the shoulder. She was dangerously close to the edge of the road and if the shoulder had been any smaller the Jeep would have continued its trajectory over the edge of the road and into the Cotton Key Basin. Fortunately, she managed to maintain control of her vehicle. As soon as there was a chance to stop Kate's Jeep ground to a halt as she slammed on the brakes. Kate looked uncomfortably at the oncoming traffic. When she thought she was safe she put on the parking brake and killed the ignition switch.

"Wow that was darned close," said Ray. "Are you okay?"

Kate muttered a few choice expletives under her breath. She was as white as a sheet. Even though the Jeep had ground to a complete halt she gripped the steering wheel as tightly as she possibly could.

"You did a great job to avoid a collision," Ray added.

"Thanks," Kate replied, her heart beating wildly with the adrenalin rush that comes from just having narrowly avoided an accident. "I'll be okay. However, I am a little steamed."

"Let's get out of here and somewhere quiet for a few minutes," Ray said.

"That sounds really good, Ray," Kate replied. "I'm either soaked in sweat or else I think I just peed in my pants. I'll be fine as soon as I can get out of these jeans."

"I'm just happy to get out of here in one piece," Ray said with a smile. He knew that Kate was doing fine any time she started talking about getting naked. She was one tough 'Wonder Woman' who could be relied upon to handle the most difficult situation without batting an eyelid. A voluptuous image of Kate, stark naked, with one leg draped over the edge of the sofa flashed through his mind. He contemplated the alternative strategies to work himself into the scene. He wondered if she spent as much time imagining him naked as he did her. "You are really beautiful," he added, reaching across the Jeep to squeeze her hand. "And an amazing driver!"

"Thanks," Kate said. She was still hyper ventilating from the experience. "That was almost as much fun as getting poked in the eye with a sharp stick!"

"I know. That was about the most reckless thing I have ever seen anyone do," Ray continued. "I didn't get a good look at the driver of the van, did you?"

"Not really," Kate replied.

They compared notes. The driver of the cargo van had a beard. Kate tried desperately to wrap her mind around the notion that she may have just passed the maniacal musician from the Swamp Shack. What in the world was he doing in Florida? If it wasn't Ken and the Frenchmen who had been stalking them through the Keys then it had to be the New Orleans Traders, the Russian Mafia, or the Chinese Consortium.

Neither Kate nor Ray could identify the driver of the cargo van. They had not gotten a good look at his appearance, or the van's license plate. They considered calling 911 and finally decided to let it go since it was no longer an emergency. Kate located the number for non-emergency situations on her mobile phone. She dialed the Highway Patrol and gave them all the information she had. There was nothing else to do. Kate restarted the vehicle and made her way slowly down the shoulder. After a half mile she came upon a strip mall with a few stores. She turned the Jeep around, waited at a traffic light, and then got back onto the road to Sombrero Key.

That must have been what it felt like in the old days when your ship was attacked by pirates, she thought. One minute you are sailing merrily along the ocean and the next minute you are in a fight for survival. She took a quick glance behind. It was reassuring not to see any pirates in the back seat. Their camping gear and the red cooler was securely strapped down behind her seat. Everything seemed to be intact.

"He looked a lot like Fidel Castro," Ray said.

"That boy needs to have a heart to heart talk with his maker," she said. "He's not living his life with much regard for his fellow man."

"Exactly what I was thinking," Ray replied. "A moving violation or two from the Sheriff might be a good thing. A few days in the cooler without any beer and a shave might not hurt either."

"We should come up with a plan to kidnap him and take him back to Texas with us. I'm sure Troy would like to have a nice long chat with him," Kate replied. "So he did have a Cuban looking beard, did he?"

"He sure did," said Ray. "He looked very Cuban with his beard, dark glasses and cap. He just needed a cigar to make it official."

"If I ever get that half assed Cuban pirate across my knee he will have no ass by the time I am finished with him," Kate said with venom.

Kate rounded the last bend in the road on her way past Duck Key and the Dolphin Research Center. In the distance, she could see the breakers in the ocean approaching the shore in a slow but steady progression from the opposite direction. It was one of those moments that take your breath away. The waves were tinged with puffs of white foam that floated effortlessly towards the shore.

They reached Marathon and paused at a gas station to fill up their Jeep. Ray studied the map. It was shortly after 1:00 pm and the beautiful Florida Sunshine seemed to make their surroundings several shades brighter than normal. They picked up a couple of sandwiches from the delicatessen that was adjacent to the gas station.

"How do you feel about stopping at the Dolphin Research Center before driving down to Sombrero Beach," Ray asked. "It's less than twenty minutes from here."

"I'd love that," Kate replied.

Just like that. Suddenly life was back to normal again. It was as if the incident on the highway had never happened. Except for the grace of God, they could just as easily be lying face down on the bottom of the Atlantic Ocean or the Gulf of Mexico. Instead, they were headed blissfully down past a long row of palm trees along the highway for another the lazy day at the beach. They stopped at a small grocery store along the highway, picked up bag of potato chips and some bottled water, and jumped back into the jeep. They purchased some fresh pineapples and packed them into their cooler. Then they hopped in and a short while later found themselves cruising along the seven-mile bridge. They were planning to stop for a picnic lunch at Bahia Honda State Park and then continue on to their hotel at Key West

They were driving along at a rapid clip when the cargo van that had almost driven them off the road a short time ago re-appeared in Kate's rear view mirror. The bright sunshine reflected off the windshield of the cargo van. Although Kate could not actually see who was behind the wheel of the cargo van. It could have been anyone. However, she knew intuitively that Fidel was back and it seemed that he was determined to get to the ocean to see the sunset before them.

"He's back," Kate said.

Ray stiffened as he glanced behind the Jeep.

Kate slowed down and moved over onto the shoulder to give him room to pass. However, instead of going around her vehicle, the cargo van smacked the Jeep from behind with a vengeance. The Jeep lurched forward and Kate fought desperately to keep control of her vehicle. Ray was halfway through his Subway sandwich. In desperation he threw it at the cargo van. Bits of lettuce and tomato splattered on the windshield of the cargo van. The move must have distracted Fidel, as he seemed to fall back a short distance behind the Jeep.

Kate felt very vulnerable and simply could not understand what was happening. "I don't believe this," she said. "You don't suppose that's our crazy buddy Louis the umpteenth from France, do you?" she asked Ray.

"It sure looks like him, but I can't tell," replied Ray. "The way he's behaving one would think that he either hates us, or he's after the warm beer and the golden delicious pineapples we have in our cooler."

"Damn!" Kate exclaimed. In that instant she realized it was all about the golden delicious pineapples!

Kate and Ray had only been on the island for about a week and they had completely forgotten why they had come there in the first place. They were so busy enjoying the landscape, the scenery and the natural beauty of Keys that they had ceased looking for pirate treasure shortly after their first snorkeling trip. Key Largo had worked its magic on them and they had succumbed to its charms.

However, getting his hands on some mythical pirate treasure had clearly become an obsession with Louis. He must have seen them carrying the red cooler between them on the way to their Jeep and concluded that they had indeed found the long lost treasure of Jean Lafitte hidden away in a cave beside Key Largo. Louis was not beyond using his field glass to spy on them. He had probably observed every step they had taken and waited for them to find the treasure before he attacked them.

Kate waited for a second tap on her bumper, checking her rear view mirror feverishly as she sped up and lurched along the one lane highway faster than she cared to go. As she drove she was surprised when she checked her rear view mirror, and did not see him behind her. She glanced at Ray. From the terrified expression on his face, she realized that Fidel was right beside her on the left side of her Jeep and getting ready to drive her off the road. Kate quickly ran through her abysmal lack of options and realized that she would have to take some action soon or else she would literally up to her ears in sand. They careened along the road like Roman charioteers going neck to neck down the stretch in an amphitheater from the first century B.C.

Kate looked up to see a small SUV coming towards her from the opposite direction. The SUV was directly in her path attempting to pass a slow moving sedan. Logic demanded that she slow down to let the SUV complete its passing maneuver and to let Fidel pass her as well. However, instead of slowing down, she stepped on the gas, and felt the Jeep accelerate rapidly. If Fidel was going to run her off the road he would have to do it now, or fall back to avoid hitting either the sedan or the SUV. The cargo van fell in behind her as Fidel decided that the odds were against him. From the opposite direction the SUV fell back into its own lane and the crisis had been averted momentarily.

Kate and Fidel continued racing down the highway. There was a red F150 in front of Kate going about its business without a care in the world. Kate approached the F150 at break neck speed. A collision with the red pick-up seemed inevitable. Kate realized that she would have to pass the F150 in front of her or else she would be sandwiched between a slow moving F150 and Fidel who was right behind her. She looked in her rear view mirror and saw Fidel in the cargo van. He was speeding up and would smack her rear end once again within seconds. "Here goes nothing," she thought to herself as she swerved out into the lane of opposing traffic from behind the F150 in front of her. As soon as she had moved out from behind the F150, the cargo van flashed into the space she had vacated and hit the slow-moving F150 instead. The driver of the F150 was having none of this nonsense. He slammed on his brakes. Fidel hit him again. Kate passed by the pick-up with relative ease and returned to her designated lane. In the distance she saw a large bulky delivery truck approaching her from the opposite direction. Glancing to look at her rear view mirror, she saw Fidel swerve from behind the F150 into the passing lane. The driver of the delivery truck raised his cap, waved and honked the horn on his vehicle as they approached each other. Kate waved back at him as they passed each other. A few seconds later Kate heard a large explosion behind her and realized that Fidel's cargo van had just collided with the delivery van while trying to pass the pick-up. The explosion the followed the collision between the two vehicles rocked the bridge and Kate slowed instinctively. As she continued down the road, Kate hoped fervently that the driver of the delivery truck had not been harmed.

"That should slow him down a bit," Ray said. "Are you okay?"

"I hope that stops him dead in his tracks," Kate replied uncharitably. Her last encounter with Fidel had left her quite shaken. "It's about time Fidel met something on the highway of life that is just a wee bit bigger than himself," Kate said. "

They traveled along silently, scarcely daring to breathe. The cargo van did not reappear in   Kate's rear view mirror.

"He must have hit the delivery truck," Kate said finally.

"Or that tour bus that was right behind it," Ray said.

"Hope the driver of the delivery truck is okay," Kate said.

"I hope so too" Ray replied. "I think he'll be fine," he added after a brief pause. "I'm not so sure about Fidel."

"Serves him right for trying to run me off the road," Kate said.

The sun slipped behind a cloud making it possible to gaze at the horizon without squinting. Kate felt an immense sense of relief course through her veins as her adrenalin rush started to dissipate.

The traffic thinned out after some time and they found themselves very close to the ocean. Kate could smell the water as a pair of seagulls flew overhead. There was a trove of trees in the distance and she made her way to it. She parked the Jeep underneath a canopy of green vines that grew alongside a small fenced area near the tree.

Her heart was still racing.

She turned towards Ray and they held each other for a long time. If Fidel was still following them, they did not plan to get back on the highway until they saw his van go past them on the highway.

"I hope nothing ever happens to you," Ray said. "I couldn't live without you."

Kate didn't say a word. She just nestled her head against his shoulder and held him close to her.

"Where did you learn to drive like that?" he asked.

"Just did!" Kate replied. "About five minutes ago." She traced her fingers down his chest and kissed him. They sat in the car for a long time to catch their breath until the sun went down over the horizon. One giant orange fireball that doused itself in the ocean.

Kate did not want to return to their hotel and live across the parking lot from the man who had just tried to kill her. Twice. She was sure it was Louis. They contemplated their options.

"Do you think we could pick up some camping gear and spend the night at Bahia Honda?" she asked.

"Sure," Ray replied.

They made their way to Bahia Honda State Park and checked into a campsite.

"Let's go into town and get us some camping supplies," Ray said. "We can leave the cooler here until we get back.

In the waning light of the day, Kate made her way back to US 1. She was quite sure that they had not been followed to Bahia Honda. She wondered how long it would take Fidel to figure out where they were. As a precaution, she drove the last stretch of road to the highway in the light of the moon with her headlights turned off. She turned them back on only after she was on the highway trying to look inconspicuous. Just another car in the ebb and flow of traffic headed towards Key Largo.

*   *   *

They drove down to Marathon and purchased some camping supplies from a discount retail store. A small Coleman tent, some air mattresses, flashlights, battery-operated air pump, sheets, etc. Then it was time to go back to Bahia Honda. As Kate drove the short distance back to Bahia Honda Key, she tried to visualize her trip down that particular stretch of road earlier that day, expecting a white cargo van to lurch out of the darkness and reappear behind her. However, the return trip to Bahia Honda was uneventful and before long, they were back at the campsite unpacking their supplies and putting up a tent. That is to say, Ray went to work while Kate sat in the Jeep sipping a bottle of Guinness and making helpful suggestions from time to time.

Ray was about as addled as he could be as he fumbled to put up the tent in the darkness. They laughed like teenagers when his first feeble attempt to put up the tent came crashing down because the supports had not been positioned properly. When he finally got all the supports in place, he unzipped the entrance to the tent and stepped inside. Kate protested that they would probably end up in the ocean if a big gust of wind came along at the right time, but she went inside anyway. It was dark within the tent and they placed the flashlight in one corner. They spread out the air mattress and added air to it with a battery-powered contraption and then they both lay down on it. There was a window at each end of the tent and they unzipped these as well, letting the ocean breeze waft through their new island home. Kate turned off the flashlight, and undid the buttons on Ray's shirt ever so slowly.

"Maybe I should go take a swim in the ocean and see if the water is any cooler than the air in this tent," Ray said. "It's getting pretty hot in here."

"If you go out like that I know at least half-dozen women on the beach will jump you before your toes touch the water," Kate said.

They could see the shimmer of the moonlight on the water in Bahia Honda Bay through the screened opening in their tent. There was a screen mesh at the top of their tent and they opened it to let in the moonlight and the sea breeze. The sky was full of stars. Kate had slipped out of her sealskin now and Ray knew it was going to be another golden delicious evening. He could feel the warmth and weight of her pineapples against his chest.

"Shhh," she whispered when he said "I love you," even as he entered uncharted territory. He pulled her down against him and could feel every inch of her flesh against his body. Kate gasped and said "je t'aime mon amour. Oh Dios Madre, I love you, I love you, I love you."

They set sail once more charting a new course under a moonlit sky, navigating purely by the reflection of the stars in each other's eyes. It was an incredible journey. Beads of perspiration trickled down Kate's back and they went slip sliding headlong down a river of emotion in a world where nothing else and nobody else mattered. With the tenderness that only true love brings to each other.

*   *   *

"What day is it today?" Kate asked as they woke up to the sound of birds making kuk-kuk-kuk sounds in the trees outside their tent.

"Not sure," Ray replied sleepily. He was not used to being asked difficult questions this early in the morning. He could never understand why women didn't understand that all a fellow wants to be asked at 6:30 am is how to measure the wave length of gamma rays under an electron microscope, not something mundane like 'What day is it today'. Besides the truth of the matter was that he honestly did not know what day it is. "Maybe it's Thursday?" he replied uncertainly.

"How many days have we been here on the beach," Kate asked.

"Gosh Kate," Ray said. "Maybe only two or three days".

After their first unforgettable night together on the beach, Kate had steadfastly refused to return to the condominium. It was nice not to have to deal with Fidel, Ken and the three Frenchmen at every turn. They ate sandwiches from the delicatessen at the local grocery store near beach, washed them down with beer, and spent their days walking along the shore, swimming in the ocean and relaxing by the water. Life was great. However, Kate knew that they would eventually have to return to reality. Besides, she had so much sand in her hair that she simply could not stand to live with it any longer. She was also getting a little weary of taking express showers in the outdoor stalls near the beach where they were camping, never sure if someone was watching surreptitiously from a distance.

"Well we are going to have to go back today," Kate declared. "I'm not spending another night with a pervert like you next to me!"

Ray protested that he was not a pervert. However, Kate had her mind made up and there was nothing he could do about it. She gave him a playful shove and moved deftly out of the way as he reached for her.

"Aren't you supposed to be out in your fishing boat catching us something to eat, instead of looking at me as if I was breakfast?" she asked.

Ray got up reluctantly. "Have you seen the spear that I was using yesterday?" he asked.

"The one that was bigger than any spear I've ever seen in my life?" she asked.

"Yes," he replied.

"No," Kate said, looking at him with a bad girl smile on her face. "I haven't seen your spear today. Now go out and come back with breakfast while I catch up on my beauty sleep."

"You look pretty good right now," Ray said, feeling an urge of desire as he looked at her sleeping on a wilted air mattress. "I'm not sure I have the words to describe how immeasurably beautiful you are." They could see the calm blue water of the ocean through the window opening in the tent.

"Not half as beautiful as I'm going to be in an hour," Kate said firmly as she turned to moon him. The tan lines where her swimsuit had covered her skin were in sharp contrast to the lightly colored flesh next to it.

"Promise me you'll still be here when I get back," he said. "Put a message in the wine bottle for me and stick it in the sand outside the tent if you decide to go anywhere before I return."

Kate gave him the bird without looking in his direction.

"Go find your spear and don't come back until you catch that giant striped zebra fish we saw when we were swimming out in the ocean yesterday," she said. "I don't like the way he blows bubbles at me when I'm swimming."

Ray put on his swimming briefs and stepped out of the tent to meet a new day. After a brief swim in the ocean, he walked over to the Jeep and put on his jeans and a shirt. He drove down to the grocery store by the highway, less than half a mile from where they were. When he returned, he had two cups of fresh coffee and some blueberry muffins.

"We need to get back to our condominium," Kate said firmly, as they finished their coffee and muffins.

"I agree," Ray replied. "Might as well check in with reality and see what's been happening with the rest of the world. I think we have put it on hold long enough. I am going to let the air out of their tires, or kick their ass, if those boys from France give us any more trouble".

"You and me both," Kate said. "I have had it with them puissant French Fries. It's time we showed them a little down home Texas hospitality".

It did not take very long for Kate and Ray to pack their belongings and get everything loaded back into the Jeep.

*   *   *

Kate stormed up to Ken Porter's room the minute they reached their hotel. She pounded her fist on the door.

"Open up Kenneth Porter," she said.

"Who is it?" inquired a muffled voice from the other side of the door.

"Room Service. Free gift from Key Largo Hotel Association," Kate said. "Full body massage special with naked woman. Must be big boy and more than fifty to qualify. Open up Papa San, if you want to see me naked with my beautiful badass twin girls. Hotel manager special. Ordered just for you Mr. Kenny.," she added in what she thought was her best Oriental accent.

The naked woman massage offer did the trick. It was either that, or the chance to see the badass twins. Kate heard the door click and Ken opened it a fraction to look at his happy hour special. He was wearing his boxer shorts, with little Ken Junior winking at her through the opening.

"Oh. It's you," he said as the anticipation on his face turned into resignation in the instant that he recognized Kate. From his gaze, Kate knew that it must have been the line about the breasts.

"Darn right it is, Ken, you miserable pervert. Just think of me as your wet dream and your worst nightmare all rolled into one," she said as she stormed into the room.

Kate lit into Ken the minute she was inside the room and locked the door behind her. She grabbed the waistband on his boxer shorts and balled it into her fist. Then she shoved him rudely against the wall.

"Oh my goodness, don't stop Kate," Ken pleaded. "You have no idea how beautiful you look when you get all hot and bothered."

"I'm beyond hot and bothered mister," Kate said and slammed him against the wall again. She was about to knee him when she paused to control herself.

"I just get all excited thinking about you," Ken said.

That did it. Kate kneed him and he yowled and crumpled into a rather large blob on the floor.

"I'll have you know that I almost got killed by your treasure hunter buddies today!" Kate said. "All on account of you! You and your idiotic yarns about pirate treasure. "They have their bird brain minds made up that if they just follow me around this island I'm going to lead them to a treasure trove of riches beyond their wildest imagination."

"I know," said Ken as he lay on the floor, trying to look up her dress. He grabbed an ankle and gave it a tug, trying to pull her down next to him.

Kate twisted her foot out of his grasp without much effort. She resisted the temptation to pound his chest with the heel of her foot. She sat down on the only chair in the room and crossed her legs when she noticed where his gaze wandering towards a parking area that was reserved for Ray. There was an ottoman beside the chair and for a minute she considered putting her feet up on it but decided that it wouldn't fit in with the message she was trying to communicate.

"There's no pirate treasure here Ken," she said. "At least there is none that I know of".

"I know," repeated Ken blankly.

"The only treasure here is the sand and the stars, the sun and the moon and the ocean. If you cannot feel blessed beyond any measure by the way the breeze brushes past your skin as it rolls over the ocean then you are missing out on the greatest treasure that this island has to offer you," Kate said.

Ken had picked himself up from the floor. He lay down on the bed breathing heavily.

"You have to persuade your friends to leave me alone, or else I'm going to call the cops and get a restraining order," Kate continued. "Kapiche! It may not do any good but it is all I can think of right now."

Ken had wilted and lay crumpled upon the bed. He looked sad and defeated.

Kate got up from the chair and walked over to the bed beside Ken. She leaned over and kissed him on the forehead, letting her breasts brush gently against his face. She had his attention and moved away deftly before he could put his arms around her.

"I love you as a friend and a fellow human being, Ken," she said gently. "Someone I have known practically all my life growing up in Goose Island. Now we are going to go home in a few days and I want that friendship to continue. I need you to call the dogs off and if I ever find Jean Lafitte's pirate treasure, I assure you that you'll be the first to know. I plan to share any good fortune that comes my way with you and everyone else on Goose Island."

"I don't feel so good Kate," Ken said, breathing heavily. "How about a little mouth to mouth?"

"You are a bad boy Ken," Kate said with a smile. She kissed him gently on the forehead again and gave him a hug. Then she stepped away again before he could reach up and grab her. She moved quickly towards the door.

Ken looked up at her gratefully.

"If you see the Oriental masseuse that knocked on my door a short while ago please tell her that I'm sure we can work things out," he said. "Why don't you come here and lie down next to me so we can talk about it?"

"Because," Kate said and she blew him a kiss and stepped out of his room, closing the door behind her.

*   *   *

Kate went down to the main hotel lobby and had the bartender pour her a glass of Kona beer in a frosty beer mug and sat at a table in the patio looking out over the ocean. Tiki torches blazed in the night and the clouds glistened with an eerie glow as the moon hid behind them. It was her last night on the island and she wanted to remember it in a different way.

When she went back to her room, Ray was reading his email. He had several bottles of

GOOSE ISLAND BLACK JACK

Sandbar beer chilling in an ice bucket on the dresser.

"Would you like a cold beer," he asked.

"No," she replied. "I'd rather have you.

"Here's an email from you," Ray said. "It looks like you mailed it to me last week before we left Goose Island." He opened the door to the patio and let the cool ocean breeze waft into their room.

"I know," she replied. "Let me tell you what it says."

When they kissed each other, it was with a passion that set her heart aflame again. As they tumbled into the chaise lounge by the window Kate felt a rush of emotion unlike anything she had ever felt before. Their bodies entwined and she could feel him against every inch of her skin. It had started to rain and Kate could hear the sound of the raindrops falling against the window. The staccato drum roll of the rain rose to a crescendo, interspersed with the rumble of thunder in the distance. Kate knew that Ray would have to return to Odessa soon, but for now he was hers and hers alone.

*   *   *

It was their last morning in the Keys. When they awoke, they headed down to the restaurant in the lobby of the hotel at Key Largo.

They sat down at a table overlooking the ocean and watched the sunbeams dance on the water.

After breakfast, they had a few hours to kill before it would be time to catch their return flight back to Texas from Miami Airport in the afternoon.

While they were waiting for their meal, Ken Porter approached their table with a dour look on his face.

"It's all over, Kate," he said. "You don't have to worry about anything."

"What's over?" Kate asked. "What don't I need to worry about?"

"Henri's gone," he replied. "You don't have to worry about him."

"She doesn't?" Ray inquired, raising his eyebrows.

"That's right, she doesn't," Ken continued. Henri drove off the road and was involved in an accident with a tractor yesterday. His brother Sebastian and son Louis are getting ready to fly home to France with his remains right now."

"My goodness," said Kate. "How on earth did the accident happen," she said.

"It seems that he lost control of his vehicle somewhere on the west side of US1," Ken said. "He was probably driving too fast for his own good."

"I'm so very sorry," Kate said, with a puzzled expression on her face. She felt a wave of relief knowing that she was not going to be followed all over town by a raving lunatic in a cargo van . The only problem was that she had expected the raving lunatic to be Louis, not his father, Henri.

"It's not your fault," Ken said.

"I know," Kate replied. "It's just that I do feel responsible. I think they must have followed me here under the delusion that I had a secret treasure map in my possession. Honestly, Ken, the only thing that I found in the antique chest that I purchased earlier this year was some sand, dried flowers, and a small flag."

"It's not your fault that you don't have a treasure map",

Ken added. "That was just something that Henri created in his mind, because that's what he wanted to believe."

"Thanks for coming by to let me know, Ken," she said. "I hope I wasn't too rough on you last night."

"It's always a pleasure to see you Kate," said Ken. "Any time. How would you like to have some Chinese food with me tonight?"

"No thanks Ken, not tonight," Kate said firmly.

Ray glanced quizzically at the two of them. Whatever it was they were discussing, it was none of his business.

≈≈≈≈≈≈

Home Sweet Home

It was time to go back to work, make some money, pay the bills and set aside a little something for the taxman at the end of the year. Kate and Ray caught a return flight from Miami back to Dallas that evening. It had rained all day and the airport was full of stranded passengers crowding all the restaurants, coffee shops, and bars at the airport. It was a huge relief when they started to board the flight to Dallas and they were finally seated on the first leg of their return trip home.

Ray opened the flight magazine and started working on the crossword. Kate leaned contentedly against his shoulder. Her proximity to him was like a drug and she simply could not get enough of him. Some day she was going to have to get him to move to Goose Island. She pictured herself with him seated on her leather sofa in her living quarters at the Goose Island B&B, with her feet upon his lap while watching a movie. The picture on the TV screen got blurry and disappeared completely as she felt his hands rubbing the soles of her feet as he gave her a foot massage. "That would never work," she thought to herself with a smile as she kissed him tenderly on the cheek. She knew that he could never resist the temptation to massage her feet, kiss her ankles, and then proceed to nip and nibble his way up her legs until she ended up tangled in his arms. Her clothes strewn on the floor next to the sofa without as much as a sip of tequila. Kate squeezed Ray's hand while he filled in another clue in the crossword. She was going to miss him when he returned to Odessa.

They said goodbye in Dallas and went to different departure gates to catch their connections to Corpus Christi and Odessa, respectively. Kate's flight to Corpus was uneventful. When she landed in Corpus Christi, she put her luggage away in the trunk of her car. She unlocked the gun case and placed the Beretta back in the glove compartment.

She traveled down the park road along Mustang Island to Port Aransas and caught the ferry at Aransas Pass before getting on Highway 35. Kate smiled when she saw a seagull perched on the sign near Copano Bay that read "No Jumping from Bridge". She looked over the top of the Copano Bay Bridge at Copano Bay to the west and Mesquite Bay and Matagorda Island to the east. She paused to watch a small fishing boat that was about to go underneath the bridge.

There was nothing quite like the familiar sights and sounds of Goose Island to make her feel at home again. Goose Island Key was nothing like Key Largo or Islamorada, but it was heaven on earth for her. Goose Island Key was her Caio, her island.

Shirley stopped by the Golden Goose to visit Kate as soon as the bakery closed for the day. She was bubbling with excitement and wanted to know all about Kate's trip as they drove back home. "Are the Florida Keys really as amazing as everyone said? Had they fed the pelicans at Robbie's Marina in Marathon? Had they seen the Bahia Honda Bridge? Was the sunset from Key West as pretty as a postcard? Had they gone surfing in the Atlantic?"

Kate tried to answer Shirley's questions as rapidly as she could. "Yes it is really beautiful in the Keys, and oh so very laid back. No! They had not had a chance to go surfing. Maybe next time she would take surfing lessons."

*   *   *

Kate couldn't wait to get her life back to normal. She compiled two small photograph albums of pictures she had taken along the trail and people enjoyed looking through these. Everyone she met was delighted to hear about her experiences in the Keys and her thrilling trip to Shell Island. She discreetly neglected to describe her hair-raising drive on US-1 to anyone. There was no need to clutter up some perfectly good vacation memories with a handful of bad experiences. However, news of Henri's demise had preceded her arrival. Everyone on Goose Island were trying to figure out what had happened. As far as Kate was concerned, it was a surprise to her as well.

"It says here that Henri died in a traffic accident on US-1 between Miami and Key West," Shirley remarked, picking up an old copy of the Goose Island News. She was clearing out a stack of newspapers left behind at the bakery by her customers. "Did you see Ken Porter or the three Frenchmen on your vacation?"

"No, not really," Kate replied. "I saw someone who looked like Ken from a distance once or twice, but I couldn't be sure."

Shirley took the news of Henri's death rather hard. "He was a really nice person," she said to Kate. "I don't know how Louis is going to get along without him."

"Yes indeed," Kate replied, thinking that he had been an incredibly dangerous idiot. "I am sure Louis is going to miss him. Do you know when he plans to return to Goose Island?" She had still not worked out how clean shaven Henri had come to resemble Fidel Castro when he had passed her on US-1.

"I don't think he is planning to return," Shirley said. "We were going to visit 'Boredough' someday," she continued with a tear in her eye. She had not seen Louis for several weeks and it was evident that he had abandoned her.

Kate smiled. Shirley made it sound like a place where the pastries were all as flat as pancakes. "You can still go there you know," Kate replied. "Perhaps you could visit Europe." There was no answer. Clearly, Shirley did not intend to traipse across the Atlantic after someone who had not shown a great deal of interest in her. Being a hunk only got you so far. Even if he could not score a home run each time he was on the plate, a fellow still had to try to bunt the ball in order to get to first base.

"Are you still planning on getting married to Troy?" Kate asked.

"Yes," Shirley sniffed.

"Have you made any plans with Troy for your honeymoon," Kate inquired.

Shirley burst into tears. "We are going to have the wedding at the stockyards in Fort Worth," she wailed. "We are going to Billy Bob's after the wedding for a reception."

"Well that's real nice Shirley. I've heard that it's a really fun place to visit," Kate said. "They have great bands, cold beer, and the biggest dance floor in the Texas. Who is playing that night?"

Shirley was un-consolable. She did not know who was playing at Billy Bobs that night. Kate looked it up.

"Well I hope you like Jerry Jeff Walker," she said.

"I do," Shirley said. Her sobs subsided and she brightened up as the thought of going around the big dance floor at Billy Bob's with Troy began to take shape in her mind. In spite of all his shortcomings, she did like the way Troy could dance the two-step and twirl her around the dance floor.

* * *

Ken Porter had travelled to France to attend Henri's funereal. He had just returned to Goose Island. Ken didn't have much explaining to do. His return to Goose Island was all the evidence everyone needed to provide the reassurance that the treasure hunt had not been successful. Any treasure that lay in the Keys was still there waiting for the next wave of Goose Island residents who wanted to take it upon themselves to find it.

Kate walked into Giordano's after leaving Shirley at the Goose Island Bakery. It felt so wonderful to be on Goose Island, without having to keep looking around constantly to see if she was being followed. Life without having to see Louis, Henri or Sebastian on the island was better than she remembered. She looked around the room at Giordano's, and noticed Ken sitting at a table near the bar. She walked over to Ken's table where he was basking in the attention that he was getting from two of the island residents, Olga and Janice.

Kate sat down at the table with Ken. With his freshly tanned face and relaxed appearance, he looked more attractive than he had ever been before. Ken was just finishing an exaggerated description about how clear and blue the water had been in Key Largo, how the fish had jumped right out of the water and straight into his hands.

"Have you told them the story about the fish you caught at Key Largo?" Kate asked. "You know the one that was so big we had to call a towing company to help get it home. I think we must have fed half the hotel with it."

"Not yet," replied Ken, his face brightening considerably. He looked at Kate conspiratorially. "I was just going to get to it."

Olga and Janice clamored around Ken for the details of the story. The fish he had caught seemed to get bigger each time it jumped out of the water. By the time he landed it on the deck of the fishing boat, it was bigger than a longhorn steer and they needed a winch to haul in his catch. Olga realized this was just another of Ken's tales.

"Let's go sister," Olga said. "We need to run or we'll miss the start of the World Cup. Mexico is playing Germany tonight and I don't want to miss a minute of the game." Olga took Janice firmly by the hand and steered her firmly out of the door, just as Troy walked into Giordano's.

"Hello Ken! Hey Kate! Good to see you. When did you get back in town?" Troy asked as he walked into Giordano's and sat down at a chair that had just been vacated by Olga.

"Just got back. It's only been a couple of days. Good to see you too," said Kate.

"Where are the boys from France?" Troy inquired.

"I haven't heard from Louis and Sebastian since they decided to return to France," Ken replied, his broad face breaking into a subtle grin. "I don't really expect to see them anytime soon. Henri had an accident while we were in Florida. He passed away in a car crash."

"That's too bad," Troy said. "I'm glad you weren't with him when it happened."

"Yes that would have been terrible," Ken replied. "I was hanging out with his son Louis at the time. We flew down to Key West to attend a musical concert together. Henri had some business to attend to in Miami and he was going to drive down later that day to meet up with us in Key Largo. All I really know is that he was involved in a head-on collision with a moving van on US-1."

"That's what I hear too," Troy said. "Hey, did you hear about Peter Scully?"

"He passed away in a car accident on Copano Bay about two weeks ago, right? Ran his tow truck right off the road. "

"That's him," Troy replied. "He drove clear into Copano Bay."

"I remember Pete," Ken said. "He was such a nice fellow. Always there when you needed him. As I recall, it happened just when we were leaving for Miami."

"Sure was," Troy said. "He and I were good buddies. We went to high school together and he didn't deserve to go like this. Left behind his beautiful wife Betty. They had only been married one year. Betty is going to try to run his tow truck business without him. That's going to be hard on her. We are all going to miss Peter. "

"We should try to do something for the family," Ken said quietly.

"I was hoping you would feel that way," Troy replied. "Betty told me that you own the mortgage to the Peter's Towing Company. She needs a little relief until she gets her settlement from the insurance company."

"Well sure," Ken said. That's no problem at all. I'll call her right away and let her know that she does not need to worry at all."

Kate sighed. All Betty needed was Ken Porter in her life.

"There is one other thing," Troy added.

"What's that," Ken asked.

"I need to have you down at the station for questioning," Troy said. "No hurry. I know you just got back in town. Talk to your lawyer first if you want to. It's just that this business regarding Peter is probably not accidental. We are treating it as a homicide investigation. I think your friend Henri was involved. His brother Sebastian and Louis are also going to be requested to appear for questioning as soon as they return to Texas. They could be tried as accomplices due to their involvement in Henri's activities."

"You know I had nothing to do with Peter's death," Ken protested.

"Sure, but we still need to find out what you know," Troy added. "Since it is a homicide investigation we want to make sure nothing is overlooked."

Kate smiled. She did not say anything. Troy was staking out his turf now and she knew that the boys from France might just decide never to return to Texas again".

Troy motioned silently to Kate that he wanted to leave the table. Kate and Troy excused themselves and moved away to a table towards the end of the room. Kate knew there was more to the story.

"This is way more complicated than it looks," Troy explained when he was alone at the table with Kate. "There's also the unfinished business regarding the deaths of Zachary and Nicole Dubois. It seems that the accidental car crash that they died in was really a homicide."

"Really!" Kate exclaimed.

"Yes," Troy replied. "I'm sure that Henri pushed them off the road."

"Wow!" Kate said. "I could never imagine he would be capable of murder," she added with just the faintest touch of sarcasm. "How did the police figure that out?"

"Well I just called the Sherriff's department to report a potential homicide when Peter died. They take that sort of thing quite seriously," Ken added. "They were able to match the damage to Zachary's car with the SUV that Henri owned at that time."

"I'm confused," Kate said. "What do you mean by 'at that time'?"

"The SUV that Peter was towing when he went over the bridge was a new, current year model. I'm sure it was the one that tried to push you off the road on Highway 35 this Spring. However, thanks to all the water damage that occurred when it fell into the bay, that may be hard to prove. When we checked the records on the SUV we found that Henri had traded in a similar two year old vehicle when he purchased this one. There was some damage to the front end of the vehicle that was traded in. It was repaired by the dealer after he accepted the trade-in from Henri. We contacted the dealer for their records and found some photographs that were taken at the time of the trade in. The repairs to the older vehicle and the timing of the trade-in overlap with the death of Zachary and Nicole. Henri must have felt very confident that he was not going to be questioned by the police or else I doubt that they would have traded in the vehicle that was used in the accident.

"Sounds to me like it was Henri," Kate said softly. "What do you think?" she asked Troy.

"Yes, it sure does seem as if Henri was behind their deaths," Troy replied. "If he was still alive we would be taking him in for some serious questioning. When I first heard about the accident on US-1 in the Florida Keys I thought it was Louis from the description we were provided. However, Louis had an ironclad alibi. He was hanging out with Ken at the time of the accident. Henri was also wearing a fake beard at the time of the accident. He may have been trying to shift attention towards Louis because he knew that Louis was sure to have an alibi. As soon as I realized what was going on, I knew that all these 'accidents' were connected with each other. I felt obligated to bring the matter to the authorities. "

Kate nodded. She was sure that Ken did not know about Henri's overly aggressive driving habits and his penchant for violence. If he had, he may have thought twice about befriending Henri. Ken could easily have become his next target. He must have felt that Ken knew something important and that was probably what was helping Ken stay alive. However, Henri was starting to get a little impatient because he had failed to find the treasure. He was clearly out of control at the time of his death on US-1.

"The Sherriff's department told me that they had been planning to bring the three Frenchmen in for questioning upon their return to Texas," Ken continued. "It seems that there may have been a small explosive device on the car that had a flat tire as it went over the causeway and ended up pulling Peter down into Copano Bay?"

"That would have to be Henri," Kate replied. "What an evil man."

"That he most certainly was," Troy said. "We are still trying to figure out exactly how it was done. My guess is that the explosion was triggered by Henri from the fishing pier just as the tow truck was going over the bridge. It could have been a lot worse. Depending on the size of the explosion, we could have lost a section of the Copano Bay Bridge and that would have resulted in more fatalities."

"My goodness," Kate said. "That's really quite a cold blooded thing to do."

"It's hard to prove that he did it," Ken continued, "just like all the other murders he committed. However, there is one other thing," he added.

"What's that?" Kate asked.

"Peter Scully's prints match the ones that were lifted from your B&B and also from Shirley's apartment, and from Charlotte and Jerry's patio door," Ken continued. "So Scully was also mixed up in this somehow."

"I see," Kate replied. "Do you think Henri hired him to do some of his dirty work for him? Later, he may have wanted him out of the way and decided that a towing accident was a convenient way to get rid of him."

"I don't know. Possibly," Troy said. "When we checked the records, we learned that Scully towed Zachary and Nicole's car to the police station in Rockport after their crash on

Highway 35. Henri couldn't grab the trunk after the crash because Peter was Johnny on the spot and showed up immediately after the crash occurred. After the accident, Henri tracked Peter down to find out what had happened to the trunk. Henri may have offered Peter a reward for finding the trunk. Scully was responsible for several break-ins. He was looking for the trunk. Not to murder somebody."

"I see," Kate said. This confirmed her suspicion. Peter was the first person to see the trunk up close. He had helped to carry it out of the wreckage of Nicole and Zachary's car and into the police station. Henri must have gotten to Peter with the idea that they could make some easy money. Peter's wife Betty might also have known about his involvement. That explained Betty's feelings about Zachary and Nicole. "But why kill Peter?"

"He probably knew too much," Troy replied after thinking it over. "Henri had to get rid of Peter because he would not go along with Henri's plans. Petty theft is one thing but murder is a completely different ball game."

"So it was Henri who broke into Lucy's studio in Galveston?" Kate asked rhetorically.

"Yes," Troy said. "Peter was at the bottom of Copano Bay by the time the break-in at her studio occurred."

Kate nodded. Peter must have connected the dots when Henri asked him to break into Lucy's apartment in Galveston.

"Exactly," Troy replied.

"Who broke into Nicole and Zachary's apartment?" she inquired.

"I don't know," Troy said. "It couldn't have been Henri. He was busy driving them off the road."

"Right, and it couldn't have been Peter," Kate said. "He was busy towing their car."

"Maybe they just forgot to close their door," Troy suggested.

"Maybe so. Perhaps their dog just opened the latch on his own and let himself out," Kate said.

"That's possible," Troy said. "Some dogs know exactly how to pull down on a door handle. Only problem is that if the wind blows the door closed it's not that easy to get back in."

Kate and Troy stared at each other for a while. "I should be getting back to work," Troy said. "I'll bring that trunk back to you. I think this mess sorted itself out. Henri was the bad apple in the bunch. The other two boys are probably innocent."

"Yes. I agree," Kate said. She felt bad for having misjudged Louis and Sebastian. "But you would still have to bring them in for questioning, right?" she inquired, almost as an after-thought. It occurred to her that Troy would not have allowed Louis to roam freely on the streets as long as he was within reach of Shirley.

"Of course," Troy said. "After all, this is a murder investigation, not a real estate deal. We have to look at every detail to be sure they were not involved."

Kate smiled. It was apparent that Troy was still very much in love with Shirley. He was a true Texan, who would never give up on the woman he loved even if she spurned him a million times.

≈≈≈≈≈≈

Spyglass Hill

Kate took the pirate flag out of the trunk and spread it out on the coffee table in her bedroom. She gazed intently at it, hoping to glean some minute detail that would help unlock the mystery. The water pouring out of the skull shimmered in the sunlight. Kate walked slowly around the table. The trunk was on the table next to the flag. As Kate studied the pirate flag for the hundredth time, she noticed something unusual. When the trunk was placed next to the flag, the ship that was carved on the trunk seemed to be floating on the water rippling out of the pirate's skull on the flag.

Kate realized that there was a connection between the etchings on the treasure chest and the pirate flag. If the pirate ship was sailing on the water then the water flowing out of the skull's mouth on the pirate flag was not a waterfall at all, but the waves rolling out of a body of water such as Copano Bay. The other side of the trunk had an etching that resembled a dragon. The dragon resembled the shape of the waterway that comprised St. Charles Bay, which lay adjacent to the north west side of Goose Island. It seemed as if the pirate ship was sailing out from Copano Bay towards St. Charles Bay.

Kate could feel the hair on her body start to bristle against her skin. She had the unreal feeling that there was another presence in the kitchen with her. It was unnerving, and Kate struggled to catch her breath. Just as she had done in the past, Kate took a deep breath and recited the Lords' Prayer to help her calm herself. "Lord have mercy," she said aloud to herself. "This simply cannot be happening." However, invisible pirates who wanted to help resolve a murder or to provide clues in finding hidden treasure were always welcome to stop by for a cup of coffee. Especially, Grandpa Jean.

The diamond that glittered on one of the pirate's teeth flashed in the sunlight. Kate took another look at it. The size of the diamond, and its prominent placement on the pirate flag seemed especially significant. The flag slipped noiselessly off the table and fell to the floor next to the treasure chest. Kate picked it up and straightened the flag upon the table once again. This time the pirate ship was sailing into Copano Bay. Did this mean that the treasure was 1821 paces from the mouth of Copano Bay?

As all the different pieces of the puzzle interlocked, Kate realized that the treasure had to located somewhere between St. Charles Bay and Copano Bay, both of which flanked Goose Island on either side. The treasure chest and the pirate flag provided a set of complementary keys to the location of the treasure. Both were essential for the solution. If the flag had been separated from the treasure chest it was unlikely that anyone would ever locate his buried treasure ever again. The misshapen skull in the middle of the pirate flag seemed to become a real person who looked back at her as she stared at him.

"Of course," Kate exclaimed out aloud. "The diamond in his eye marks the location of the treasure. If only I knew where that is supposed to be. What do you think, Jean?" She asked this question rhetorically. She did not really expect an answer. "If you were sailing from St. Charles Bay into Copano Bay what would you be looking at?" Kate paused as she paced around the coffee table. She put her foot up on the table and leaned forward to look out the window with the spyglass in her left hand. She closed her left eye as she tried desperately to concentrate on the images that appeared before her. She closed her right eye slowly and surveyed the coastline in her mind. She was now a pirate captain checking out the coastline. She paused to look twice at something that caught her eye. It was the unmistakable profile of a naked mermaid sun bathing on a rock on the prettiest beach on the Gulf Coast!

Kate could not decipher the meaning of the eye sockets in the pirate skull depicted on the flag. However, they did not appear to describe the shape of one of the islands in the Pacific, the Atlantic Ocean, or the Texas Gulf Coast. It had never been a body of water such as Copano Bay, Mission Bay, Mustang Lake or Mesquite Bay. The key was the water flowing out of the pirate's mouth. The pirate's mouth represented the mouth of the water flowing out of the mouth of Copano Bay. A seafaring vessel that travelled into Copano Bay entered pirate territory immediately after entering the mouth of Copano Bay.

Kate picked up her beach bag and towel. She rode her bicycle slowly down to Shipwreck Beach in a daze. She parked her bicycle and made her way past the sand dunes to the boulder that she liked to lean on whenever she went down to Shipwreck Beach. It was her favorite spot. It was a warm sunny day and Kate left her shoes on the boulder, next to her beach bag and towel.

Kate turned towards the direction of Copano Bay and began taking large measured strides as she walked. About 15 minutes later she he was standing directly underneath the Copano Bay Bridge, just where the mouth of the bay curled upward in a wicked smile. This was the entrance to Copano Bay. She turned around and walked back in the direction she had started from. After 1821 paces, she found herself standing at a familiar spot on Shipwreck Beach. About twenty paces behind her was her beach bag and towel exactly where she had left them a short time ago. Kate walked over towards her belongings and put on her tennis shoes.

As she studied the boulder, Kate realized that it was almost certainly made of granite. She felt a shiver of electricity course through her veins. Although the granite boulder blended in with the sand colored hues on the beach, it was distinctly lighter than the dark brown rocky outgrowths nearby. Not exactly something that was native to Goose Island. And there was another small detail. The baguette diamond that glittered on the tooth in the pirate's mouth was similar to the shape of the large brown boulder.

She looked at the boulder in a trance. The more she studied it, the more Kate became convinced that it must have been transported to the spot where it lay. "It must weigh a thousand pounds," she thought to herself. If the treasure was buried underneath the rock then it would require a small army and some type of earth moving equipment to budge it from its position. Jean Lafitte must have hauled it with him to Goose Island.

Kate went home. She tried to gather her thoughts as she drove her bicycle down Marlin Avenue. When she reached home, she brewed a cup of fresh coffee. Then she dialed Ray's telephone number. She called Ray and explained everything in detail. Ray was skeptical. He knew the spot on the beach that Kate described to him all too well. He had sat on the boulder with Kate any number of times, holding her hand and watching the waves roll on to the shore. It was a good spot for a beer on a moonlit night in a romantic sort of way. He could hardly believe that it marked the location of the pirate treasure. Meanwhile, Kate was getting more and more animated as she described her suspicions to Ray. He could not ignore how charged and passionate she was. He longed to be with her and promised to visit Goose Island at the earliest opportunity. In a convoluted way, it made perfect sense that Jeanne Lafitte would place the treasure exactly where his sweetheart liked to spend her time when she was at the beach. Ray suggested that Kate should get some legal assistance and contact her ex-husband James just in case there was something of value underneath the rock.

*   *   *

"Did you find the treasure yet?" James asked when he answered the phone. He was only half-serious.

"You're never going to believe me, James," Kate repeated. The words had scarcely left her mouth before she realized her life would never be the same again.

Kate did not say another word. The silence at Kate's end told him all he needed to know. James knew Kate well enough to pay careful attention to everything she told him. He had been doing a fair bit of analysis and research since Kate had contacted him about the phone calls she had received from the New Orleans Traders. It did not take him long to figure out that something phenomenally stupendous had just taken place.

"Oh my God!" James replied. "I'll be right over".

Kate hung up the phone. She called Ray and explained everything in detail. He could hardly believe it himself.

James caught the first flight to Corpus Christi the next morning. He ran into Ray at the airport at Corpus Christi. They rented a car together and pulled into the driveway at the Goose Island B&B just as Kate was waking up for breakfast. A short while later they were seated around the table next to the pirate trunk and the pirate flag.

"Wow!" James whistled under his breath.

"I know," Kate said. She proceeded to fill him in on the details.

"It's absolutely fantastic Kate," James said.

"That it is," Ray said in agreement. He walked over to the window and looked outside at Copano Bay. "We are going to have to call this the house on Spyglass Hill."

"Arrr! Now that's an idea," Kate said. Everyone laughed.

"But there's just one small problem," James said.

"What's that," Kate asked.

"Just that you have no actual proof that the treasure is under the rock," he said. "Not that I have any doubts in your deductive abilities. You do understand, don't you?"

"Of course, James," Kate said coldly. "Well in that case, there's no problem at all if there's no treasure, is there."

"True," James replied. "I had assumed that you had actually found the treasure."

"I have, James," Kate replied.

"Uh huh," he grunted.

The enthusiasm that had preceded James' comment disappeared from the room.

Treasure or no treasure, it seemed to make sense to let the recovery effort be conducted by a team of professionals.

"We don't need any redneck cowboys trying to move the rock with their pick-up trucks," James said, looking at Ray.

Ray didn't say a word.

Kate agreed.

Ray didn't say a word. For some reason it seemed that they had both decided to pick on him. He didn't care. He had Kate. There would be plenty of time for him to settle personal accounts with her in private.

James shared a few details from his research. If the treasure was found on public property, by law the treasure belonged to the State Of Texas. The laws governing the discovery of buried treasure on land are quite different from those regarding the treasure contained in a shipwreck. The difference is attributable to the intent of the person whose actions resulted in the creation of the treasure trove. Items that have been hidden deliberately are treated differently from a shipwreck destroyed by accident in a storm.

With James' assistance, legal documents were drawn up so that all of the treasure, if any, was donated to Texas A&M University in return for their assistance in the recovery. One of Kate's guests from the Goose Island Bed and Breakfast was a professor in the Marine Biology Department at Texas A&M University. Dr. Dean McCoy knew Kate quite well, and he helped convince some of his peers that she was not a delusional woman who had been mentally unsound for decades. Kate had to turn over the pirate trunk and the flag. It would end up in a glass case at the Texas A&M Maritime Studies Center in Galveston.

The Aggie network came to Kate's assistance in a big way. The cost of the recovery effort was provided by a group of benefactors who were just as eager to see what lay underneath the rock on Shipwreck Beach. The University supervised and oversaw the recovery effort at virtually no cost to the school. The contractual agreement stipulated that any items of value recovered by the team were to be housed in a special maritime museum in Galveston. The only thing that remained to be completed was to uncover the treasure that surely lay buried beneath the granite boulder on Shipwreck Beach.

It turned out to be a bigger challenge than expected. Word of the pirate treasure that lay buried on Shipwreck Beach had spread like wildfire throughout the area. Before any serious attempt could be made to recover the treasure, the area surrounding the granite boulder had to be cordoned off from a horde of independent adventurers who were determined to find the treasure on their own. The spectator gallery that came each day to observe the beachfront excavation grew to rival the crowds on the 18th hole at the PGA Championship.

Once the end of the beach had been secured and the sand around the boulder was excavated very carefully. Then the boulder was shifted carefully off to one side. It was wrapped with large straps and raised upwards in slow motion with the help of a large portable crane. It seemed as though the whole town had decided to turn out in force every morning with binoculars and beer to watch the proceedings. An extra detail of police security was provided around the clock. The land was excavated very carefully so as not to damage anything that lay buried underneath the soil.

The recovery effort continued for days, and then weeks. The area that had been excavated grew larger and larger. The townsfolk complained that they had lost use of the beach for the best part of the summer and were anxiously awaiting an end to the foolishness so that life could return to normal. After the initial excitement, anticipation wore thin and the crowd of onlookers that turned out every day grew smaller and smaller. Finally, it had dwindled down until the primary audience consisted of Kate, Shirley, Charlotte, Troy and

Jerry and Ray who came down to Goose Island on weekends, just as soon as he could get away from work. It was enough for him to hold Kate's hand through the proceedings and to enjoy her company when they went home to the Golden Goose at the end of each day. He was not looking for any treasure that remained to be found underneath the rock.

"I just don't understand," Kate said to Ray as they were walking back home after another despondent day watching a painfully slow excavation effort.

"Well they have been very thorough, Kate," Ray replied. "If there had been any treasure present, it would have surely been found by now".

Kate had to agree. She was starting to feel like an idiot whenever they stopped by the Swamp Shack for dinner. Despite all her personal convictions, she had to accept that the treasure must have disappeared a long time ago. She wracked her brain to try to understand that there was no treasure. She just couldn't let it go. It had to be there. It had to.

*   *   *

The next day Kate requested permission to examine the boulder itself. Since the search had not uncovered anything of value for several weeks, granting access to the boulder was hardly an issue. Next to the large gaping hole that had been excavated, the boulder looked like a small insignificant pebble. The supervisor in charge of the recovery effort waved her past the makeshift fenced area. He had just received word that the recovery team was to get ready to pack up and go home within a few days.

Kate ran her hands along the surface of the boulder. She had sat on it so many times that she already knew every inch of the surface without having to look at it twice. However, it was not the same. In the past, she had been a mermaid sitting on a rock next to the ocean. Now she was a pirate. The boulder was no longer just a chunk of quartz, feldspar, and other minerals from the earth.

It was not until Kate ran her hands along the surface of the rock that had once been on the underside of the boulder that she found the anomaly that she was looking for. There was a small bump on the rock that was the exact shape and size as the black onyx stone that the mermaid had been seated on inside the pirate trunk. Pressing the onyx rock in the trunk had revealed the pirate flag. Kate wondered what would happen if they could press the bump on the boulder. She pushed it as hard as she could with her thumb and fore-finger. It did not budge. One of the men on the recovery team came over to help her. He brought a small mallet and gave it several solid, hard whacks, without making a dent. "Thwack, thwack, thwack," went the mallet. Pieces of sand flew in the air. The man from the recovery team started to sweat with beads of perspiration running down his forehead. Kate looked at the bump expecting it to shear off the rock any minute. Then, after what seemed like an eternity, a small seam appeared along the belly of the boulder.

"Holy smoke! Would you look at that?" remarked the fellow from the recovery team.

"Yes indeed," said Kate who was transfixed with astonishment for the moment.

Once the seam appeared, it was only a matter of time before they tapped their way carefully into the mother lode. The rock split open effortlessly, and the contents within it spilled out upon the ground. At first glance, it looked like rubbish. A large number of small dark pebbles fell to the ground. They were covered with barnacles. Some of the pebbles disappeared noiselessly into the sand. If they had not all been almost the exact same shape and size Kate would have probably tossed them into the ocean. However, something in their weight and their symmetry that caught her eye. Someone brought a pocketknife and carefully scraped off the tar and the barnacles off one of the pebbles. It sparkled brilliantly in the sunlight. A closer look revealed a Spanish Doubloon from the sixteenth century. There must have been hundreds of gold coins within the rock. The rock itself had flecks of gold within its grains and Kate wondered if she was looking at the largest piece of Amarillo Bamboo quartzite granite that she had ever seen.

The pirate treasure had always been inside the rock, not underneath it. It had remained there for almost two hundred years. Hidden from view so that vandals and other treasure hunters would never find it without the map he had left behind. Safe from hurricanes, storm surges, the power of the sea and other ravages of nature that could easily have relocated the boulder. The rock had probably ben hollowed out and outfitted in South America. Jean Lafitte had sailed back to Texas and filled it with all the valuables that he owned. He had sealed the rock shut and placed it on the beach that he liked to visit with his wife. If she had studied the map carefully from the proper perspective she would instantly have known exactly where the treasure was located. For all she knew there were several more treasure filled rocks scattered along the Gulf Coast! The treasure was probably worth a few thousand dollars in the sixteenth century. However, almost three hundred years later it was worth almost five hundred million dollars.

Kate had made an agreement with the State of Texas to turn Shipwreck Beach into a protected State Historical area that extended along the entire length of Goose Island, providing parking facilities, restrooms and other modern conveniences befitting its revised status. Residents of Goose Island were exempt from the fee that had to be paid by visitors for access to the facility. The fee helped to prevent Goose Island from being swamped by hordes of treasure hunters who would otherwise have descended on the island armed with shovels and metal detectors.

Kate's personal share of the settlement with the State of Texas left her a very wealthy person. She placed her portion of the reward money in a trust created for the benefit of the residents of Goose Island. The trust agreement constrained the manner in which the corpus of the trust was to be invested and the amount of money that could be withdrawn each year. Otherwise, the trustees were free to spend the money as they saw fit. It was quite acceptable for them to come to the aid of a single individual, or to invest the money in a public works project benefiting the City of Goose Island in any manner that was deemed appropriate. One of the first acts of this organization was the creation of an Art Museum dedicated to the memory of Zachary and Nicole Dubois whose deaths had precipitated the events that led to the biggest find of hidden treasure along the Texas Gulf coast.

Lucy Dubois realized that her family members were probably descendants of Jean Lafitte. Her paintings of Goose Island hung proudly at the entrance to the museum. There was one large painting of an early nineteenth century sailing ship with its Jolly Roger unfurled as it sailed rapidly towards Copano Bay. Lucy had captured the white flecks of surf on the tips of the waves so perfectly that you could picture yourself on the deck of the pirate ship and taste the salt water . Lucy was given the authority to select all the artifacts inside the museum, including the pirate flag and steamer trunk that had belonged to her late Great Grandpa Jean.

Ray suspected that Kate was as much a descendant of Jean Lafitte as Lucy. Ray knew that Kate could only have accomplished the task of finding the treasure with the natural abilities and instincts that she had inherited from Jean Lafitte. Kate's discovery of the treasure was staggering.

"Grandpa Jean would have been proud of you," said Ray as they sat on Kate's porch drinking a glass of red wine.

"Thanks Ray," said Kate dreamily. "You do know that the real pirate was Grandma

Eloise. She's the one who enticed him to settle down Texas in the first place."

"I have no idea whom you are talking about," Ray said, puzzled at not being able to grasp the reference to Grandma Eloise. "Whoever it is, you are definitely his next of kin and you know it."

"I couldn't have done it without you Ray," Kate said. Her chest swelled up with pride at his remark, threatening to pop the buttons on her shirt. Maybe she was related to the pirate king. Maybe not. However, she had definitely walked the plank a few times to find the treasure he had left behind.

"Thanks," Ray replied. He was basking in the pleasure that comes from being with the woman of his dreams. His personal treasure chest was overflowing with her love.

Kate could see the pirate flag fluttering excitedly in the breeze as it flew above Jean Lafitte's schooner. The three diamonds sewn into the fabric glittered in the sunshine. She had found the treasure trove that glittered in the pirate's mouth. Now if she could only find out where the treasure that glittered in the pirate's eyes was located!

In Kate's mind, the real treasure had always been in walking barefoot on the sandy beach near Goose Island. It lay in every golden sunrise when the sun burst through the clouds in the morning and every burnt orange sunset after a day spent looking for seashells. The treasure remained in walking in the surf that washed up along the shore and watching flocks of geese on their migratory journeys through the area each year. It would live forever with every flash of blue on the horizon at sunset when Kate took off her jeans to retire for the evening. She reached over and nibbled gently on the tip of Ray's ear.

"Love you too, you pirate!" he whispered.

≈≈≈≈≈≈